By ZAHRA OWENS

NOVELS
Clouds and Rain
Earth and Sky
Floods and Drought

Diplomacy
Façade
The Hand-me-down

NOVELLAS
Balance
Charity Starts at Home
Happiness for Beginners
I Can See Right Through You
You Can Choose Your Friends
You Can't Choose Your Family

Published by DREAMSPINNER PRESS
http://www.dreamspinnerpress.com

The Hand-me-down

ZAHRA OWENS

Dreamspinner Press

Published by
Dreamspinner Press
5032 Capital Circle SW
Ste 2, PMB# 279
Tallahassee, FL 32305-7886
USA
http://www.dreamspinnerpress.com/

The Hand-me-down

Cover Art by Paul Richmond
http://www.paulrichmondstudio.com

ISBN: 978-1-61372-763-8

Printed in the United States of America
First Edition
September 2012

eBook edition available
eBook ISBN: 978-1-61372-764-5

To Saura, who, both as a translator and as a friend, fueled my love for Spain enough to write about it.

Thank you my beautiful friend!

To everyone who has ever needed to explain his relationship to his friends. Relationships, like people, come in all shapes and sizes, and sometimes, even your friends just don't "get it." But all that matters is LOVE.

Chapter 1

WHEN the plane touched down in Barcelona, it was the middle of the night, but I was still on New York time, so I was actually less tired than I would be after a hard day's work. Traveling first class had its perks, not least the almost personal service the airline provided in the form of a charming and rather buff male flight attendant who made sure my every need was met. Okay, maybe not my *every* need. His service didn't provide *that*. He did, however, make sure I slept soundly for a good three hours in a seat that was more comfortable than the one in my own living room, and that when I woke, the meal I'd skipped was still hot. He also made sure the cabin lights were low, and the only sound was the humming of the engines. His perfect service even made sure I barely registered there were other businessmen sharing the cabin with me. For once, during my waking hours I actually got some work done. I kept thinking the flight attendant could make some rich guy a very attentive but inconspicuous butler. And he was a treat to look at as well.

Walking down the concourse on route to the baggage claim, I felt more invigorated than a transatlantic passenger had the right to be, and as I passed the droves of cattle car passengers and their tired kids, I tried not to smile too much. At least they didn't do this once a week. I was so used to the time change it no longer bothered me. If all went well, I'd be back in the Big Apple before the weekend with time off to go clubbing. That was all in my future. For now, it was business all the way.

At immigration, a few words of Spanish, a stern, businesslike look, and my almost-full passport made the immigration officer put aside his prejudice against my shaven head and muscular bad-boy physique as he returned my passport to me, and let me enter the country. Luckily my numerous tattoos were covered by my travel attire, or he might have had a different reaction. I picked up my garment bag and the small suitcase I could hook my laptop bag to, and briskly walked toward the terminal's outer lobby, where a portly driver stood with my name printed on a placard. Jeremy Robinson. But friends call me Jez.

"Good flight, sir?" the driver asked in heavily accented English after I had settled in the back of his car.

"Perfect, thank you," I answered. I recognized the logo on his lapel as the one from the company I was going to visit. "Will you be picking me up in the morning?"

"Yes, sir. When would you like me to be there?"

"Eight is fine." That would give me time to review some of my notes while driving, and would take into account that traffic in downtown Barcelona was notoriously difficult to predict. Also, I preferred to arrive early and see how ready they were for my arrival. I admit that seeing them scurry around nervously while I keep my notorious cool strokes my ego.

As I settled into my hotel room and hung up my suits, I mentally went over my agenda for the next few days. I was invited to a company where the CEO was looking for "a new challenge." Officially I was contracted to review which of the VPs could be promoted to a higher position, but unofficially I was bringing several lucrative offers from other companies to the CEO. Meeting with everyone, and drafting an official report, would take three days. The networking necessary to do my job would occupy just one night. The date for my visit had been chosen to include an evening of brushing shoulders with a whole dining hall full of captains of industry, so I hoped I'd meet prospective customers there. I was always on the lookout for the next lucrative job.

For now I ordered a room service dinner of chicken Caesar salad and turned on the TV while I took my laptop out. After flicking through numerous channels of loud and chatty debate programs and frantic news, I settled for a nature channel and turned the TV to mute. The sudden silence in the room helped me focus on the e-mails that popped up on my laptop.

ALTHOUGH my job rarely bored me, this trip was more of the same. I always did my best to look focused, asked all the right questions, and in this case interviewed all the people at the VP level, but they all tried too hard to suck up to me, so I found my mind drifting off. My last interviewee was a particularly good-looking young man who turned on the charm. He was one of the most junior VPs and only in his position for a meager three months, but I caught myself imagining what he'd look like without his dark grey suit, and wondered what he did to get to the position at his early age. The CEO looked like the type who could bend a guy over his designer desk before offering him a promotion.

"Mr. Robinson?"

Damn, I never did this. There was a wall the caliber of the Berlin one between my private life and my business persona, and nothing penetrated it. Usually. So I had to excuse myself and left the guy behind looking stunned. I made my way to the restrooms and entered a stall where I sat on the closed toilet. Wiping my hands over my shaved head, I knew what I needed. I took out my cell phone and searched for leather clubs. I was sure that twinky VP had a twin in some club in Barcelona, and nailing him would make maintaining my wall so much easier. Just a few more hours of work and an evening of networking, and then I'd get to do my favorite kind of networking. Making a connection of the physical kind.

Maybe I needed a vacation? I knew myself, though. I'd still be working if I booked a cruise or paradise holiday. Nothing better to do anyway.

WHEN I woke up on my last day in Barcelona, my body was still humming. I felt invigorated. The club I'd found online turned out to be a gem and then some, with tight male bodies eager to please. My favorite was probably the muscle guy I ended up fucking in full view of about four or five other guys, two of which took over the show after we were finished. Not that I asked his name or had any intention of ever meeting him again. There was no need. I got what I wanted, and I was pretty sure he did as well.

While packing my bags, I turned the TV to CNN. There was an item about a volcano in Iceland erupting and spewing ash into the atmosphere, but it only drew my attention because they were talking about closing airports. My flight to NYC was in twelve hours, and I hoped the cloud wouldn't interfere with the path my pilot needed to take.

By the time I'd finished submitting my report to the CEO and discussing his personal options with him, he told me that all transatlantic flights were canceled. He offered me accommodation at his country home, but I declined. Like I said, I don't mix business with pleasure, and my work there was done. I called my office in New York, but they already knew the score and told me to enjoy some time off. What the hell was I going to do with myself in a city I'd only ever been to for business?

When I arrived back at my hotel, the manager came over to me, smiling apologetically. Apparently they were swamped by all the tourists stranded in the city, and they asked me whether I'd consider moving to a smaller room so they could use my suite to house a family. Of course they would foot the bill for this. I didn't care much for luxury, so I agreed, figuring it would last one or two days at most. My new room was tiny but comfortable, and I got a bottle of cava as a thank you.

I decided to surf the net for porn, but after the live action of the night before, it bored me to tears. When I opened Twitter, I came across a few haphazard posts from a man I hadn't seen in years: porn star Nick Stone. The pictures he tweeted looked vaguely familiar, and then he talked about his villa outside Barcelona. I smiled when I realized we were in the same city, and I had time on my hands.

Nick and I went way back. When I met him he was this godlike creature with seven percent body fat, tirelessly worked muscles, and a cock that always seemed ready for action. In the days before Internet porn, he was everywhere and worked for the biggest gay porn production houses. He even managed to make the transition to the

Internet, starting his own site and selling his videos there. I got to know the man behind the larger than life persona and found a man who had a voracious appetite for life and fun but could just as easily enjoy silence and sitting on a couch reading a book. And then eight years ago, he went off the grid. I only found him again when someone retweeted his messages.

A few phone calls to mutual friends later, I had Nick's cell phone number, and I was starting to feel excited about catching up with him again. Being a no-holds-barred kind of guy, I didn't hesitate to dial his number.

"Nicky?"

The silence at the other end made me uneasy for just a moment.

"Who is this?"

"Jez Robinson," I answered calmly.

"Oh. My God. The Red Robin."

I chuckled at my old nickname. "Not so red anymore, Stud Muffin. I got hair with character. It'd rather fall out than turn grey, so I shaved it all off."

"Your leather boys should appreciate that look."

I drank in Nick's cultured English accent, which he'd always kept up even though his vocabulary over the years had been peppered with American words. "Oh, they do."

"My hair is almost white," Nick replied.

"I saw your pictures," I admitted. Some of his tweets had contained a link to a fashion website where I found pictures of him fully clothed, and looking stunning. "So you turned into a bona fide fashion model in your old age?"

"Who are you calling old?" he asked with a hearty belly laugh. Then he coughed. Repeatedly.

"Ever thought about quitting those cigarettes?" I quipped.

"Quit six years ago," Nick said after he finally got his breathing under control. "Hey, a guy's got to do something to keep the money flowing in, Jez. So what made you call me?"

"I'm in Barcelona," I said softly. "Stuck here by that volcano. I should be on a plane back to New York right now, but it's canceled." There was a silence at the other end of the line, and I could almost see Nick smile. I imagined him reclined on the sofa, stretching out his long, elegant limbs.

"You have to come see me. You can stay over. I have plenty of room. We can catch up. It's been way too long, Jezzie."

I decided this was the best offer I'd had in a while. "Tell me where I can find you."

Chapter 2

NICK'S villa was about a half an hour's drive outside the city limits, but it felt like I'd left the smells and noise of the city behind hours ago. The hotel driver who brought me had to navigate his car up a hill and through streets clearly not made for a motorized vehicle until the road opened up into another street, this one lined with rhododendrons. About halfway up the mountain and to the right was a gate, just like Nick had explained. I tipped the driver after he took my two bags out of his car, and then I pulled the string to ring the old fashioned bell at the top of the gate.

Through the gate I could see the stone villa with its many whitewashed corners and a little tower at the side, and beyond it I saw a glimpse of a gorgeous vista. As I reached for the bell again, the front door opened and out walked a young man who looked exactly like Nick's type: average height, more than average body, a beautiful round face with a luscious mouth and framed by short medium-brown hair. Underneath it were shoulders that looked nicely muscled but were, sadly, covered by a shirt. When he came closer, I managed a brief look into eyes the color of Mediterranean seawater. He didn't look at me very long, though.

"Buenos días," I managed. "Me llamo Jeremy Robinson." My Spanish was limited, but I figured I might as well try it out on Nick's… whatever he was. He nodded at me as he opened the gate and let me in, then walked away to let me close the gate myself. So maybe he wasn't a servant after all? I followed him toward the house, careful not to feast my eyes on him too much. He was wearing a white shirt and black dress slacks that fit him perfectly. Somehow it didn't surprise me that Nick would employ eye candy. I didn't have time to wonder longer about the young man's place in Nick's household, because as soon as my eyes adjusted to the relative darkness of the cavernous hallway inside the house, Nick walked up to greet me.

"Jezzie! It's been too long!"

I smiled automatically, hiding the fact that I thought Nick looked a lot skinnier than when I last saw him. He was still taller than me, but not by much, and he still dressed impeccably, but he looked a little… frail.

"You've met Jamie," Nick stated rather than asked. "Jamie, darling, can you take Jez's bags upstairs to his room?" As Jamie took the garment bag from me, Nick enveloped me in a tight hug, and I was glad to feel his strength, which apparently hadn't disappeared along with his old physique. Other than that, in the past years he'd changed from stud to distinguished gentleman. It was almost hard for me to think of him as Nick Stone, the porn star. Now he fit the mature fashion-model look to a tee.

Before he let go of me, I ran my hand through his floppy white locks. "When did this happen?"

Nick pulled back just enough to look me in the eye. "Long story, but I was dyeing my hair long before I quit performing."

"And now your chest hair is as white as the rest and it's too cumbersome?"

Nick tsked me. "A little respect, please!" The sparkle in his eyes betrayed that he was enjoying the teasing. "The pubes are more salt and pepper now, and I always got waxed, which I don't do anymore." He let go of me, but kept his hand on my upper arm. "Well, I still trim, of course. I haven't lost all my pride yet." He squeezed my biceps. "You're keeping up with your weight training, aren't you?"

I chuckled. "Like you, I do it so I can get laid."

Nick rolled his eyes and gestured toward the back of the house. "Let me give you a tour." He sauntered off in front of me, and I realized he hadn't lost any of his elegance. He was probably the only man I knew who could glide through a room and still make it look manly. The kitchen we walked into was light and airy. Behind the counter stood Jamie, and I speculated for a moment about the alternative route he must have taken to bypass the hallway.

"Stop ogling my boyfriend," Nick said good-naturedly, which immediately made me look away from the handsome young man. So Jamie was Nick's lover. I admired his good taste. I had to look at Jamie again when Nick leaned against him to whisper something in his ear. There was clear intimacy between them, and I knew Nick was showing Jamie off to me when he unbuttoned the top of Jamie's shirt and slipped his hand inside.

Jamie barely reacted, save for the fact he was clearly leaning into the touch. He smiled just a little when Nick whispered something else in his ear and then nodded before Nick let go of him and walked away. With his hand on my arm, Nick guided me through the french doors to the garden, where I was immediately consumed by the majestic view.

"Oh, wow."

"Isn't it the best?" Nick asked. "The house itself is not that special, but this view is why it just said 'buy me!' Between London, Miami, LA, and New York, I always considered myself a city boy, but here I find peace." Nick leaned a little closer. "Having Jamie here helps, of course."

"I can see how he'd have that effect, yes. Where did you find him?"

Nick cocked his head. "That's another long story. If you stay sufficiently long, you might find out."

I shook my head. "As soon as the skies clear and planes start flying west again, I'm off."

"Thought so," Nick replied.

Was it wishful thinking, or did he sound regretful? Maybe I should take that offer of vacation time and stay longer? Then again, I was sure Nick would tire of me soon enough, and he'd want the house to himself and Jamie again.

Nick took me to a secluded area in the garden where a long table, a bench, and four chairs occupied most of the space. Vines were directed to grow along a trellis and it offered shade to sit under.

"Jamie's fixing us a light lunch," Nick remarked as he gestured me to sit down. Then his cell phone rang. He fished it out of the pocket of his slacks and looked at it. "Sorry, but I need to take this."

I sat down and expected Nick to walk around the garden talking to whoever had called him, but he sat beside me on the bench facing the pool as Jamie came from the kitchen with a tray.

As Nick talked on the phone in what sounded like near-perfect Spanish to my ear, I had time to observe Jamie. He looked like the ideal servant. He moved almost silently, avoiding eye contact and using easy, fluid actions to set the table for us, taking great care in placing the cutlery and glasses. I noticed he set only two places, for Nick and me. He walked away and almost immediately returned with a bottle of Rioja. He showed it to Nick and Nick returned a look to Jamie that made my stone-cold bachelor's heart flutter. After just a flick of a finger—a gesture I didn't understand, but Jamie obviously did—Jamie expertly opened the bottle and poured about half an inch of deliciously burgundy red into my glass. Nick gestured at me to taste it and I took a small sip. I'm not much of a wine drinker, but the wine tasted pretty amazing and almost immediately seemed to fuse into my body.

"Excellent," I said. "Great choice, Jamie."

Jamie met my eye so fleetingly it almost seemed accidental. He nodded ever so slightly and added more wine to the glass still in my hand. He then filled Nick's glass and walked back to the kitchen.

As Nick put down his phone, I gestured at him with my glass. "Amazing wine."

Nick raised his glass and twirled it before smelling the wine and finally taking a sip, which he rolled around in his mouth. Once he swallowed, he lay back in his seat and looked utterly satisfied. "It was a great year. If I knew you'd be staying longer, I would have made arrangements to visit the vineyard. I know the man who makes this wine."

I was sure from the way he looked at me that he meant "know" in a biblical sense. I looked at the bottle again and noticed the label was handwritten.

"Of course this isn't the Rioja region, so he can't officially sell it as Rioja," Nick said after he noticed my suspicious look. "But he uses the right techniques and grapes, so for me he calls it Rioja." Nick smiled contently. "It's amazing wine, so who cares."

"Is Jamie not joining us for lunch?"

Nick sighed. "No. I asked him this morning, but he didn't want to interfere."

I shrugged. "He wouldn't be interfering. He's your partner. Call him and ask him to join us."

At that moment Jamie arrived with two plates full of assorted goodies. I noticed tomatoes and mozzarella sprinkled with basil and olive oil, the Spanish anchovies they call boquerones, green and black olives, dried and cured pata negra ham and spicy salami, and a basket of bread and cheese. Nick exchanged tender touches with Jamie and thanked him, but didn't ask him to stay. I couldn't leave it like that.

"Jamie, why don't you make yourself a plate too and come and sit with us?"

I thought Jamie looked trapped. As if Nick had not invited him, or had expressly forbidden him to sit with us. Could this be the case? Jamie briefly looked at Nick, grabbed Nick's glass of wine, and finished it off before fleeing back toward the kitchen. I followed the young man with my eyes and then felt Nick's hand cover mine. There was compassion in his face, for whom, I didn't know. Then it dawned on me that I'd never seen Jamie speak, and Nick often gestured at him, even when he asked him something. Was Jamie deaf?

"I didn't mean to make this awkward, Nicky," I said by way of apology.

Nick shook his head. "He didn't want to sit with us, because—" Nick paused as if he didn't know how to explain. "—he doesn't speak to strangers." He refilled his glass of wine.

"So he's not deaf?"

"Oh Lord, no." Nick laughed. "No, there's nothing wrong with Jamie's hearing. He's just been through a lot, and it takes him a long time to get to know someone, and even then he only talks to them if he really trusts them."

I nodded, not because I understood, but because it offered an explanation for Jamie's strange behavior. It still didn't feel right. "Listen, I practically invited myself over here. You should eat with Jamie and I'll eat in the kitchen."

"Don't be silly, Jez. You're our guest." He took my hand again to prevent me from getting up. If anyone knew how stubborn I was, it was Nick, and he knew I wouldn't take this lying down. "Jamie's fine. He knows he's allowed to join us. He chose not to. He also knows I'll make it up to him." Nick let go of my hand and picked up his knife and fork to start eating.

I looked at the kitchen and then dug into my plate as well. The food was even more scrumptious than it looked, but I couldn't stop feeling like the big bad intruder who was keeping the couple apart by my mere presence. Although Nick was doing his utmost to make me feel welcome, I knew I was going to have to make myself scarce for a while after lunch.

When we were done eating and had finished the bottle of wine—mostly via my glass, I admit—I was surprised that Nick didn't seem in any hurry to rejoin Jamie. I decided I'd give him a nudge. "I'm still kind of jetlagged, Nick. Mind if I go to my room and have a nap?"

Nick sat up. "Of course not. It's through the hallway, up the stairs and to your right. Jamie put your bags in your room so if you find them, you're in the right place. Live the Spanish way and have yourself a nice siesta."

"I will," I said as I got up and walked through the kitchen, where Jamie was eyeing me as I passed. I smiled at him and gestured with my head that the coast was clear. He nodded, but still didn't smile.

Chapter 3

THE guest room was light and airy and very tastefully decorated. I was used to living out of a suitcase, so other than hanging up my suits, I didn't bother taking out the rest of my stuff since I was only going to be there two or three days at best. There was a large bed, nicely made up with pristine white sheets, and a comfortable sofa next to a small table and chair. I decided to take out my laptop and sit on the sofa to check my e-mails and do a little work.

To my surprise, I woke up some time later to sounds coming from one of the other rooms. I looked at my watch and saw I'd been asleep for the better part of an hour, my laptop having gone into hibernation since I'd clearly not closed it when I'd dozed off. As I listened to whatever had roused me, I realized that Nick was definitely making up to Jamie for the separate lunch. Since I had history with Nick, I knew the small whimpering sounds I heard weren't coming from him. They were definitely turning me on. From time to time the whimpers were interspersed with Nick murmuring something I couldn't understand, but that didn't diminish the delicious sex sounds coming from down the hall.

I imagined Jamie on all fours and Nick rimming him. Although it'd been at least ten years, I remembered vividly how talented that man's tongue was, and it made me hard instantly. I put down my laptop and unzipped my pants. The whimpers next door became grunts and as they were accompanied by thumping noises from the bed, I could easily imagine Nick fucking Jamie. I took myself in hand and wiped the beads of precum already seeping out of me around the head of my cock. I didn't know which one I wanted to be, Jamie who was being expertly nailed by the biggest living porn star on earth, or Nick because he got to fuck such a gorgeous, responsive man. Since I knew firsthand what it was like to have Nick's massive cock up my ass, my attention was drawn to Jamie's rhythmical grunts. I timed my strokes to Jamie's delicious noises and kept my fist tight so I could imagine it was Jamie's firm body I was pushing into. My hips veered up of their own accord and I tried not to join their chorus for fear they'd catch on how much this was arousing me. The grunts became faster and more urgent, just like the need for me to come became more pressing.

"Right there," I heard from the other room. Just when it dawned on me the raspy, low voice wasn't Nick, the same voice groaned, "Close!" and I shot my load all over my own hand. Next door I heard a few quick jabs and then a long drawn out grunt which I recognized as Nick's before the room went silent. Just as I started to get up to clean myself off, I heard murmured conversation. As much as I tried, I couldn't make out what was being said, but I knew, despite the fact that Nick had always made a living in the sex industry, away from the camera, he was a big softy who loved to cuddle for a long time after sex. I could imagine Jamie being pretty receptive to that as well. All of a sudden, I felt envious of what Nick and Jamie had together. Where did that feeling come from? I couldn't figure it out. Nick was one of the few men I'd had sex with more than once, and I knew that if he asked, I'd let him fuck me again. It had always been casual between us, with neither of us demanding anything from the other, but then Nick was in no position to demand anything from his lovers anyway, since he was the one who got paid to fuck around. Surely it wasn't jealousy of Jamie that made these feelings bubble up suddenly?

I got up and found my way to the bathroom, where I cleaned up before returning to my room to change my clothes. The house was quiet by then, and I opened my laptop to do the work I'd started out doing, but my mind wasn't on working, so I quietly made my way downstairs and took a book to read into the little vine-covered alcove I'd had lunch in. Our wine glasses were still there, and I finished the last gulp still left in my glass. About an hour later, I spotted Jamie through the window to the kitchen. When he noticed me looking at him, he retreated inside. I decided to bring the glasses in, and he took them from me, simply nodding his thanks. When he turned away from me, I grabbed his wrist and he pulled away violently.

"Jamie, I'm sorry," I said softly, letting go of him. "I didn't mean to do anything to upset you, and I'm certainly not here to encroach on your territory. I'll be leaving as soon as the planes fly again to take me to New York."

As our eyes met, I noticed Jamie didn't look away immediately like he had before. He seemed to be checking me out, sizing me up. I decided to talk about something we shared— our love for Nick—and hoped he wouldn't take it the wrong way.

"I don't know what Nick has told you about me, but he and I have a history together. It was always casual between us and we were never exclusive. Back then, neither of us wanted it to be anything more than what it was. I don't know if you and he are exclusive now, but I'm not about to find out. I can see what you two have here and you make him very happy, Jamie. I'd never come between that."

Jamie seemed to like what I said, because the smallest hint of a smile played around his mouth and his eyes started to sparkle.

"Do you trust me when I say I won't make a pass at Nick?"

After what felt like forever, Jamie nodded. Not with a lot of conviction, but at least we'd established some sort of communication, and all I wanted was for him to feel more comfortable around me.

"Now will you please join us for dinner tonight?"

The smile disappeared and for a moment I feared I'd screwed up, but then Jamie nodded again, a little hesitantly.

"Anything I can help you with?" I asked him as he started rummaging around the kitchen.

Jamie shook his head, and I felt like he just wanted me gone. I didn't want to try my luck, so I went back to my space in the shade where I could enjoy the peace and quiet of the Catalan countryside.

When Nick joined me there, he was in good spirits. "Had a good nap?"

I nodded. "Don't let me get used to it. I can't afford to sleep the day away."

"So we didn't keep you awake then?"

"Uh?" I replied, feigning innocence.

"Jamie and I… we didn't really sleep this afternoon." Nick said it with such pride in his voice that I almost wanted to go on teasing him by telling him I had no idea what he was talking about, but Nick and I went back a long way and I knew how proud he was of his sexual prowess, so I didn't have the heart.

"Judging from the noises you wrung out of Jamie, I'd say you've lost none of your old magic."

Nick grinned like the Cheshire cat, but it didn't last long. "I'm feeling my age. He's hard to keep up with sometimes."

"But not today."

"Maybe that had something to do with you," Nick hinted.

I snorted. "Oh, come on. What am I when you have this Greek god walking around your house?"

Nick didn't answer, but I could tell what he was thinking. Having me around spiced up his monogamous life, a life he'd never been accustomed to and maybe hadn't chosen willingly.

"I still think this is doing you a world of good," he said, gaily changing the subject. "If I were you, I'd buy myself a house somewhere nice and go there a few times a year. Doesn't have to be long. Just a week here and there, you know, to recharge the batteries."

"I'm fine," I said, not even convincing myself. "Besides, I'd get bored and just start working."

Before I could stop him, Nick took a grab at my book, turning it over. "That doesn't look like work. You're reading a crime novel. Pure escapism for you. I bet if you keep that up for a few days, you'll return to New York a changed man."

I knew there was some truth in what Nick was saying. I'd only been there for a few hours, and already I felt like some heavy weight had lifted off my shoulders. Although I barely admitted it to myself, I hadn't even checked the airline's website yet, for fear that it would say my flight had been rescheduled and I'd have to leave. I'd even left my cell phone and my laptop upstairs, which was unheard of.

Jamie appeared from the kitchen, carrying a tray. He put it down on the table in front of us and poured us each a glass of sangria from a carafe. He also put down two bowls, one with carved fruit and one with olives. I again noticed there were only two glasses.

"Jamie?" I said to grab his attention. "Get another glass for yourself and come join us. It's lovely out here."

Jamie shook his head.

"Nick and I are just talking. Unless you need help with dinner? I'd love to make myself useful."

Jamie looked at Nick, not for confirmation, but for help, so Nick turned to me. "Jamie might join us later, but for now he's more comfortable inside."

"Fine, then I'll go upstairs and do some work. The last thing I want is for Jamie to feel out of place in his own home." I got up, but as I reached for my book, Nick took my wrist.

"Sit down." He looked at Jamie. "You too. Come sit by me." He draped his arm over the edge of the bench, making a comfortable space for Jamie to sit. Jamie looked at me for a moment, probably to judge whether or not I was too close for him to sit between us, but it was a long bench and I was sitting at the other end of it, tucked into the corner. Jamie sat down and leaned his back against Nick's chest. Nick kissed his hair and wrapped his arm over Jamie's shoulder so his hand could rest on Jamie's chest. They made a beautiful couple, and Jamie seemed to relax somewhat.

"Jamie isn't so much uncomfortable around you, Jez, as he is around me."

I mentally checked whether my mouth had fallen open, because I could tell from Nick's face, my expression must have shown considerable surprise.

"Jamie's worried about what I'm going to talk to you about, since it's probably his least favorite subject."

This was corroborated by Jamie, whose eyes travelled across the wide expanse of the olive groves in the distance.

"Jez, when you called me, I told Jamie this was our opportunity to set a plan in motion that we've been talking about for a while now. He doesn't particularly like it, but we're running out of time."

I didn't catch what Nick was getting at and looked at him, then at Jamie. Jamie's eyes were going watery, which worried me. What plans? Running out of time? What could possibly be so urgent?

Nick continued, but he too stopped looking me in the eye. "I hinted at you buying a property to get away to if things were getting too hectic. Would you consider buying this house? If you do, I can give you a good price."

I shook my head at the turn of events. "Why would I want to buy your house? This isn't a vacation place for you. This is your home. Yours and Jamie's." Then it dawned on me. I was really slow sometimes. "You need money?"

Nick chuckled, but not as if he found something funny. Jamie turned his head so his cheek was resting against Nick's chest, and Nick kissed his hair again. Then Nick looked me in the eyes. "I'd like you to buy this house as an investment, so Jamie will always have this as a home. He'll take good care of you when you come here to rest and recharge your batteries."

"And you? Where will you be? Are you going back to London?" I still didn't get it. Somehow I had the feeling I'd missed some vital piece of information that would allow me to fit the puzzle together. The only clue given to me was a single tear running down Jamie's cheek, one he was quick to wipe away.

"I'm dying, Jez."

Chapter 4

"WHAT?"

Jamie jumped up, shrugging Nick's arm off his shoulders as he determinedly paced into the house. I jumped up along with him.

"Leave him. He'll be okay," Nick said, raising his hand at me. I sat down on the bench again, feeling defeated. "He's known for a long time, but he can't accept it."

"I'm not surprised. Nicky, I...." I didn't know what to say, except, "How long?"

"We found out how sick I was almost two years ago. I had treatment, but they eventually gave me three months to live. That was more than a year ago." Nick's voice was calm, like he had accepted it a long time ago, but to me this was new, and it hit me like a tsunami. Nick, the only man I'd ever come close to loving, was now dying?

"I have lung cancer, Jez. I had surgery, then radiation, then low dose chemo, just to prolong my life. I'm living on borrowed time. Jamie knows it, and I've accepted it." Nick's voice was calm, a lot calmer than I knew I'd be if the shoe were on the other foot. "But Jamie, well... he doesn't know anything about business, or managing money, so even if I leave him my estate, he probably won't be able to live off it. He needs... help."

I nodded, wondering exactly what Nick expected of me. "So you want me to buy this place and manage Jamie's inheritance?" Nick nodded, although I had the feeling this wasn't all he needed me to do.

"He can't even talk to *you*, Jez. How is he going to talk to my banker or even my delivery man? I've organized as much as I could, but there's always going to be unexpected events. Given time, he'll learn to trust you and then he'll talk to you, but he needs to know he's not alone in this."

My mind boggled at the turn of events in the last twenty-four hours. Less than a day ago, Nick was just a distant memory to me, and now I found myself executor of his estate. I needed time to think. "Maybe you should go see if Jamie's okay?"

Nick got up from the bench, and I thought he suddenly looked tired and worn out. Was it simply the fact that I knew how sick he was? Or was it that he'd kept up the façade this morning and now found no more need for it?

As I walked into the kitchen a few minutes later, carrying the tray with the leftover sangria and the olives and fruit we hadn't touched, I caught Nick consoling Jamie under the archway that separated the kitchen from the dining room. Jamie wasn't crying, but he did look distressed, so I decided to find the alternative path to my room instead of disturbing their intimate moment.

Once upstairs, the responsibility Nick was thrusting on me became clearer. If I bought this house, I'd have a house-sitter, but I would need to come here several times a year to make sure the house, and especially Jamie, were all right. This was a lot to take on for a guy who was always jetting around the world and didn't even own a pet because that was too much to be responsible for. And Jamie was more than a pet. Then again, he could feed himself, so maybe he could be left alone for a while.

Just to be sure life outside this little dot on the map of Spain hadn't warped into something else, I opened my laptop and scanned my e-mail. There was no news from the airline and just one message from the office. Clark, my personal assistant, had sent me a short note saying everything was under control and my clients of next week were notified that my visit might have to be postponed. On my cell phone was a message stating that my flight had not yet been rescheduled and they would call me again in the morning.

Maybe Nick was right and I just needed to clear my head. Easier said than done when I'd just found out that the only man I ever gave a damn about was going to die, and I'd wasted years thinking I'd just bump into him again when our paths crossed. Well, they'd certainly crossed now. With very little time left, it seemed.

I knew I wouldn't be able to concentrate on work, so I picked my book up again and went in search of another secluded place where I wouldn't disturb anyone. Near the end of the corridor I found an unused room. A door, locked but with the key on the inside, opened onto a small terrace, and when I walked outside I found a worn wooden chair with an old, empty wine bottle next to it. There were leaves from last fall swept against the side of the house and it was dusty, to say the least. It didn't look like anyone ever came here. When I looked over the edge, I could see the unusually lush, overgrown garden beneath and could get a pretty good idea of how the house was built. It seemed to be the sort of house that had started small and simple, possibly even as a one-story, and then had rooms added onto it.

In the garden below, I saw Jamie swimming in the azure pool.

His movements were slow and deliberate as he swam back and forth. It only took him a few strokes to get across to the other side, but I could tell he was enjoying the coolness of the water on this balmy day. After a little while, pushing himself out of the water and onto dry land in one swift movement and causing a sudden rushing sound of water, Jamie jumped out of the pool and stood tall, stretching himself as rivulets of water ran down his gorgeous body.

I couldn't have looked away if I'd tried.

Jamie could have been a model, with long legs and narrow hips, a washboard stomach and shoulders that broadened considerably near the top. He was wearing every man's dream: a red Speedo that left nothing to the imagination.

Even from my perch, high up the villa, I could see Nick's boasting that he was a size queen was not just said in jest. Jamie looked like he was built to be in porn. Maybe that's where Nick found him? I knew Nick still worked in his old industry. Although he no longer performed and his own website had long ago shut down, I knew from the Internet research I'd done before coming here that he recruited and occasionally directed for one of his old employers. In that world, Jamie's considerable shyness and seeming inability to talk to strangers wouldn't be much of a hindrance. Porn actors with substantial assets were rarely employed for their ability to deliver lines.

Jamie ran his hands over his short-cropped hair and pressed the excess water out of it before walking to where Nick was resting on a lounge chair. Nick held out a towel to Jamie and Jamie grabbed it before leaning over Nick to kiss him. Just before Jamie obscured my view, Nick smiled at his young lover.

The sight was sickeningly sweet and at the same time, I was sort of jealous. I'd never been a one-man guy, but there was no mistaking the fact that Jamie made Nick very happy, and Nick wasn't a believer in monogamy either.

As I watched their exchange, I was almost ashamed to wonder how Nick's illness panned out for them in bed. Jamie was young and beautiful. Surely he wanted a man who could treat him right in bed. I'd heard their exchange earlier today, but how often was Nick able to indulge in that with his young man? I shook my head. I knew firsthand what Nick used to be able to do in the sack, and that was definitely worth something at the time, even outside of a porn set. I was sure Nick would have some tricks up his sleeve, but I couldn't imagine a young, healthy gay man settling for cuddling and kissing. Then again, what I'd heard earlier was definitely more than a little heavy petting.

I tried to return to my book, but Jamie's display as he dried off and then wrapped himself in the towel to snuggle into Nick's embrace made me feel horny and uncomfortable at the same time.

I WAS called down to dinner by Nick as the sun was setting, and this time Jamie joined us to eat a simple dinner of Spanish omelet and mixed salad, accompanied by the ever-present glass of Rioja, although I noticed Jamie drank water. Jamie still didn't speak, but as Nick and I never seemed to run out of things to say, it wasn't a problem. It was strange for me to see Nick so attentive to Jamie, especially since Jamie acted like Nick's servant, anticipating his needs and almost attending to them before Nick could want for anything. Although that evening we didn't talk about Nick being ill, I accounted for Jamie's behavior in that context. I was a little unsettled by the unspoken tension, but I couldn't help being touched by Jamie's plight as I couldn't imagine what it must be like to be so devoted to a partner you know might not be with you anymore in the near future.

I didn't sleep well that night, although the bed was comfortable and my constant travels generally made me used to diverse sleeping conditions. The house was quiet, though, and as I woke up early the next morning and walked to my secret vista point on the unused terrace, I spotted Jamie already at work in the garden. The temperature was rising quickly and by the time I'd taken my book out he'd taken his T-shirt off and was on his knees weeding. I put on my rarely used glasses to see the beads of sweat roll down his suntanned back. Needless to say, I barely read a paragraph in my crime novel and jacked off in the shower to images of Jamie before going down to breakfast.

Life around the house was slow and low-key, and I was surprised how quickly I adapted to it. After breakfast, Nick drove us into town, where we bought some bread and simply walked around for a short stroll, then had a coffee at what seemed like the only café in the sleepy place that hadn't been discovered by tourists yet. We talked about unimportant stuff, clearly avoiding the tough subject of Nick's impending death. Then again, although Nick was substantially less muscled than he used to be, he didn't look like he was about to drop dead, so I didn't want to treat him like that.

After lunch, Nick took a nap on his lounge chair and when he woke, he called me into his office, which was the only messy room I'd seen in the entire house.

"Sorry for this," Nick apologized. "Jamie takes care of the house, but he doesn't come in here. Which is obvious." He moved a pile of papers from a chair so I had someplace to sit before powering up his computer. "I wanted to show you a few things about my finances," he said casually.

The tension in the room doubled instantly.

"Jamie will inherit the lot," Nick continued, as if he hadn't noticed. "We got legally married, not because we absolutely wanted to, but because I wanted him to be provided for in case anything should happen. Less than a year later, I got sick, so you can imagine I was glad that was out of the way. You'll need to keep an eye on the money, though."

I shook my head in disbelief. "Nick, you haven't seen me in what, eight years?"

Nick took my hand, which I'd laid casually on a stack of paper. "Like I said, Jamie isn't interested in all this." He sighed. "He doesn't have a head for figures. He'd be duped out of money within a week if I let all my well-meaning advisors step in."

"And what makes you think I'd be any better than them?"

"Because you have no financial stake in this. You have your own money, so no need to benefit from my inheritance, even indirectly. And you're loyal."

I raised an eyebrow. "What makes you think that?"

"You're in an extremely high-powered business, where it's dog-eat-dog. You steal people away from multinationals to put them in other high-octane jobs, yet you've worked for the same company for how long? Fifteen years?"

I nodded. Of course Nick was right. "You don't know what it's like, Nicky. They have my balls in a vise."

Nick laughed. "So that's why you like it there? Torture is one of the on-the-job perks?"

"You know me too well." If they knew just how well, even the best employer in the world could easily fire me. Luckily they didn't know that in my younger years, I'd starred in a series of Nick's videos, catering to the leather crowd. That was where our trust had been cemented. We were occasional lovers at the time, and Nick had finagled to bring his own whipping boy to the shoot. Afraid to be exposed, I was fitted with a leather hood, which was never taken off. The type of video didn't require me to do more than be subjected to Nick's "torture," tied up, whipped by Nick's bare hands or with paddles, and fucked roughly. I wasn't supposed to display emotions other than grunting or crying out, and there wasn't even a need for me to come, which I couldn't have anyway. Nick had even arranged for a guy to give me a good fucking afterward, since even the best porn star couldn't perform anymore after six hours of keeping it up for the shoot, but I'd always declined, preferring to wait for the real thing. Invariably, Nick would get horny again a day or two later and thoroughly reward me then. Those were fond memories, but not something I could ever share with anyone but Nick.

I sighed deeply. "Okay, show me where everything is."

Chapter 5

ON MY third day at the house, I called my New York office and officially asked them to reschedule my meetings for the next week. There were rumors that the airlines were getting ready to start flying again, but I'd barely checked my e-mail, let alone done research on the company I was supposed to visit, and I knew my heart wasn't in it. I wasn't yet ready to tell them to send a replacement, but the mere fact that I'd entertained the idea told me that for the first time in fifteen years, I'd finally found something more pressing to do than work.

No doubt the company I was keeping had something to do with that. Despite their physical and emotional closeness and the passing of time that for the first time in my life felt excruciatingly fast, Nick and Jamie had found a way of no longer making me feel like the fifth wheel on the wagon.

Jamie still didn't speak to me, but he looked less troubled or shocked when I spoke to him directly, and he had an uncanny way of communicating with his surroundings; one I, as a lifelong student of non-verbal communication, was endlessly fascinated with. Under the guise of offering to help Jamie around the house, I found myself seeking out his company whenever Nick was taking a nap. He always declined with a barely there smile, but tolerated my presence nevertheless. Occasionally I'd refill the bottle of water he took everywhere, just to see him smile at me when I handed it back to him, and one time he drank from it right away, turning me on with the bobbing of his Adam's apple.

One morning, Jamie accepted my offer of help when he was changing the sheets on the bed he shared with Nick. I'd never been inside their room, but just like every other room of the house except Nick's office, it was light and airy, and exceptionally clean and clutter free.

I was therefore a little surprised when, as we ripped the dirty sheets off the bed, a well-shaped, ivory-colored dildo sprang from under one of the pillows. Jamie was quick to hide it, and despite my pretending not to have seen it, he blushed profusely. If he'd just gone about his business, I would have been able to go on pretending, but he remained frozen, as if he was afraid of my reaction.

Moving around to his side of the bed to add my empty pillowcases to his pile of laundry, I tried to put him at ease. "It's okay, Jamie. We're all gay men here. I stopped taking my toys with me on long-haul flights after airport security made me unpack a suitcase once. It's embarrassing around strangers, but we're friends, right? And I won't tell anyone."

When he looked up at me, I couldn't help meeting his gorgeous aqua-blue eyes. As he moved closer, I didn't step back, although my instincts told me he was entering my personal space. To my considerable surprise he grabbed me, one hand on the back of my neck and one on the small of my back. I froze, but he thawed me with a kiss. It was so unexpected; I didn't know how to react. For a moment I didn't, but then he opened his mouth and I just had to kiss him back. He still tasted of the herbs from the white cheese he'd put on his breakfast toast and he smelled like a man should: clean, with just a hint of musk. He ground his body against mine and I could feel he was as hard as I was. My hands, which had remained limply by my side until now, moved of their own accord to his sides, which felt every bit as lean and muscled as I'd expected. For an instant I wanted to push him on the bed and have my way with him, and then my guilty conscience took over.

This was my best friend's man, my dying best friend's lover, and I was kissing and groping him. It didn't matter that Jamie had been the one to take the initiative. All that mattered was that I wanted Jamie so much I would have betrayed Nick for it.

So I pushed Jamie away. We were both panting. I could see Jamie's erection through the loose jogging pants he was wearing and I could feel the heaviness in my own, knowing we'd come *this* close to bringing each other off, *this* close to crossing the line. And in the bedroom he'd shared, for God knows how long, with Nick.

I moved to the other side of the bed again, determined to help Jamie finish making it, but Jamie simply stood there and I fled. When I got to my own room, I started packing, but stopped myself when I realized I'd have to explain to Nick why I was leaving so suddenly while Nick knew perfectly well I'd already called my office to extend my absence. I couldn't justify telling Nick a lie, but there was no way I could tell him the truth, so I decided to stay and keep my distance from Jamie.

Later that afternoon, from my perch on the now no longer unused terrace, I saw Jamie putter around in the garden, pulling out weeds and clearing the path, while Nick took a nap on the reclining chair just next to the rain barrel. A little bit later, they were both on the patio.

Nick was lying on the recliner, his long limbs even more elegant now he was less muscled than in his porn days. His once gorgeously flawless face was marked with lines that gave him character and framed by a nicely trimmed, almost white, full beard. His hair was equally devoid of color, but it still had its seductive wave which, despite the potential to look feminine, didn't do anything to dispel Nick masculinity.

Jamie was sitting on the side of the recliner, facing Nick. I couldn't see Jamie's face, only Nick's tender loving gaze at the younger man. As Nick stroked Jamie's forearm, it struck me how much love I could feel from the gentle exchange. It felt strange to remember how shamelessly Jamie had seduced me earlier, and I tried to make sense of my conflicting emotions. Nick was speaking in hushed tones, so I couldn't hear what was being said, and as far as I could tell Jamie only nodded or shook his head. Then Jamie lay down beside Nick, who pulled the young man closer, his hand caressing Jamie's short-cropped hair. There was a faint smile on Jamie's face and when he closed his eyes, he seemed blissfully happy. Nick kissed the top of Jamie's head and then looked straight at me. Nick was smiling and I felt caught, so I scooted back into my chair, depriving myself of the peaceful view below. I was startled by my own rush of emotions.

Why was I letting my heart influence me now? How much did I really know about the relationship Nick and Jamie shared? Were they even exclusive? I remembered Nick once telling me that the sheer mention of monogamy made him run for the hills. That he'd always wanted a relationship, but it was hard to find a man who could cope with the fact that Nick would always have sex with other men. On *and* off camera. Nick had often lamented to me that he craved a true emotional connection with another man, but that it wouldn't and couldn't include physical monogamy. But that was eight years ago, and at the time Nick was a virtual god, powerful and immortal. Now he was confronted with his own mortality, which had undoubtedly changed his perspective somewhat.

The conversation I'd had with Nick hit home now. How was Jamie, painfully shy and selectively mute, ever going to survive without Nick? Jamie never left the secluded villa as far as I could tell. Although I had gone out for drinks and the occasional stroll with Nick, Jamie never joined us. Groceries were delivered, and even the occasional letter was taken back to the post office by the local mailman. Whenever we went into town for groceries, it seemed almost more an excuse to get out of the house than a necessity. And I still hadn't been able to coax as much as a few mumbled words out of Jamie, although I knew from that first afternoon that he could talk.

Could I take care of Jamie? I peered over the edge of the terrace down at the lovers. They were lying together peacefully, seemingly asleep if it weren't for Nick's hand slowly caressing Jamie's back.

Life simply wasn't fair. Nick had done everything to screw up his life, including a risky and no-holds-barred lifestyle, yet he'd found a totally devoted young lover, or at least that's what he pretended to be in Nick's presence. The idea that Nick was simply handing Jamie over to the first man who came knocking made the bile rise in my throat quite unexpectedly. Jamie wasn't a favorite pet you found a new home for. He was a man who had to be allowed to make his own choices. My mixed feelings about the whole affair confused me to no end. On the one hand I understood Nick wanting to put his affairs in order, and I "got" that he wanted someone to keep an eye on Jamie, but surely Jamie should be the one to choose? Or was that what Jamie had done by kissing me?

I knew I'd have to find a way to coax Nick into telling me exactly how he saw this business of taking care of Jamie and could only hope I wouldn't need to bring up the pass Jamie had made at me.

To my surprise, Nick took me out to dinner at a local restaurant later that night. Jamie didn't join us, and though all through the evening I tried to bring the subject of Jamie up, Nick either ignored it or changed the subject outright, telling me we were there for my sake so we could get reacquainted. Nick almost seemed happy for the distraction when we were approached by a short, tubby man with dark, curly hair he introduced to me as Pablo Quintana. He turned out to be the man who'd made all the delicious Rioja we regularly consumed at the house. Pablo extended an invitation to visit the vineyard, and I made a point of congratulating him on his vintage, at the same time explaining that I wouldn't be staying long enough to drop by. He was graceful and left us alone to eat.

When Nick continued redirecting the conversation whenever it came to Jamie, I started to feel very uncomfortable, as if I was being played, but I couldn't for the life of me get to the bottom of it.

After midnight, I was still lying awake when there was a knock on my door. Figuring it was Nick, I got out of bed and put on my boxers before letting him in. To my surprise, it was Jamie, dressed in boxers and a T-shirt.

Chapter 6

"WHAT are you doing here?" I asked blankly, knowing pretty much Jamie wouldn't answer me.

Instead he pushed the door completely open and stepped inside. I didn't know how to react, and then he kissed me again. It still felt amazing, but now the guilt was there immediately.

"We can't do this, Jamie." I pulled away from him.

Jamie didn't reply. Instead he looked toward the hallway and closed the door. I reached to open it again, afraid it would create unwanted intimacy, but he stopped me.

"We can't do this to Nick."

Jamie nodded as if he wanted to tell me that "yes, we could."

"Nick loves you. He's devoted to you, Jamie. He asked me to take care of you after his death."

Jamie's eyes went watery, but he didn't cry. Instead, he nodded again.

And then something clicked. "Does Nick know you're here?"

Again the nod.

If Nick knew, then…. Jamie slowly closed his eyes and all I could do was wrap my arms around him. There was nothing sexual about our embrace this time. He hugged me back and we stood there consoling each other, and Jamie put his head on my shoulder. After a while we sat down on the bed and he took my hand.

"You love him, don't you?"

Jamie nodded, wiping his face with his hand.

"I love him too, Jamie. I'd do just about anything for him. Up until eight years ago, we had a pretty intense friendship, and as you know it was a friendship with benefits, but then he disappeared. He even stopped making movies. It was as if he'd gone underground. I never knew what happened, but I figured we'd sort of drift into each other's space again somehow, like we had on and off for years."

Jamie looked up and pointed at his own chest.

I narrowed my eyes. "You? You happened? Is that when you met Nick?"

Jamie nodded, and he was smiling just a little.

"Wow, you've been together for eight years?" I could swear Jamie looked proud. "And he gave up performing for you. He always said it would be hard to sustain a relationship as long as he was working in front of the camera."

Jamie put his head on my shoulder again and then shivered. I wanted to drag him under the bedcovers with me, but I figured we'd end up doing something we'd regret, so I opted for putting my arm around him instead. He turned in my embrace and kissed me again. The friendly, casual air was immediately cranked up to red hot as he straddled me and ground himself against my body. For a few seconds I gave in, simply because he made lust boil up in me just as he had when he was outside weeding his garden, but I knew I had to stop this sooner rather than later. Jamie was a strong man, though, not that I'd ever doubted that.

"Jamie. Jamie, please. Please stop." I admit I didn't struggle too powerfully, but I didn't lead him on any more than I already had and eventually, he gave up and got off my lap.

"Go back to your own room, Jamie. Snuggle up to Nick and make love to him. He's your lover. He's the one who should get this from you."

I could see Jamie's disappointment. After all, he was nothing if not expressive, but I couldn't let myself feel it. I would simply not be able to live with myself. Even if what Jamie had told me was true. Even if Nick knew Jamie was here seducing me, I still couldn't bring myself to go through with it.

After Jamie left, I closed my door and tried to sleep. It wasn't easy. Even jacking off to relax wasn't without its struggles because all I could see when I let my imagination run wild was Jamie in the throes of ecstasy and me bringing him there.

THE next morning, after a fitful sleep, I found Nick in the garden, having breakfast all by himself. Jamie was nowhere to be found

"Nick, what is this?" I hissed.

Nick smiled and took a small bite from his toast and marmalade. "What?"

"Don't act all innocent with me."

Nick shook his head, maintaining he didn't know what I was talking about.

"Jamie told me you made him come to my room to seduce me."

"It didn't take a lot of persuading, Jez." There wasn't even a hint of repentance in his voice.

"But you made him do it?"

Nick threw me a look that I could only read as pity. How dare he give me one of his condescending, oh so British stares? "What kind of pervert are you? Sending your innocent, shy, reticent *lover* over to another man's bed."

"Jamie likes you. All he wanted was my consent and I gave it to him. And he's *not* innocent, darling."

"I'm disgusted by you."

"Why, Jeremy? Because you lust after Jamie, and you can't understand why I'd willingly share him?" Nick laughed out loud, the sort of belly laugh I remembered from much more carefree times.

"I don't *lust* after him."

Nick shook his head. "You're an open book, Jez. I see how you look at him when you think I don't notice. I've seen you up on your perch, looking down at Jamie weeding the garden, and I've seen you eyeing his arse. You want to nail him so badly, I can almost taste it."

"I don't," I hissed between clenched teeth. "The days when we shared men are long gone."

"Good days, though."

I gave him the death stare. Even if it was true, it didn't mean I had to admit it. How would I feel if I found Nick eyeing my lover with a lustful eye? I'd be green with envy. Not that I had a lover, or knew firsthand what it was like to feel jealousy, but I could imagine it.

Nick put his hand over mine. "Jamie deserves a lover who can give him everything. I can barely get it up these days. He's only got half a lover and even then, only if I'm not too tired."

So I was Nick's substitute? A cock for Jamie? "Doesn't Jamie get a say in this?" *Or me. How about my feelings in all this?*

Nick laughed. "He may seem docile and easygoing, but I've never been able to make Jamie do anything he didn't want to do. And that includes *ordering* him to sleep with you."

When I didn't respond, Nick threw me another one of his compassionate smiles. I could almost smell the condescension.

"He may take instruction exceptionally well, but he's no pushover, and even if he was, I'd never do anything to harm him. You see, in some ways he's a total innocent. He doesn't grasp the concept of fidelity, but he does know loyalty. He wanted to sleep with you and doesn't understand that it could make me jealous, but he does know that he'd never do it without my permission."

"All the more reason for him to seduce me simply because you suggested it," I was quick to reply. "He's loyal to you, so if you ask him to come to my bed and suck me off, he'll do it, simply because you asked him. No wonder he looked so hurt when I told him to stop. It wasn't because I rejected him, but because he would have to go back to your bed and tell you he'd failed."

Nick's eyebrows rose up. "He told me you didn't have a lot of stamina. That you came very quickly."

Now it was my turn to look surprised. "You mean the little shit lied to you?"

"He's not such a little shit, Jezzie. I'm nothing if not a size queen."

"But he lied to you!" As soon as the words left my mouth, I felt like a twelve-year-old again and Nick chuckled. Judging from his expression, he knew what I was thinking about too. Sometimes I felt Nick and I went back too far. It made me relax, though.

"He's proud, Jez, despite appearances. Guess he didn't want to admit he'd been unable to pierce your armor."

"And you're fine with that?"

"There are more important things in life than little white lies. He came back to our bed and slept next to me. I got to wake up next to a beautiful warm body with a big, hard cock, an eager mouth, and a delightful arse. What more could a man possibly want?"

"You haven't changed one bit, have you?"

Nick shook his head, delight sparkling in his eyes. "Just because the equipment malfunctions more than I care for, doesn't mean I can't still enjoy him. But I know he wants to be thoroughly fucked again. By a hard cock, not a few fingers or a dildo." Nick looked at me from under his floppy white hair. "And you're the only man I know who can do that and will allow me to watch."

I rolled my eyes, but I had to admit my anger had abated. "You could pay a guy to come in and perform for the two of you. He'd let you watch as long as you forked out the cash."

Nick's face grew serious. "Jamie needs trust. I won't let a stranger fuck him. That's what I rescued him from, and I promised him I'd never let another guy fuck him without his consent."

"Oh, as if I'm a friend of the family's."

"Listen, Jez. I didn't suggest you to Jamie. He knows about our history and he knows I trust you, but that didn't have to mean he'd trust you too. But he does. I told you. He's the one who suggested he try to seduce you to see if you'd want to fuck him."

"And you agreed with him? You think it's normal that he just seeks out other men because he can't get from you want he thinks he needs?" My righteous indignation shone through, I'm sure. "Is that what you think love is?"

Nick chuckled and threw me a thoughtful look. Was he thinking about what I'd said? Or just pretending to? He may only have acted in porn, but I always thought he was the finest actor in that business. "You're a fine one to talk about love, Jez. You never wanted it. For the longest time I thought you had a problem with my job, but after a while I realized you just couldn't stomach the idea of commitment. This is commitment too, Jez. My commitment to making Jamie happy is that I let him find his own way. He trusts you, although I've told him you'd rather run than take care of another person. He wanted to see if he could force a connection. For him, this connection runs through the bedroom. He's not hindered by his shyness there, because he knows what he can do to another man. He wants to see if he can trust you enough to let you take control of him, and at the same time he wants to see if he can make you do to him what he wants."

I felt my cock stir at the idea of Jamie wantonly seducing me to go all the way. I just couldn't reconcile the idea with the obvious love, affection, and dedication Nick and Jamie shared. Although I was certainly no expert on relationships, or particularly interested in a monogamous relationship for myself, what Nick and Jamie had bordered on my ideal of a dedicated, monogamous partnership. But how did Jamie wanting to sleep with another man and Nick's unquestioning permission for Jamie to do this figure into this ideal? "Doesn't it bother you to think of Jamie with someone else?"

"Christ, Jez, you're not just someone. I've known you for ages. I gave you your first decent blowjob. I fucked you God knows how many times. Of course I trust you with Jamie. Does it bother me? Well, I'd prefer it if I could do it and I probably wouldn't let you if I could keep up with him, but I can't, and he deserves more than I can give him. Okay, so maybe it bothers me enough to want to be there when you do it, but if Jamie doesn't want me there, I'll be fine with that too. Because I know he'll always come back to me." Although Nick's voice was calm, I could see him getting worked up and his rant ended with a coughing fit, one for which I got up out of my chair so I could rub Nick's shoulder blades like I'd seen Jamie do a few time. When Nick's breathing finally calmed down, I looked in the direction of the kitchen and saw Jamie standing in the doorway, one hand holding the screen door open. When he noticed he'd been caught, Jamie stepped back quickly and let the door fall shut.

"Go see that he's all right," Nick said, pointing at the door.

I hesitated for a moment, feeling like I could do more for Nick than for Jamie, but I saw the determined and worried look in Nick's eyes and decided I could go after Jamie and bring him out to see Nick if he didn't want to listen. "You'll be okay?"

"Yeah, yeah, I'm not dead yet."

The kitchen was dark compared to the sun in the garden, and I had to wait for my eyes to adjust. Jamie wasn't there, so I walked through the house in search of him. It took me some time to find Jamie in the last place I looked: the upstairs bathroom. He was on his knees, wearing bright purple rubber gloves and scrubbing the bathtub.

"There you are," I said in as soft a voice as I could manage. "Nick was worried about you."

Jamie didn't let on he'd heard. He continued vigorously scrubbing the already pristine surface of the large tub.

"He asked me to come get you."

This time Jamie nodded, but he didn't stop working. When I put my hand on Jamie's shoulder, he froze for a moment before continuing, so I pulled my hand back.

"It's clean enough, Jamie. You always keep this place spick-and-span. Come downstairs with me. Everything will be okay, you'll see." Why I felt the need to reassure Jamie as if he was a child was beyond me, but I wanted to protect Jamie from harm and seeing Nick riled up so much he ended up in a coughing fit obviously upset Jamie too. Jamie didn't answer me, though. The only sound was of his scrub brush rubbing across the surface of the white tub. I eventually left Jamie alone and went back downstairs where Nick was still on the recliner, enjoying the evening sun with his eyes closed and his breathing back to normal.

"He won't come down," I said.

Nick opened his eyes. "Was he scrubbing the bath? I told him he's going to scrub right through the glaze one day." Nick sighed. "That's what he does when he's upset. He cleans. Is it any wonder you can eat off the floors in this house?"

I smiled. "There are worse things than obsessive cleaning. He could have gone upstairs and trashed a room."

"Oh no, that's not Jamie. Sometimes I think he's as emotionally unstable as his mother was, but he learned to suppress it, because if he got carried away as well, she'd be worse than normal. So he learned to control himself. He learned to cope."

"By cleaning?"

"He couldn't run away because she was too paranoid to keep the door unlocked and she didn't clean, apparently. I don't know. I don't think he's told me all that went on in the House of Horrors."

"I'm surprised you know that much. You have actual conversations?"

Nick laughed, almost sending him back into a coughing fit. His breathing was labored enough that it stopped me from asking more about Jamie's past, although I wanted to know everything Nick knew. Instead, I focused on Nick, hoping the chance to talk about it would present itself again sometime soon. With my soothing hand on his shoulder, Nick's breathing quickly turned calmer again, and we continued the friendly banter as if it'd never turned serious at all. "Do you really think he's just a pretty piece of arse for me? That wouldn't leave much now I can't fuck him anymore, would it?"

"I figured you just liked the care he bestows on you. You always were a sucker for attention."

"And I never fell for a nice piece of arse attached to a moron, Jez. At least give me that."

I nodded with a smile.

"That's why I always had a soft spot for you. You could talk me under the table."

"Or wrestle you under it," I added.

"That too. Don't underestimate Jamie's strength either. He's had to support me more than once when I was sick."

We both looked in the direction of the kitchen when we heard pots clanging and cupboards opening and closing.

"We're having mushroom risotto tonight. I better go see if Jamie needs any help." Nick got up with some difficulty but resisted my offered arm. "Can you set the table out here? Looks like a lovely evening."

"Sure." I watched Nick walk inside and, through the kitchen door, saw him wrap his arms around Jamie from behind. As I walked into the living room to retrieve the plates and cutlery, I couldn't help overhearing Nick's voice.

"I'm fine, sweetheart. And you know you can trust Jez."

"He's okay," Jamie replied in the same sexy, low voice I'd heard that first day.

"He's kind and sort of a gentle giant. He's strong but not afraid of showing his softer side. He's like me in that way."

Jamie smiled and although I could only just make out his expression, it warmed me up from head to toe.

"I don't see you bending over for anyone, Nicky. Not even now that you can't fuck me anymore. That means he bottomed for you. Repeatedly."

"And what an amazing bottom he was. But not like you, darling. Nobody does it quite like you."

They kissed in what looked like a strange mix of tenderness and passion. I couldn't help but stare at the grinding motions of Jamie's groin against Nick's lean body as Jamie tried to get as close as he could to Nick, and at Nick's hands groping Jamie's buttocks. I wasn't sure I could resist the next time Jamie was offered to me. I made my way out to the patio again, willing my erection to subside. When I walked back inside, the men were laughing.

"I'm never letting you in my kitchen again," Jamie was saying. "Every time you come in here, I burn something." The pan ended up in the sink with a clang. "Now I need to start all over again. Luckily we didn't ruin the mushrooms yet." There was more amusement than anger in Jamie's voice, but I couldn't get enough of the sexy rasp and surprising darkness of the otherwise mute young man. I could only hope that one day Jamie would be able to talk to me like that too.

Chapter 7

ABOUT twenty minutes later, Jamie and Nick joined me at the table outside. The risotto was perfect and Jamie was quiet again. All during the animated conversation with Nick, I couldn't stop looking at Jamie. I knew I couldn't let my eyes linger too long because Jamie often looked uncomfortable if he spotted me gazing his way, but most of the time I couldn't resist either, especially when Nick looked at his young lover. By the end of the evening, Nick had consumed one glass of wine and Jamie and I had shared the rest of three bottles of red.

I felt comfortably buzzed as I undressed in my room and was just slipping under the blankets when Jamie entered without knocking. The only light still on was the lamp at my side of the bed, but it was enough to see Jamie was only wearing a short bathrobe. This was the second time Jamie had entered my room like that, and I was no longer surprised or standoffish, thanks to my earlier conversation with Nick. I'd never been adverse to one-night stands, and if Nick was right and Jamie only wanted a thorough fucking, I could give that to him.

When Jamie opened his robe, I feasted my eyes for the first time and saw that Nick hadn't boasted. Even flaccid, Jamie's cock was long, beautiful, and perfectly formed. His pubic hair was neatly trimmed.

"Does Nick know you're here?"

Jamie nodded.

"Is he asleep?"

Jamie nodded again.

I held out my hand, inviting Jamie into the bed. He walked closer and took the offered hand, but instead of following it, he pulled me to him.

"You want me to fuck you?" I asked, resisting getting up.

Jamie shook his head.

"What then?"

Jamie pulled on my hand again until I complied and got out of bed. We were about the same height, and I pulled Jamie toward me to try and kiss him, but Jamie pulled away.

"Too intimate?" I asked. "Is kissing only for Nick all of a sudden?"

Jamie shrugged, smiling teasingly.

"Okay," I replied softly, intrigued by the rules changing. "Tell me what you want, then."

Jamie kept eye contact as he sank to his knees and took my flaccid cock in his mouth. It grew heavy so fast I almost felt dizzy. I watched Jamie take me deep and tried to keep some semblance of control as Jamie broke eye contact and continued to lavish himself on my now fully erect cock.

"If you want to get fucked you better stop now, Jamie." My voice was unsteady, but Jamie didn't relent. "Jamie? Stop, please." I gently rubbed my hand over the soft bristles of Jamie's short hair.

Instead of stopping, Jamie looked up at me. He took my free hand and placed it on his head as well, then resumed sucking me off.

"You want me to fuck your mouth?" I asked with a slight tremor in my voice. I felt a curious mix of emotions running through me. On the one hand, I wanted to do it. Nick, who rarely took a passive role when it came to sex, had taught me how gloriously liberating it was to fuck someone's eager mouth, and to my surprise he'd been the owner of that eager mouth. My problem with Jamie was that I didn't know him well enough to be able to gauge how much he could take.

Jamie nodded eagerly.

I looked down over Jamie's curved back to his ass and the hand with which he appeared to be fingering himself. "Wouldn't you prefer a good fucking?"

Jamie shook his head "No."

I pushed forward slightly until I thought I'd just about reached the back of Jamie's throat, but Jamie didn't gag. "Have you been practicing this with Nick?"

Jamie swallowed around my cock before nodding affirmative.

I pulled out and pushed in again, a little faster this time. Again, Jamie didn't gag; in fact, he moved forward, meeting me halfway. I lifted my hand. "I won't hold your head. I want you to be able to pull away."

Jamie shook his head just a little and used one of his hands to fix mine to his head. Although he hadn't said a word, Jamie's pleading look told me what I needed to know. Jamie actually wanted to be restrained. He wanted his mouth fucked until saliva was dripping from it and his eyes were bloodshot. I vowed to myself I'd stay in control, that I'd try to judge how far I could go with Jamie, how much he could take.

Jamie slowly let go of my hand and brought his hands back down, one behind him, one in front. Although I couldn't see either, I could imagine that Jamie would be jacking himself off and fingering his hole. I knew that's what I'd do and had done on the occasions when Nick had shown me how good it was to be in Jamie's position. There was no doubt in my mind that Nick had also instructed Jamie. The thought alone made my cock fill up even more. As I started slowly fucking Jamie's mouth, I could see Jamie undulating at the same rhythm. Jamie's mouth was hot and wet and he urged me on to make me speed up. He was looking up at me and moaning around the welcome invasion, and I tried hard not to let my body take over.

Control. I had to stay in control.

As I pulled back I saw a glimpse of Jamie's erection, hard, glistening, and pointing straight up. The head was dark and purple, and Jamie was cupping his sac rather than fisting himself, pushing the inside of his wrist against his belly, trapping his ample cock. There was no doubt in my mind that Jamie was enjoying this. "Fuck, Jamie," I mumbled.

Jamie's response was a moan that fanned out from my cock to my shoulders and knees and made my breathing quicken. My groin thrust forward, almost out of reflex, and Jamie started gagging. Instead of pulling against my hands, Jamie pushed forward. I saw tears streaming down his cheeks as his body resisted the invasion even more than before and saliva started gathering at the edges of his mouth. Just when I let go of Jamie's head, Jamie convulsed, shooting ribbons of cum all over his hand and belly. Almost immediately Jamie latched onto my cock again, raising his hand to smear his release all over my erection and taking it into his mouth again where I lost it, thrusting deeper as I came down Jamie's throat.

I'd lost control. I'd promised myself I wouldn't but I did anyway.

I sank down to my knees and took Jamie in my arms. I cradled the young man and caressed his hair. Jamie was still in ecstasy, his body shaking in my arms. I tried to look him in the eye, but it wasn't until Jamie looked up at me that I saw he was actually laughing. "This what you wanted then?" I asked, unable to contain a smile.

Jamie nodded, erasing any lingering doubt from my mind. Jamie led my hand to the crease of his ass.

"Fucking hell, you're plugged up. No wonder you came so hard."

Jamie launched himself at my mouth and kissed me as if he wanted to return my cum to me. I didn't resist, just like I let Jamie lead my hand to push against the plug. Although it was hard to think clearly, it was no real surprise to feel Jamie coming again as our combined movements sped up.

"You youngsters," I murmured. We were both sweaty and sticky, but I didn't want to let go of Jamie just yet, so we continued to kiss and cuddle in front of the bed. "I thought kissing was only for Nick?"

Jamie smiled enigmatically and promptly launched himself at me again. I had to admit I enjoyed it, but I needed to get more comfortable, even if that meant Jamie was probably going back to Nick's bed. I pulled back and got up while I helped Jamie off the floor as well.

"Don't look at me that way," I said, seeing Jamie's disappointed look. "Come take a shower with me. I can't let you return to Nick smelling of sex and spunk."

We continued kissing under the spray of the walk-in shower, and Jamie made a show of dislodging the butt plug in full view. I knelt down to get a better look and couldn't resist kissing the birthmark on his left buttock. It looked like a lopsided star, and he laughed when I nipped at it. All through the shower he was playful and flirty and ever kissing me, but I could tell his shyness was returning. I wondered when it would start feeling awkward again.

After drying each other off, I got back into bed. Jamie seemed to hesitate as he made up his mind, but eventually crawled under the covers with me.

"Don't you have to get back to Nick?"

Jamie shook his head and burrowed deeper, his cheek resting on my chest. He was asleep almost immediately, but I couldn't stop my mind. Should I wake Jamie up to go back to Nick's room? Had Nick instructed him to stay over? I had to admit Jamie was totally my type, at least physically. He wasn't as tall as Nick, but had a nice tight body, with muscles that showed he used the weight room in the attic. His round face harbored small but bright eyes, and his short-cropped hair betrayed not even the hint of a bald patch over his crown. Jamie had a widow's peak that intrigued me, and I loved rubbing my hand over his soft hair, not in the least because I expected him to start purring with delight. For now, the silent Jamie just leaned into the touch, even as he slept.

My feelings for Jamie were part fatherly/brotherly protectiveness and part animalistic lust. Although I'd been a part of the leather scene only because I had the perfect look for it and not because I liked dominating other men, Jamie's almost total surrender to me made my dormant inner Dom growl with delight. Jamie trusted me. Jamie wanted this. Only briefly did I entertain the idea that the only reason Jamie did these things with me was because Nick had instructed him to do them. I tried to forget that maybe Jamie wasn't submitting to me but to Nick.

Chapter 8

WHEN I woke up in the morning, I was alone in bed. I didn't mind. For a one-night stand sort of guy, this was business as usual, and I preferred guys not to stay for breakfast anyway. In this case, I could only hope that Jamie had slipped away in the middle of the night to continue sleeping in Nick's arms, where he belonged.

When I made my way downstairs, it was eerily quiet, so when I walked into the garden thinking I'd be alone there, I jumped when I heard Nick's voice calling my name.

"Ooh, I love a guilty conscience," Nick said with a broad smile as he watched me catching my breath. "No need to feel guilty. I got the play-by-play from Jamie this morning. Of course, after last time, I don't know how much of it was true, but he'd clearly enjoyed himself."

It was strange for me to feel shy about my sexual exploits, especially around Nick. We'd shared men before, had played tag for a willing bottom who could easily accommodate two, or had sent men to each other after we were done with them. This was different, though. This was Nick's lover of eight years, the man he'd left the porn business for, the man he clearly had an almost symbiotic relationship with.

"He was plugged up. Horny as shit," I eventually said. Even the memory made my cock fill up again. "I thought he wanted to be fucked, but... well, he wanted to be fucked all right. He wanted me in his mouth. He surrendered to me, Nick." God, when did this happen? I couldn't even look Nick in the eye.

"I remember making you do that to me. And you know I don't give up control easily. I must have told Jamie at one time how amazing it was to have you fuck my mouth." When I looked at Nick, he had a faraway look in his eyes, as if he was remembering something good.

"In fact I'm sure I must have, because he asked me to teach him. Had to get him over his gag reflex, but that was the best lesson I ever taught him." He turned to me. "Especially because he likes it."

"He does seem to." Damn, it was strange to talk about this with Nick.

"We've already discussed how he's going to let you fuck him. That is, if you're still up for that?"

I nodded, trying not to look too eager. I was helping them out, right? My own feelings toward the whole thing were inconsequential.

"And are you okay with me being there?" Nick didn't wait for me to answer. "If you'd prefer me not to be, I understand. I trust Jamie and I trust you. I'm just an old perv."

"No, that's okay. You can… be there." Oh, what the hell. "You can even participate if you like. Wouldn't mind getting my hands on you again."

Nick chuckled contently. "I'm not as buff as I used to be, Jez."

"I never just fucked you for your body, Nick," I said confidently, because it was true. "Or your cock." Okay, maybe that was a half-truth. I did love Nick's cock, and what he used to be able to do with it. There was a reason he was destined to become a big porn star, and it wasn't just the size of his instrument, but the fact he had amazing stamina, great rhythm, and a sort of warped, wild imagination in bed. I'd never been an eager bottom before or after Nick, but during, well, let's say that even if Nick had wanted to, I would never have suggested topping him because taking that amazing cock up my ass was all I could ever think of around him. Even now.

Nick looked smug. "I guess I'll let Jamie tell you what he wants from you. But I think I can tell you I'm going to take out the blindfolds tonight."

I wondered how Jamie was going to explain his ideas when he didn't want to talk to me, but then we'd gotten pretty far last night without words. I figured if something got lost in translation, Nick would gladly play interpreter.

The one thing I was sure of was that it was going to be a long day. Jamie cooked lunch and dinner for us, as normal, and I couldn't miss the fact that they were lighter meals than usual. Jamie and I had our fair share of wine again, and as I was helping him with the dinner dishes that didn't fit in the dishwasher, I was surprised to hear him speak to me directly.

"Jez?"

"Yes," I said, hearing my voice betray my surprise.

"Nick said I was to invite you to our bed tonight, so there would be no misunderstanding."

"I believed Nick when he said you wanted this."

Jamie nodded shyly, but the wine had clearly made him bolder. "I do. I wanted it last night, but then I wanted Nick to be there with me. There are no secrets between us."

"I can believe that."

Jamie smiled and God, how I loved that smile, probably because he didn't show it very often. He invaded my personal space and I let him. He leaned closer to whisper in my ear. "I've been horny all day. I can't wait for you to fuck me. To feel a real live cock inside me again. It's been so long."

"I heard you and Nick that afternoon after I arrived," I said, looking sideways.

Jamie was still pressed against me and his warmth seeped through our clothes. "That's why I was so ashamed when you saw that dildo. That's what Nick needs to use if I want to be fucked these days. I don't mind too much. Nick tries and I can get *him* off sometimes, but he can't stay hard anymore. Not to fuck me. And sometimes I really need it."

I wrapped my arm around Jamie and he melted into my embrace. When I caressed his soft, bristly hair, he dove into the nape of my neck and kissed me there, sending shivers down my spine, right to my cock.

"Why don't you go to Nick and get ready? I'll take a shower and join you later. Do you want to do it in my room?"

Jamie looked up. "No, let's do it in our room."

"Okay."

WHEN I walked into the master bedroom, freshly showered, Jamie was on his back, arms raised over his head, shielding his eyes. His legs were spread, knees bent, with Nick lying in between his legs.

I felt like an intruder, but then again, I'd been given a clear-as-day invitation and I had said I'd come, so I cleared my throat to announce my arrival.

Nick's head popped up. "Ah, there you are. I'm sorry, we started without you, but as you know already, this one"—he pointed at Jamie, who had opened his eyes and was looking at me—"is good for at least two, sometimes three rounds."

To my surprise, Jamie held out his hand to me. When I didn't react immediately, a shy smile spread across his face and he crooked his finger at me. I walked closer and took Jamie's hand. As soon as Jamie got a good grip, he pulled me to him and kissed me hard. When he pulled away, I looked at Nick and how Jamie pushed Nick's face back against his groin. Then Jamie kissed me again. If I'd had any doubt before who was in charge in bed, I now knew it was Jamie, like Nick had always told me.

Despite Jamie's tendency to be incredibly withdrawn and shy in social situations, I had already found out that in a sexual context, there was barely a trace of that. Jamie knew exactly what he wanted from a partner, and he always got what he wanted, even without speaking. For a fleeting moment, I wondered where Nick had found Jamie in the first place, and then Jamie stole any coherent thought from me by first palming my cock through the thin cotton fabric of my boxers and then, quite slowly, covering my clothed erection with his mouth. The heat felt incredible and combined with the slightly coarse fabric, I felt myself hardening very quickly. When I looked over at Nick, he was hungrily blowing Jamie while using his fingers to open him up, and Jamie started humming. I didn't think I could stay in control of my own body much longer, so I pulled back. I felt slightly embarrassed to be this close to coming, at my age and without even having pulled my cock out of my boxers.

Nick seemed to find it amusing as well, since he stopped what he was doing. "He's good, isn't he?" he said, with his best cat-that-got-the-cream grin. "And we've barely gotten started." Nick got up from between Jamie's legs and moved closer to me. He put his hand on the back of my neck and looked me in the eye. I thought he was giving me time to pull away, but I couldn't. I'd always found Nick incredibly handsome. When he was still working in porn fulltime, he was a true Adonis, with muscles in all the right places and barely any body fat. He usually had a waxed chest and meticulously trimmed pubic hair that seemed sculpted to perfectly frame his larger-than-life, uncut cock. Now he was definitely older, more sinewy, but I found myself hoping I'd age half as well as Nick had. Despite the hideous scar running around one side of his chest, it was impossible for me to imagine Nick was ill. His wavy hair had turned almost completely white, but instead of it making him look older, it gave him a distinctively regal air. He had a beard, also white, and his body hair was all natural now, very salt and pepper and sort of randomly spread across his chest and stomach, right down to his belly. There were still no signs of love handles or belly fat. I figured Nick had won the genetic lottery, if you forgot about his illness for a moment.

In fact, the only sign of illness I saw in Nick was that his cock was only just slightly more filled than it would be in a totally flaccid state. Nick was aroused all right. His eyes were dark with lust, his neck and chest were flushed, and his nipples were tight, but like Jamie had explained, he could no longer get it up. Hence the reason I was in the room with them.

I had seen Nick and Jamie make out. I'd seen them kiss and caress. One afternoon, I'd also been witness to Nick bringing Jamie off with his hand on the lounger in the garden. Jamie seemed quite content with the state of their relationship, but this was Nick's gift to Jamie: a man Jamie could trust to fuck him into oblivion and then quietly sneak out of the room to let them sleep. After all, there was only one thing Nick could no longer give him: a hard cock.

I thought I should feel offended, but I didn't. I was the one who didn't want a relationship, who felt content with carefree hook-ups and occasional one-night stands, so why should I feel offended that this was all I was getting?

When Nick pulled me into a kiss, I felt myself submitting to him. I didn't question it. This was how it had always been between us, those numerous times we'd sought each other out for a casual romp. I now realized it was never that casual. I didn't do boyfriends and rarely allowed seconds, as if a guy was burned after he'd slept with me once, but I honestly could no longer count the number of times I'd had sex with Nick. From our first acquaintance, when I was just a fan, there had been electricity between us, and tonight was no different. I knew we were both kinky enough to find Jamie's presence anything but a hindrance.

It was strange to be in the position I was in. Although I never bottomed for my casual hook-ups, if it had been just Nick, I would have, eagerly and without question. Toward Jamie, my position was also clear. I was here to perform for both men, by fucking Jamie into oblivion while Nick watched. The only thing that remained to be seen was how Nick would react to seeing someone else in the place where he was supposed to be. I didn't know Nick as the kind of guy who took things lying down, and despite his earlier lifestyle, where physical monogamy was completely impossible, Nick did have a jealous streak. I thought he was just possessive enough about Jamie to have it surface at the most inopportune moment. Luckily, I felt confident enough in my own strength and powers of persuasion to know I'd be able to deal with it as long as I left either Jamie or Nick in charge.

As Nick let go of me, he looked at Jamie and couldn't help return the young man's smile. Jamie was slowly touching himself and no doubt enjoying the view.

Nick reached over to the nightstand and took out a long lace sash. "I think it's time for this."

"You mean you won't let me watch you two anymore?" Jamie asked.

"This isn't about us," Nick replied. "We're here for you."

"I will feel the difference, you know," Jamie teased. "Between you"—he pointed at Nick—"and him." He pulled me down to give me a sloppy, open-mouthed kiss. "Although I'm so going to enjoy him." He let go of me and turned to kiss Nick again. I could see the difference between the kiss he'd given me and the kiss that was now bestowed on Nick. Jamie had kissed me to arouse me. He was kissing Nick as if it was just the two of them in the room and I no longer existed. I didn't take it personally. It was enough for me to see Nick so totally consumed by his boyfriend, and Jamie so completely into Nick that he didn't really need to reassure him what was about to happen wouldn't change anything between them.

As Nick came up for air, he put the sash over Jamie's eyes and Jamie lifted his head so Nick could tie it.

"Comfortable?"

"Hmm." Jamie nodded.

"Can you see anything?"

"Who turned off the light?" Jamie joked.

Both Nick and I laughed, and I couldn't help but wonder which was the real Jamie: the boisterous, uninhibited sexual animal, or the quiet, shy, selectively mute young man. I was sure the truth was somewhere in the middle.

Chapter 9

WITH the three of us in bed, Jamie blindfolded between Nick and me, Jamie wasn't anything like the shy and quiet man I'd met just a few days earlier. For one, he wouldn't stop talking.

"That tickles!" he practically screamed when Nick and I used our tongues to trace the nicely defined muscles that made up his six-pack, side by side, painting his stomach with saliva.

"A little more to the middle!" he commanded when we nicked his hip bones with our teeth, one of us on either side.

Nick and I barely needed to talk. We could still communicate with looks and gestures as if we'd never been apart for so long. We didn't set out to tease Jamie, but the stars in Nick's eyes were enough to tell me he was enjoying it at least as much as me. Yet, it was just as hard a struggle for Nick as it was for me not to take Jamie's long, hard cock into our mouths. We did eventually, but only to stop Jamie begging so loudly. When we caved, Jamie started moaning and we were enjoying that too, letting our lips touch at either side of the pulsing column.

"Fuck, I want to see! I want to see both of you blowing me!"

Nick moved up Jamie's body. "You will. One day."

"Not fair!" Jamie shouted. His protests were just for show, though. His hands weren't tied up so he could pull off the blindfold if he wanted.

"Admit you like it," Nick said, just loud enough for me to hear.

"You know I do," Jamie replied, a lot softer than before. They started kissing and I started blowing Jamie in earnest. I could taste his arousal as he moved his hips to thrust in and out of my mouth. It brought back memories of the night before, but Jamie's moves were a lot smoother than mine had been. Nevertheless, they helped the heat rise in me too. Not that I wasn't already aroused by the situation. The idea that I was going to get to fuck Jamie was enough of a turn on.

Nick played the great distracter, though. We fooled around some, with Nick calling most of the shots. At one point we dragged Jamie out of bed and turned him around so he'd lose his orientation, then pushed him into a corner of the room where we continued to touch and kiss him. He never lost his erection. As soon as it waned, there would be something else going on that made it return and we'd be off again. Eventually, Jamie grew tired of the teasing and ripped off his blindfold.

"I guess we're done then?" Nick said with a glint in his eyes. He was panting, and I knew we'd have to take it down a notch if we wanted him to keep up with us. He tugged at his barely hard cock and I felt sorry for him, but I tried to look at the bigger picture.

Jamie knew Nick was teasing but he didn't take the bait. Instead he looked at Nick with defiance all over his face.

"Let's get back to bed," I suggested. "Take a breather."

"You getting tired, sport?" Nick asked.

"A bit," I replied, although I could have easily gone on for a little while longer. Nick threw me a grateful look.

"I want to watch the two of you together," Jamie demanded as he flopped down on the bed. "I keep hearing about how great you were together, so now I want to see it for myself."

Jamie's suggestion worried me a bit, since Nick could no longer fuck me and I was not about to fuck him. To my surprise, Nick took it all in stride. "Whadda ya think, Jezzie?" he said in an exaggerated American accent. "Shall we give the youngster a show?"

I shrugged, ready to go along with just about anything Nick suggested.

Nick sat down next to Jamie and gestured for me to join them. As Nick stretched out on the bed, I leaned over him and let him kiss me. Damn, that man could still kiss like nobody's business. I was almost jealous of the fact that Jamie got to do this every day. While our lips locked, he took my erection in hand and rubbed it, bringing it back to full arousal. I tried to reciprocate, but felt very little reaction from him. When we stopped kissing and I traced his chest with my lips, licking along the half-faded scar on his chest, I felt him give in to the touch. He soon pulled me up again and took my face in his hands. "Get him ready. I want to see him writhe on the bed."

I could tell Nick was growing tired so I didn't hesitate. After all, I wasn't just here for Jamie. Pleasing Nick with our show was part of the deal. Jamie smiled as I grabbed the lube from the nightstand. He was still hard. Youngsters. I knew how receptive he was, so it wouldn't take long to prep him, especially since Nick had started before I'd arrived.

"How do you want me?" Jamie asked. Nick shrugged and I didn't really care.

"It's your call, Nicky," I suggested.

Nick looked at Jamie for what felt like a long time. To kill the time and prevent me from urging them on to make up their mind, I slipped on a condom and tried to keep my erection from fading.

"Come here," Nick eventually asked Jamie. "Let us give you the best of two world. You like a good pounding doggy style, but you also like it lovey-dovey. I'll cuddle and kiss you while Jez fucks you."

Well, that's how I would have done it too.

Jamie smiled, giving his silent approval as he crawled to straddle Nick's supine frame. I'd had a chance to admire Jamie's beautiful ass the night before in the shower, but not like this, displayed for my pleasure. I bypassed his birthmark this time, but couldn't resist licking the little rosette between his perfect ass cheeks as Jamie pushed toward me and I made him moan into Nick's mouth. I continued tasting his musk as I opened the lube, squirted it on my fingers, and warmed it before replacing my mouth with my slicked-up digits. Although he let me inside easily, he remained tight as I tried to open him up more. My free hand felt for his erection and I was delighted that he was so hard it stuck to his stomach, barely flopping around as he writhed against my fingers.

Nick was holding Jamie tight, kissing him and rubbing his nipples. I could see them exchanging looks, conveying things to each other I couldn't begin to fathom as Jamie pulled away from Nick's mouth to catch his breath. I knew I was the cause of that as I was rubbing along Jamie's prostate. I didn't persist too much, since Jamie reacted very swiftly to even the most casual of touches, but as he raised his ass in the direction of my fingers, impaling himself, I could see the lines he'd been painting on Nick's hairy stomach.

Nick was moving alongside Jamie, taking both their cocks in his hand when I pushed the head of my cock against Jamie's entrance.

"Fuck, yeah. Inside," Jamie groaned, moving back and forth between Nick's hand and my cock until I felt myself slipping past the first ring of muscle. I stopped when I saw Jamie's body go rigid, but he reached for me. "More. Fill me up."

"Be patient," I whispered in his ear. "Give your body time."

"God, you know… how long it's… been?"

I looked at Nick, but he smiled at me. "Go on. He can take it."

I slowly pushed in, feeling the resistance, and just as I thought I'd almost hit rock bottom, Jamie stopped moaning. He threw his head up, curved his back, and stopped breathing. I swear I could feel his channel pulsating around my cock.

"Did he come?" I asked Nick, my voice strained from holding back.

Nick was supporting Jamie with one hand, his other hand lodged between their bodies. "I think it feels that way for him. He looks amazing from where I am."

At that moment Jamie gasped for air and started shaking all over his body. "Oh God, so good."

"Stay inside him," Nick asked me gently. "It's not over yet, but he needs a little time."

"No, don't pull out, please," Jamie pleaded. "You feel so fucking amazing."

I had a hard time keeping still, our position not the most comfortable as I was trying not to put all my weight on Jamie. "Just roll with me," I suggested. "We'll be more comfortable on our sides."

Jamie hesitated, then nodded and grabbed behind to grasp my hip. Nick held on to Jamie so we could move, little by little, until we were on our sides. Jamie relaxed as soon as he realized I was still inside him, and he twisted to give me a chaste kiss. "Who says size doesn't matter, hey?" he whispered to me. I smiled and moved closer to lie against his back. Jamie lifted his leg over Nick's side and started playing with Nick's salt-and-pepper chest hair. Without looking at me, his free hand urged me to start moving again. From time to time, Nick would look at me, and I felt strange because I couldn't read his expression. Was he proud of Jamie? Envious of me? Was he trying to encourage me to give pleasure to his boyfriend? My own feelings were muddled with everything else, and I decided to push them aside because they were interfering with my ability to hold my erection.

Jamie pushing himself away from Nick and against my chest brought me back to reality. Nick was fondling Jamie, judging by his amused look at their more or less connected groins. When I kissed Jamie's neck, he moaned softly and leaned into my touch. It felt very relaxed and laid back as I started slowly moving again.

"Oh, fuck, Nicky. This is so much better than a toy."

I couldn't help chuckling and took it as a compliment.

"Can I keep him?" Jamie asked playfully.

"Of course you can," Nick replied. "But you'll have to give him a reason to stay. He's a bit of a wanderer, our Jeremy."

"Are you?" Jamie asked.

"'Fraid so," I said, although right now staying here and making love to Jamie was something I'd consider.

Jamie was lying with his eyes closed, all senses directed at the slow-building pleasure we were creating, so I nuzzled his neck and closed my eyes too. To my surprise, I soon felt soft bristles against my lips and as I opened my eyes, Nick was close enough to me to kiss him.

"Are you okay with the slow pace?" Nick asked me.

"For a while, yeah. Until Jamie recovers."

Nick led my hand between their bodies before returning to give me a peck on the mouth. "He's still bone-hard, Jez. He doesn't need more time to recover."

Jamie's erection moved against my hand, seeking friction, making my hips push forward of their own accord. Nick opened his mouth between mine and Jamie's and I imagined our tastes mingling. It made me feel included and less like the human sex toy Jamie had implied he saw me as. Not that I was taking his comments personally. He was moving with me languidly and it felt pretty good to me too.

When I changed my angle just slightly, Jamie started moaning, and he raised his hand to grab the back of my head and pull me closer. "Right there. Don't stop."

"Want me to go faster?" I was having a hard time holding back now we were all more or less in sync, and the delicious noises Jamie was producing, seemingly unconsciously, added to the heat rising between the three of us.

Jamie shook his head, not at all convincingly, without interrupting his rhythmical chant so I kept the pace easy, knowing I wouldn't be able to hold back indefinitely. Then Nick laced his hand underneath Jamie's knee and pulled his leg up and the angle changed again. I pushed in harder and Jamie pushed back, making me feel like I could up the tempo. Just when I thought it couldn't possibly get any hotter, Nick's fingers rubbed the distended muscle surrounding my cock and I feared I was going to lose it. This had all been about Jamie's pleasure, though, so I pushed my hand down and squeezed the base of my cock.

Nick must have felt my movements, because he smiled and then winked at me. His hand was still where I was joined with his boyfriend, and I gave him an exasperated smile. He just nodded and I moved a little faster.

"Oh God, yes," Jamie sighed more than said. "Fuck, this is… going to be… a good one."

And then one of Nick's fingers slipped inside Jamie alongside my cock and I needed to squeeze harder to hold myself back while Jamie totally lost it. Clinging to Nick, he thrust forward, ribbons of cum coating Nick's belly. The spasms kept coming with every time I thrust into him until I stopped squeezing myself and lost it too.

I don't know how long we lay like that, panting, kissing sloppily while we caught our breath. When I slowly pulled out, holding on to the condom, Jamie gasped and I felt the need to soothe him. It was Nick who got up off the bed to get a washcloth. He walked back into the room, wiping Jamie's release off his own belly before doing the same to Jamie. When he handed me the cloth, Jamie made a miraculous recovery, pushing Nick to lie on his back on the bed. Since I was close to him, I wrapped my arm around Nick's shoulders and nuzzled him, asking silently whether he was okay. He seemed to understand, because he nodded at my unspoken question. I watched while Jamie took Nick's flaccid cock in his mouth and went to work. It didn't fill up much, but Jamie obviously knew what did it for Nick, since Nick was panting in no time. I enjoyed holding Nick like that, caressing his beard and listening to his incomprehensible mumbling while Jamie blew him and massaged his sac and taint until his stomach muscles contracted and he came.

The look of bliss on Nick's face was priceless, but it was matched by the pride in Jamie's smile. He eased himself down, half on top of both of us, and kissed Nick. "Thank you."

The words, so simple, held so much. Thank you for letting Jez fuck me. Thank you for being here while he did it. Thank you for enjoying it too. Then he kissed me and repeated his words. This time I heard: thank you for making me feel good. Thank you for allowing Nick to be a part of this. Just thank you.

I'd never felt so linked to anyone, and I didn't want to get used to the emotional connection I knew was forming between the three of us. I was outstaying my welcome. Our unspoken agreement was that I'd make Jamie feel good and leave him satisfied, then make my getaway to leave him and Nick to enjoy the afterglow. As I started worming myself from under Jamie's bulky frame, he stopped me.

"Stay. Please?"

"I... There isn't enough space in this bed for three." Part of me wanted to stay, but I knew it wasn't my place. This was the bed Nick and Jamie shared every day. I had my own bed across the hall.

"Sure there is," Nick said in his no-argument manner. "You'll have to contend with Jamie, who can't lie still to save his life, but stay." Nick caressed one of my pecs and the muscle underneath contracted reflexively, so I swatted his hand away. He grabbed my wrist and kissed the palm of my hand. It was hot in the room, but I pulled the sheet over us anyway, and we dozed off after taking some time to find a comfortable configuration.

Chapter 10

THE next morning I called my office to ask them to assign another agent to my next client. They didn't argue and asked how long I'd be unavailable. I took a swing at it and told them I was taking the next month off. I had fifteen years of vacation time saved up, and I knew I wasn't irreplaceable for ninety-five percent of my clients. I got confirmation of my leave of absence on my cell phone straight from the CEO that afternoon. Still, it surprised me how relaxed I felt knowing I wouldn't need to think about work for the next thirty days. Spain, and more precisely Nick and Jamie, had certainly changed me, and for now it felt like it was for the better.

I spent the next few days having long meal conversations with Nick, interspersed with solitary walks through the olive grove when Nick rested. Sometimes Jamie would join me, but we didn't talk much. For some reason the silence felt comfortable. Occasionally he'd take my hand as we walked and even that felt easy.

At night, after we'd all gone to bed, Jamie would come to my room and we'd either have a quick fuck or a longer make-out session, but he always went to his own bed to sleep with Nick. There was no doubt in my mind that Nick knew where Jamie snuck off to at night, but we didn't really discuss it in detail during our private conversations. Every so often Nick joined us, but he didn't participate anymore like that first time. It changed the dynamic, but I didn't want to overthink trying to figure out whether this was because Jamie liked to perform for Nick, or whether it was because Nick knew I was turned on by being watched.

Nick's health had its ups and downs. There were days that he seemed lively and invigorated, and others when he'd cut our discussions short to either go to his room to rest or sleep on the lounge chair.

One afternoon, he asked me to go into town with him. I caught him writing up a list of things to do for Jamie.

"What's this?" I asked innocently, reading over Nick's shoulder. "Change sheets, do laundry, sweep the path, weed the vegetable patch," I read. "Doesn't Jamie know to do all this by himself?"

Nick looked serious. "He won't come with us, and he's not very good on his own, so I give him a list of things to do while I'm not here. See." He handed me the list. "He's got a choice. The ones with the little stars need to be done today and the rest is for when he has time left over."

"Ooh, paella for dinner," I joked. I could tell Nick took this a lot more seriously than I did. And I found it strange. Why would a grown man like Jamie, who obviously wasn't stupid, need a list of things to do when he was left alone for a few hours? Surely he could figure these things out by himself? Jamie seemed happy enough with his list.

"Will you be okay on your own?" Nick asked. "You can leave the house if you want to, but I'd like you to be here when I get back."

Jamie nodded and then kissed him. "Have fun." He smiled at me, but I didn't get a kiss.

We left in Nick's old VW bug, a car that seemed older than me, but still managed to crawl up the steep, narrow roads without too much cranking. To my surprise, we drove to the next town, one barely larger than the one nearest the villa. I had no idea what Nick wanted to do there until we stopped at a place that had *Servicios Funerarios* written on the marquee. My Spanish wasn't great, but the demure shop window told me enough. The fact it was situated next to the cemetery was a giveaway too. This was a funeral home. My chest grew tight.

"Does this make you queasy, Jez?" Nick looked to be completely relaxed about it, although I had a pretty good idea why we were there.

"No, I'm fine," I replied none too convincingly.

Nick raised an eyebrow as he moved into the shade of the marquee. "I need to arrange a few things, Jeremy." His voice sounded serious and a little solemn. Nick using my full name told me something as well. "Jamie can't handle all the arrangements on his own. I need to make it as easy as possible for him. I'm still hoping you'll be here then."

I swallowed away my emotions. "Nicky…. I can't stay that long. I'm sorry. I'm all for you getting your affairs in order, but this"—I pointed at the little shop—"I don't know if *I* can even do this."

"Okay, wait in the car then." I saw the disappointment in his face.

"Fine, I'll go with you," I conceded, not wholeheartedly.

We walked inside and I was surprised to feel the chill of air-conditioning. Nick's house didn't have any, and I hadn't felt the chill in the restaurants around town either. The artificial cold made me realize I really didn't miss it.

A man came up to us and bowed solemnly. Because he spoke to Nick in Spanish, I couldn't quite follow the conversation Nick had with him, but I was glad. The last thing I wanted was to hear Nick talk about his own death and what had to be done afterward. Nick didn't look like he would be dying any time soon, and I wanted to keep that thought with me. As much as I didn't want Jamie to have to go through that moment, I didn't feel all that selfish wanting to save myself the experience as well.

When we walked outside again, Nick was quiet, and I didn't try to strike up a conversation. He led me to a small café with just two tables outside and ordered us each a coffee. Our cups were almost empty when Nick took a deep breath.

"I arranged to be cremated," he said. "I don't want Jamie to have to maintain some pompous grave, and besides, where would I be buried? I can't tie him to Spain forever, and I don't want to arrange for an international transfer. Also, no announcements until all the funeral arrangements are over. Jamie will have a hard enough time with the few people who are on my list to be notified. The last thing he needs is some fans showing up wanting to pay their last respects. They're strangers, and Jamie doesn't like strangers in our house."

I nodded. I couldn't have said anything if I had to anyway. My throat was constricted and I was willing it to go away, but not succeeding very well. Damn, I loved that man and never took the time to show him properly.

Nick took my hand, right there in full view of everyone walking by. Not that there were any tourists or even that many locals outside. It was the hottest time of day, when everyone preferred to stay inside. "I know you can't stay, Jez, but you're at the top of the list to be notified. I'd appreciate it if you could fly in for a few days. For Jamie, of course."

I nodded again and squeezed his hand by way of acknowledgement. We sat like that for a while, hand in hand, like an old married couple. Then again, although our get-togethers had always been few and far between, Nick and I had a twenty year history and I couldn't just sweep that under the rug. And then there was the request that I look after Jamie after he was gone. I hadn't exactly told him I'd do it, but I knew I'd have to at some point before I returned to real life. Maybe I was just holding back telling him because I was afraid it was the last thing he needed to arrange and somehow he was holding on living until he'd finished his bucket list.

We picked up some groceries and Nick took us home via the scenic route. He stopped the car at a vista point overlooking the sea and we made out like teenagers, kissing and groping in the front seat of the tiny car with the stick shift and the hand brake getting in the way. Neither of us got off, but then it wasn't necessary. I realized I wanted this intimacy with Nick one more time, and for the first time in our lives it wasn't all about the sex. Afterward, we sat looking at the sea, smooth as a mirror. I told Nick I wanted to cook tonight, and after expressing his rather flamboyant surprise, he told me to put it on Jamie's list for tomorrow, because the paella would be all but done by the time we got home. We were laughing when we crossed the threshold to the villa, but I could tell the excursion had worn Nick out.

When we walked in we were greeted by a dark house and a pathway of candles reaching from the hallway, through the kitchen, to the back patio. The sun was going down and the sky was turning orange. I put my hand on Nick's shoulder as we admired the setting.

"Where's Jamie?" I asked. We hadn't seen him in the kitchen, where I'd expected to find him since the house smelled of food. Nick shrugged and remained silent but his eyes were all starry.

"How was your trip into town?"

We both turned around to find Jamie standing in the doorway to the kitchen dressed in a very tight white wife-beater and the kind of cut-up jeans I'd never liked on anyone before I saw Jamie in them. His feet were bare and his hands tucked into the pockets of his jeans.

"Productive," Nick said before moving to his lover and kissing him. It wasn't just a peck on the lips. Although I shouldn't, I felt like an intruder.

"Good," Jamie said as he looked over to me. "Are you hungry? Paella's done, I think."

We sat on the patio to eat, and it was the best paella I'd ever had in my life. Nick and Jamie were very touchy-feely with each other, more so than other times. They fed each other and Nick complimented Jamie repeatedly on the food. Jamie blushed every time. I felt like a mere observer, although both men tried to include me, but I didn't mind. I may have been a small part of their relationship, but I was in no way part of the intimacy they shared, and I didn't carry the history or share their particular connection. I was, however, warmed by the care Jamie showed for Nick and the gentleness with which Nick responded to his boyfriend.

Little did we know, things would change very quickly.

Chapter 11

IN THE middle of the night, Jamie bolted into my room.

"Jez, help me!"

I jumped out of bed and pulled on a pair of boxers even before I'd opened my eyes. "What's wrong?"

"Nick."

I followed Jamie to their bedroom and found Nick on the bed. The sheets were strewn around the room and Nick was shaking, seemingly unable to control his movements, his body in rigor. I tried to hold him still, but he was too strong. When I inadvertently blocked the light from his opened eyes, he seemed to calm down a bit.

"Turn off the light, Jamie," I demanded.

"But then we can't see what's wrong."

"We have the hall lights. This is bothering him."

Jamie did as I asked, and although it didn't happen immediately, the shaking became less. I cradled Nick's thin body in my arms and tried to soothe him by rubbing his hair. It seemed to help some, but he didn't become more responsive, so I was afraid we were nearing the end.

"Call an ambulance, Jamie, and the doctor."

Jamie left the room and returned with the telephone.

"The numbers are on speed dial," I reminded him.

"I don't speak Spanish," he said, pushing the phone in my direction.

"Neither do I, but I'm sure they'll understand you."

Jamie's face remained neutral, but I could see the fear in his eyes and I understood he wasn't going to be able to conquer his fear of strangers, not even to call for help, so I took the phone.

Both the ambulance dispatcher and the doctor spoke enough English to understand my plight and help was sent to the villa while the doctor promised to meet us at the hospital.

IT TOOK them several hours to stabilize Nick, and while we waited, I kept hearing Nick tell me he'd signed papers so no heroic measures would be taken to keep him alive. I feared that any time now, the doctor would come out to tell us it was hopeless and we would have to go in to say good-bye. All the time we waited, Jamie sat next to me, stoic and silent. Whenever I tried to touch him, he pulled away without malice, and I stopped insisting. I walked down the hall to get coffee for me and bottled water for Jamie and then sat back down next to him. Every effort on my part to talk was ignored. I knew it had to do with Jamie's inability to verbalize in public so I didn't push him, but I didn't stop telling him things, in the hope that he'd keep his head up. For some reason I expected him to cry, but he didn't. I realized that this was how Jamie always reacted after the most acute part of the crisis was over. It was as if he was just waiting for the inevitable, certain that it would happen whether he protested it or not.

After what felt like hours, a doctor came out to tell us, in broken English, that Nick was okay now and we could go home. Knowing Jamie would comply, even if he didn't want to, I explained to the doctor that Jamie was Nick's husband and that I was a family friend and we wanted to see Nick first. He reluctantly agreed.

He didn't seem impressed with Jamie's status, but eventually told him Nick's cancer had spread to his brain, and this had caused a seizure. He couldn't tell us how long Nick still had, but we both knew he was already living on borrowed time, so any extra was welcome.

When we walked into his room, Nick looked pale and worn out, lying unresponsive on the white sheets of the hospital bed. Jamie seemed afraid to come closer so I urged him to take Nick's hand and pulled up a chair so he could sit next to the bed. Jamie didn't move or talk for all the time he sat next to Nick, and I felt his pain, although his face remained unreadable.

WHEN I took Jamie home in the afternoon, he disappeared. I finally found him wiping the path in the garden, although there was barely any dirt there. I brought him a glass of water and he drank it quickly, but then continued his chores. Later, he caught me starting to cook and got upset.

"It's my job to cook," he said softly, although I could hear his restrained emotions fighting to come through.

"You were busy, so I figured this would be something I could help you with."

"It's my job to cook," he repeated, so I left him to do what he wanted. He made paella again, but it didn't taste quite as amazing as the night before. I suggested he sleep in my bed, but he refused, so I helped him make his bed and let him sleep there.

The next day when I woke, Jamie was already cleaning the pool and sweeping the path. After that he cleaned upstairs and then the kitchen, although both were spotless already because he'd cleaned them the day before. We visited Nick, but his condition hadn't changed much. The doctor still couldn't tell us anything more than that he was stable, but he slept almost all of the time we were there and when he woke, he barely seemed to know where he was or why he was there. I was glad he recognized Jamie and smiled at him, because it lit up Jamie's face to see his lover's more typical behavior.

It wasn't until we got home again that Jamie's mood changed. I was in the patio setting the table when I heard a cupboard door slam shut. I ran inside and found Jamie breathing hard.

"What's wrong?"

"Nothing." Jamie's voice jumped when he said it, convincing me that something was definitely wrong.

"Talk to me, Jamie," I urged gently.

"There isn't any saffron left. I can't make paella without saffron."

"There are vegetables and chicken in the fridge for a stir-fry. Shall I make that instead?" I tried.

"No!" Jamie said, like a petulant child. "I need to make paella, so I need saffron." I could tell he was getting worked up.

"Jamie," I said softly. "We've had paella two days in a row. We can eat something else."

Jamie frantically shook his head. "We can't." He pulled out a rumpled piece of paper and pushed it at me. "It says 'Make your paella for us' so I need to make it!"

I looked at the paper and recognized the list Nick had written up for Jamie to do while we were out. All his chores were on there, including the paella and "Welcome us home with candles" scribbled at the bottom, but the paella had the stars, making it mandatory. I didn't dare take it from him, but grabbed Nick's notepad from the kitchen drawer instead. On it I wrote, "Rest. Let Jez comfort you if you feel sad. Let Jez make stir-fry chicken. Sit on the patio with a glass of wine." I handed it to him.

"This isn't right," Jamie said after he read it. He seemed calmer, though.

"What's wrong with it?"

"I can't have wine."

"Why not?" I asked. He'd had wine a few times, usually at dinner.

"I can't have wine, because it makes me horny and I don't want to have sex with Nick in...." He didn't finish, but I knew what he meant, so I pulled him into my arms.

"It's okay, you can have a glass of water."

"There are no chores for me to do," Jamie continued.

I took the paper back and added, "Play some of Nick's favorite music."

After Jamie read it, he looked at me, and for the first time since we'd taken Nick to the hospital, tears welled up in his eyes. When I wrapped him into my arms again, he cried.

Chapter 12

LIKE we'd promised Nick, we brought him home as soon as they thought we could handle it. The doctor at first didn't want to let us go, but I could be very persuasive when called for. And I had promised Nick on the first day he remembered where he was that I'd move heaven and earth to get him out of there as soon as possible.

So one sunny Tuesday afternoon, almost two weeks after Nick had been brought to the hospital at death's door, we transported him back to the villa. Nick was significantly thinner and a lot weaker than when he'd left, but we brought home a lot more weight than we'd taken there with all the equipment we needed to take care of him, from an oxygen cylinder for sleeping to a feeding pump to give him extra calories when he couldn't find the energy to eat. Both Jamie and I had been given lots of instruction on how to care for Nick and how to tell when it was time to call the doctor.

To my significant surprise, Jamie took it all in stride. Although I had seen him cry when Nick wasn't watching, around his lover, Jamie was a ray of sunshine. And Nick reciprocated by bestowing hugs and kisses on Jamie whenever the young man came close enough for Nick to touch.

I kept my distance, always staying within earshot in case Nick needed me and engaging in conversation whenever Nick wasn't too tired and Jamie was elsewhere in the house. Jamie and I hadn't shared a bed since Nick's departure, and to be honest, sex was the furthest thing from my mind anyway, so when Nick regained his place in his own bed, not a lot changed besides the fact we didn't need to drive into the city every day anymore.

Two days after we'd settled at home, Nick was asleep on the lounger and Jamie was doing laundry. I got up from my seat near the garden table to move the large parasol so the sun wouldn't burn Nick's delicate skin, but the base was a large heavy thing and it scraped along the concrete floor of the patio, waking Nick from his slumber.

"Didn't mean to wake you," I said by way of apology.

"I'm sleeping my last days away," Nick said without a hint of self-pity.

"I think you have more than a few days left, Nicky."

"Sometimes I hope so, for Jamie's sake more than my own, but other times I think it would be better for me to go sooner. I know he cries a lot. And he's got you now. It's not like I'm leaving him all by himself."

I felt the pit in my stomach again. "It's a big responsibility."

Nick looked out over the olive field. "Sit down here, Jez. It hurts my neck to look up at you like that."

Nick was so skinny, I had plenty of space to sit next to him on the lounger, but it felt funny. This was Jamie's place to sit, where Nick and Jamie had long, intense conversations and even longer comfortable silences. Although I knew Nick didn't agree with me, I felt like an intruder in their safe little cocoon.

"If Jamie wants to sell the house, make sure he gets a good price for it, okay?" Nick asked, not looking at me although I was now more at his level.

"He may not want to sell. It's his home," I replied, although I didn't like the "death" conversations, as I classified them in my own head.

"He doesn't speak Spanish."

"As little as he converses with strangers, I don't think it matters much."

Nick gave me a stern look.

"He's very expressive. I've never known anyone who could get exactly what he wanted by pointing and looking, even if what he needed was nowhere in sight."

"Don't mock him," Nick said softly.

"I wouldn't dare mock him, Nick. Jamie and I probably had more conversations before than after he uttered his first word in my presence."

"Not to mention you'd already fucked him by then."

I thought I heard bitterness in Nick's words. "Well, you asked me to."

"He wanted to."

"Let's just leave the sex out of it, okay?" I didn't like where this conversation was going.

"Don't leave him out in the cold when I'm gone, Jezzie. I'll come back to haunt you if you do."

I looked down when Nick put his hand on my wrist. I expected Nick to say something profound or intensely emotional, but he didn't, and I wondered if he just needed the touch. Nick was always the touchy-feely kind. "I don't love him the way you do, Nick."

"I know."

"Don't get me wrong. He's gorgeous, but he deserves more than a man who likes a live-in housekeeper. I need more too. I need someone I can have a decent conversation with. I prefer a lover who can make his own decisions, live his own life. Jamie's like a child."

"He's no child, Jez. I thought he proved that to you all those times you fucked him. He gave you total consent and you trusted him to make up his own mind then. So he's hardly a child."

"I'll never be completely sure he didn't just do it to please you."

"Do you honestly believe that with his history, I could make him seduce his way into another man's bed, just because I asked him?" Nick veered up as a coughing fit overtook him. I jumped up to reach for the portable oxygen tank standing next to the lounger and cranked it on, pushing the mask against Nick's face. Nick tried to take a breath, but it took a few tries for him to actually get enough air into his lungs to feel the effect of the extra oxygen.

"I didn't mean to upset you," I said, running my hands over Nick's almost white, wavy hair until he finally calmed down. Nick had hinted more than once about Jamie's past, but with Jamie usually within earshot, Nick had never elaborated. I was pretty sure Jamie was nowhere near close enough to overhear us, since he was upstairs in one of the spare rooms watching TV while he ironed. We could hear the chatter of some Spanish telenovela drifting down to where we sat. I wasn't sure if asking Nick about Jamie's past was a good idea right now, but we didn't exactly have all the time in the world, and Jamie didn't speak to me enough to give me a first person account. "Do you think you can tell me a few things about Jamie's past without it resulting in another coughing fit?"

Nick smiled. "It used to upset me a lot more than it does now. After eight years, I know getting all worked up about it doesn't change anything. All I can hope for is that with a lot of love and patience, he can still have a good life. I just wish I could be here to see it."

"So you know why he is the way he is?"

"I'm sure I don't know the whole story, but I know some." Nick took a deep breath and then exhaled slowly. "When I found him, he was a fuck boy at an illicit sex club in Brooklyn. Illicit because they weren't taking care of their boys in any sort of way. There was nobody to make sure they didn't get hurt by some freak and nobody to urge patrons to practice safe sex. In fact, part of the appeal was the bareback sex and the fact that it opened at a different location every night. The fuck boys were used until they couldn't work anymore and then they were discarded like an old racing dog who could no longer run. The patrons got off on abuse too. Jamie had broken ribs when I found him, and a cracked eye socket. It wasn't until I took him to see a doctor that I found out he also had anal fissures and an untreated case of syphilis. It took him weeks to recover. Weeks of him sitting in a corner, arms wrapped around his knees, rocking himself. It took him almost four months to speak for the first time. I thought he was autistic or something. The doctor who treated him told me he had PTSD."

"Post traumatic stress disorder? Like the war veterans? Is that why he barely talks?"

"No, his not talking has a deeper cause. He was never given a chance to learn to socialize. His mother…." Nick looked at where his hand lay on my arm and squeezed it, then he looked straight at me and I could practically feel the sadness in his eyes. "She wasn't well in her head. Nowadays she'd probably be kept far away from society in some psychiatric hospital, but in her case she was taken care of by her father, who put her in a trailer in the back of his garden and brought her food. Jamie said most days she would tell her father to leave the food outside the door, and then she'd wait until it was dark and everything was quiet before opening the door to take the food inside. Sometimes the dogs would beat her to it and they wouldn't have anything to eat. One time Jamie opened the door during the day because he was hungry and she screamed for hours without stopping. He never did it again."

"Wow." I didn't know what to say. Not that I'd had a perfect childhood, but at least I'd had the chance to go to school and I'd had friends. I couldn't imagine growing up in a self-imposed prison. "So how did he get out?"

"His grandfather died and the food source dried up. His mother still wouldn't leave the trailer, so they were starving. She grew weaker faster than him. One day when she was asleep he managed to break the lock and get out. They found him wandering the streets. They called him "the wild boy." It was in all the papers that they'd found this young man who looked like he was raised by wolves. He was dirty and had long hair and a very thin build, no muscles to speak of and no fat anywhere. They thought he couldn't talk. He went crazy if someone tried to touch him. So you can imagine."

"Must have been hard for him to adapt to society."

"The strange thing was he could talk just fine. And he could read and write. He told me his grandfather had taught him those things, that on his mother's good days he'd be allowed to come inside the trailer and he'd read to Jamie from old books. Jamie's read some real literary giants, but there are strange gaps in his education. He doesn't know how to handle money, for instance. He's by no means stupid, but he just doesn't grasp the value of money. I've tried to teach him, but eventually gave up."

"So how did he end up in that club?"

"There are gaps in that story too. He told me about a man at the shelter who took care of him, gave him chores to do, and taught him how to cook for the other residents. He made him feel useful and probably helped his self-worth quite a bit, but then he left. It was a youth shelter and eventually Jamie was too old to stay, so they threw him out on the street. My best guess is that he came across some very shady people."

"How old is he now?"

"According to the records we managed to piece together, he should be about thirty-one. That's what they put on his passport. He got to pick his own birthday."

I was glad Nick was smiling. I couldn't imagine what Jamie had been through and was still going through every day. "So when's the celebration?"

"February 29th." Nick chuckled and stifled another coughing fit. "He doesn't like birthdays, but he said he could put up with one every four years."

"I'll make sure he gets a nice, quiet celebration next year."

Nick squeezed my hand again and then closed his eyes. He'd told me a lot today, and it helped me understand Jamie a bit more. I could imagine it had taken a lot out of him, though.

I startled when I felt a hand on my shoulder. When I looked up I saw Jamie's beautiful aqua-blue eyes, but they were gazing at Nick, and the love in them almost made me choke up.

Chapter 13

WHEN I woke up, it was still dark outside. For a moment I didn't know what had roused me, but then I heard frantic thumping against my door. I'd gotten used to sleeping in a T-shirt and boxers, knowing that if Jamie or Nick needed me, there was no time to lose. It seemed that this was one of those nights.

"I'm awake. Be right there!" I shouted at the closed door. The thumping stopped and I heard footsteps. I threw back the covers and opened my door. The corridor was dark, so I turned on the lights and almost immediately heard Nick's strangled voice shouting "No!" I turned them back off and tried to make my way through the darkened corridor I really didn't know well enough. Jamie met me outside their bedroom. He was carrying a flashlight and directing its beam at the floor.

"What's wrong with Nick? Another seizure?"

Jamie shook his head. "His head hurts and he can't stand the light. He can't stand me touching him either. I tried, Jez."

"I know," I answered, putting my hand on Jamie's shoulder. "Can I go in to see if there's anything I can do? Should we call the doctor?"

"Doctor, maybe," Jamie replied with a shrug. He didn't seem as calm as he usually was. "But go see first."

I briefly pointed the flashlight into the room and then pulled it away again before entering, treading carefully because I didn't know if there would be any obstacles along my way. It was eerily quiet in the room, and stiflingly warm. I found the bed and felt around for Nick, afraid that if I spoke his name, Nick would cry out again. I eventually found a cold hand and it made my breath hitch. "Nick? Nicky?" Nick didn't answer, so I followed the arm higher until I found Nick's neck and could feel around for a pulse. To my relief there was a heartbeat. I must have sighed audibly because Jamie put his hand on my shoulder. "He's alive," I said to reassure Jamie.

"He's not crying anymore," Jamie said with clear worry in his voice.

"I know. What happened, Jamie?"

"He didn't want his pain patch. He didn't want to sleep yet. He was in pain, I could tell, but I fell asleep next to him and when I woke he was crying out for me to close the curtains because he couldn't stand the light. But it was dark already."

I took Jamie's hand and put it in Nick's. "I'm going to try and let some air in this room. I can barely breathe, and Nick needs all the oxygen he can get." On my way back from the window, I went into the ensuite and retrieved Nick's Fentanyl patches. My eyes now adjusted to the darkness, I opened one, took off the protective film, and found Nick's shoulder to stick it on. At that moment, Nick inhaled sharply and cried out.

"Make it stop! Please!"

Instinctively I wrapped my arms around Nick and tried to get him to stop fighting me. "Give the patch time, Nicky!" I shushed him, holding him tight. Jamie was strong, but Nick's emaciated frame felt incredibly delicate, so I could easily imagine that Jamie was afraid to fight Nick when he was flailing around like this. After what seemed like forever, the tension in Nick's muscles eased some and he started growing heavy in my arms.

"That's it. Relax. Let the drugs take effect."

"Didn't want to be drugged," Nick replied, his speech a little slurry. "I wanted one more time… with Jamie."

I swallowed the emotions away. I couldn't even try to imagine what it must be like for Nick to feel that way. Was he aware that the end was so near he had to say his good-byes? I looked up and didn't see Jamie anywhere in the dark room. The door to the corridor was ajar, but there were no lights on there either. I knew Nick would want Jamie near. "I'll go see where he is, okay?"

"Don't leave me alone!" Nick pleaded.

Nick felt hot and sweaty in my arms, so I decided to change my strategy. "Let me get you a nice, cool cloth and I'll be back in less than a minute. No longer, I promise."

Nick relinquished his grip and I slipped off the bed. In the ensuite I flicked on the smallest light there and found the stack of washcloths all depleted, so I returned to the bedroom. "Have to go get some stuff in the hallway," I told Nick. "One minute."

As soon as I rounded the door, I literally almost fell over Jamie. "Hey," I greeted him, crouching down. "Nick's a bit better. The patch is helping with the pain."

Jamie nodded, but remained seated in his typical frightened position, arms wrapped around pulled-up knees.

"He needs you in there. Why don't you go keep him company? I'm going to hunt down some more washcloths."

"I forgot them in the laundry room downstairs. They're clean and dry. I just forgot to bring them up. I'll go get them."

I pulled Jamie to his feet, but pushed him in the direction of Nick's bedroom. "You take care of Nick. I'll go find the washcloths."

Jamie shook his head vehemently.

"Okay, stay here and go in if he calls for someone. I'll be right back."

"I'm scared, Jez."

I wrapped my arms around Jamie and hugged him tight. "I know. It's scary business. But he needs someone with him. He's scared too." I held Jamie at arm's length and then turned around to run downstairs.

When I returned, Jamie wasn't still in the corridor like I'd expected. When I crossed the bedroom on route to the ensuite, I saw Jamie lying in Nick's arms. They both had their eyes closed, but I didn't think either was asleep. The cloth wetted, I came to Jamie's side and softly touched him. "I'll put this on the table here if he needs it."

Jamie nodded, but he called after me when I tried to leave. "Please stay. The couch is reasonably comfortable and there's a blanket on there to keep you warm."

"Is that where you've been sleeping?"

Jamie nodded and snuggled closer to Nick again.

I settled in for the night, but only fell asleep when I was sure Nick and Jamie had dozed off as well. When I woke the next morning, it was to the two of them quietly talking. Somehow last night felt like a nightmare.

Reality hit when Nick seemed too weak to get out of bed for washing and changing. To my surprise, Jamie took it all in stride and washed Nick in bed, only helping him up to go to the toilet and so Jamie could change his sheets.

I stayed with Nick while Jamie jumped in the shower.

"You don't have to keep me company, Jezzie."

I threw Nick a "yeah, right" look from behind my book. I put my literature down and leaned my elbows on my knees. "Are you sick of my company already?"

"Nah," Nick replied, a faint smile making the corners of his moustache curl up.

I had to admit that, despite a fairly relaxing second part of the night, Nick looked exhausted from his morning bath so I tried to keep the conversation light. "I don't mind. Last night you were pretty desperate not to be left alone and between Jamie and me, we can keep you company."

Nick sighed. "Will get kind of boring. All I do is sleep."

"And when you wake up, one of us will be here."

Nick didn't acknowledge the statement and gave no indication whether he liked it or not, so I picked up my book again, listening to the shower shutting off next door.

"He's throwing himself into taking care of me," Nick said out of the blue.

"It gives him comfort to know you're well taken care of and that he can do things for you that make you feel better."

"I'm never going to get better, Jez. It's only going to go downhill from now on."

I inhaled deeply, trying to keep my emotions level. Just after I'd decided to take time off from work to stay the duration, that is until Nick died, I'd started reading up on hospice care and what to expect. Some accounts had talked about the dying person becoming very frank and forthright, ignoring what could be considered the proper way to talk around difficult subjects, but tackling them straight on. Maybe that's what Nick was doing.

"He knows," I answered. "But it still makes him feel good. He's your husband, Nick. Nothing's going to change that. Not even you dying."

"So you don't think any less of me for letting him do this?"

"Why would I?" I asked. "You're both grown men. You make your own decisions." *And I'm here too, aren't I?* I wanted to add, but I didn't want to sound selfish. In truth, I understood Jamie more than I cared to admit. I was only partially here because Nick had asked me to look after Jamie after his death. Another part of me was here out of loyalty to Nick, who was probably the closest thing I'd ever had to a partner, albeit in the loosest possible sense. I knew no matter how hard the foreseeable future was going to be, I couldn't leave until I was sure Nick had left this world as comfortably as possible.

Jamie walked into the room wearing only a towel. He was drying his chest with another towel, and I could see that the one around his hips was clinging to them precariously. Despite —or probably because of—the laden conversation I'd just had with Nick, Jamie had become a sexual object again, and I had to prevent my body from reacting. Luckily I was sitting down, but it amused me that Nick was eyeing him lustfully too. It broke my heart as I remembered his confession from the night before, of how he'd wanted to make love to Jamie one more time. I decided to change the subject.

"So what are we going to do today?"

Both men looked at me as if I'd lost my wits, but I didn't let it stop me. I was never Mr. Happy in everyday life, but it suddenly dawned on me that we needed to make the most of whatever time Nick had left. He might not be able to make love to his husband anymore, but that didn't mean he couldn't feel loved.

"Why don't we get you downstairs to your lounge chair?" I looked at Nick. "You can lie there and we can watch Jamie do his weeding." When I looked at Jamie, he was smiling. "Then we can have lunch and when it's too hot to sit outside, we can move to the living room and watch one of Nick's favorite movies. And if we fall asleep, we fall asleep, right?" Jamie nodded happily.

I sat next to Nick on the bed as we watched Jamie get dressed and then helped Nick get up. He was slow, but we took our time. For a moment I thought I was going to have to carry him, but his pride took over and the three of us made our way down the stairs to the patio and his lounge chair, which we padded with a thick blanket and some pillows. I couldn't get over how thin Nick had gotten over the course of three weeks. I shook away the thought as I got us some drinks from the kitchen. By the time I returned, Nick was asleep, but he needed to take his pills, so I wiped a strand of hair away from his forehead and he opened his eyes.

"Sorry, I keep falling asleep. It's the pain meds."

"No need to apologize." I handed him a glass of water and his tablets. He took them one by one and then handed me back the glass. "It's getting hot already," I remarked, pointing at Jamie, who was on his hands and knees and had already taken off his shirt.

"Down, boy," Nick said, not without a certain glee in his voice. He didn't hide the fact he was looking at my groin either.

"I can restrain myself," I teased.

"I bet you can," Nick replied, and for a moment, his eyes sparkled again. Then he became serious and his voice softer. "Is he still visiting you at night?"

"No," I replied honestly. "Not since we took you to the hospital."

Nick sighed. "I'm sorry."

I shrugged. "Wouldn't be right, Nicky."

"For him or for you?"

"For *you*." I couldn't believe Nick didn't get that. Or maybe he did, but just decided not to acknowledge it. "Sex is the absolute last thing on his mind, Nick. He knows he's losing you, and he's holding on for as long as he can. That means staying with you until you fall asleep and sleeping on that damn uncomfortable sofa next to your bed just in case you might wake up and need something. That's what he's living for right now."

"I don't want him to sacrifice himself for me," Nick said, trying to keep his voice even.

"Trust me, it's no sacrifice for him. It's his way of dealing with it. You keep telling me he needs to feel useful. Well, he can't just sit and watch you die. He wants to make sure you have the best possible ride, all the way to the end." *And so do I,* I wanted to add, but didn't. If Nick felt bad about being waited on by Jamie, he'd feel just as bad about me, and I wasn't legally required to.

"So what do I do, then?"

"About what?"

"Making it easier on him."

I didn't know how to answer that. What was Nick getting at? I decided to circumnavigate the question. "It would probably be more comfortable for you if we moved the bed downstairs. That way you don't need to climb those stairs every day."

"I don't want it to get so bad I can't talk to him anymore, Jez. Promise me if it becomes unbearable you'll slip a few too many pills into my food pump, okay?"

I knew we weren't talking about the same thing, but was Nick asking me to kill him?

"In my night stand. There's a stash of sleeping pills. With all the pain medication, I don't need to take them so I save them up. I'm scared to leave him right now, but if it becomes too bad, if I'm not really there for him anymore, please help me end it, Jezzie. On my own terms."

My throat was so constricted I couldn't even swallow anymore. I had to get up and find a place where the air wasn't so thick it would make me choke, so I fled. I knew it wasn't fair to Nick to leave him after a request like that, but I didn't know how to answer him. I understood his plight, but at the same time I couldn't kill him. And it had nothing whatsoever to do with the legal implications. I knew I'd never be able to live with myself, and neither would Jamie. Was I actually contemplating taking care of Jamie after Nick's death? For some reason it calmed me to think that after Nick was gone, I'd still have Jamie. When did that happen?

I walked into the kitchen and made us sandwiches. Big, sturdy ones with tomatoes and cucumber and ham and cheese for Jamie and me and thin, neatly sliced ones with gooseberry jam for Nick. When I returned to his side, he was still awake and peacefully looking at Jamie working the garden. I gave Nick his plate and he looked at it.

"Eat," I commanded. "I know you're not hungry, but you're not starving yourself."

"It only puts off the inevitable," Nick answered blandly.

"That may be, but Jamie deserves a beautiful corpse." Now where did that come from? Since when was I able to joke about death? To my surprise, Nick laughed, sending him into a coughing fit. He got out of it without help, though, and bit into his sandwich. I knew appealing to Nick's sense of aesthetics would persuade him, but I wasn't prepared for how happy it made Nick look or how relaxed it made me feel. I was just glad Jamie hadn't heard me.

Chapter 14

AS IT turned out, the day we fixed up a bed for Nick in one of the rooms downstairs was his last good day. After that he wouldn't eat, but would let us feed him through the tube in his stomach. I'd mix his anti-seizure medication with the off-white, strange smelling liquid that passed for high calorie food, and he was reasonably comfortable that way. Our talks became more infrequent as he slept most of the day, sometimes with Jamie lying next to him, sometimes with Jamie or me on the day bed beside him. At night, it was always Jamie, and I'd sleep upstairs in my own room. Jamie was frantic about not leaving Nick, even for a minute, and he would only take a shower or clean the upstairs bathroom if he knew I was there to stay with his husband.

I read about a book a day during that time, on top of helping Jamie with the day-to-day chores around the house. Everything revolved around Nick.

Almost two weeks after we'd brought him home from the hospital, Nick started slipping in and out of consciousness. The first time Jamie couldn't wake him, I found him sitting next to Nick with a blank expression on his face, so I taught him how to tell if Nick was still alive. It became harder as Nick's breathing started to become more erratic, slow and shallow one moment and deep and faster another. Sometimes he'd stop altogether, only to start again with a gasp. I'd read up on this on the Internet, but it still scared the living daylights out of both Jamie and me.

The only consolation was that when he was unconscious, he didn't seem to be in any pain. His rare lucid moments were another thing altogether, and one day he asked me again to help him end it. To my surprise, I actually contemplated it, understanding how he no longer had any quality of life left.

The doctor came by every day, but he offered little consolation other than to up Nick's pain medication to keep him comfortable. It only made him sleep more, and I consoled myself with the fact Nick seemed to suffer less. Meanwhile, Jamie was wasting away in front of my eyes. I had to force him to eat. For Jamie alone, I prayed Nick would die peacefully in his sleep sooner rather than later.

It was also for Jamie's sake that I'd started sleeping downstairs in Nick's room.

Therefore, when I stepped out of the shower one morning and found Jamie standing in the bathroom, I knew it was all over. Jamie's face was unreadable as usual, but I didn't bother drying off before pulling him into my arms. This time it was me who cried, while Jamie simply stood there with his arms around me.

Eventually I dressed and we went downstairs. Nick looked like he was asleep, but he was no longer breathing. For a short while I hoped he'd start up again, but I knew he was at peace. It showed in the way his face was relaxed now. I took the phone but Jamie stopped me.

"Not yet."

"We need to call the funeral home."

"Not yet," Jamie repeated.

"Okay," I gave in. "The funeral home can wait, but we need to call the doctor. That's our one legal obligation." I could tell Jamie didn't even want that, but he didn't protest. He sat down next to Nick and took his hand and raised it to his mouth to kiss it, like he'd done so many times, and all I could do was sit next to him and put my arm around Jamie. Jamie put his head on my shoulder and we sat with Nick until the doctor came. Nick's doctor was soothing and calm as he examined his body and drew blood to clear us all of any wrongdoing, like the law stated he needed to do. We thanked him for all the care he'd bestowed on Nick and after he left we continued to sit with Nick for a long time before Jamie got up.

"What are you doing?"

Jamie looked at me. "I need to wash him one more time. And put on his suit. He told me which one."

For the first time I realized that Nick had found the courage to have his death talks with Jamie as well, although I'd always figured Nick would want to spare him those.

"He wants to wear his Armani. It'll be way too big on him, though."

"I know," was all I could say.

We didn't talk and took our time taking care of Nick. Beforehand, I'd always thought I wouldn't be able to touch a dead body, but this was our Nick and it was our last chance to take care of him. Jamie and I both knew that. In the afternoon we finally called the funeral home to set in motion all the things Nick had arranged for himself. It seemed it was the custom that friends and family could still view the body before cremation, and because Jamie rarely left the villa, Nick had asked the funeral home to make sure the viewing could be held at home. I wasn't sure how Jamie would endure having Nick's body with us for the days to come, but my fear seemed unjustified.

Chapter 15

THE day before Nick's body was taken away for cremation was a blur. I called the people on Nick's to-notify list, and some people came to say their farewells to him, mostly neighbors and the people from the restaurants and cafés Nick used to frequent in town.

Jamie stayed next to Nick, his face blank, totally silent. Some people would put their hand on his shoulder, some would talk to him, but he didn't acknowledge any of them. He didn't acknowledge me either. I tried to coax him to eat, but he wouldn't. He drank from a glass of water on the table next to him and got up to go to the bathroom occasionally.

I was worried he'd crack when they took Nick away, but he didn't. He remained seated next to the empty bed. When I went up to sleep, I gave him a hug and told him to come upstairs as well, but he didn't react. I was surprised to feel him crawl under the covers a few hours later.

"Jamie?" He didn't react so I put my hand on his shoulder, but he shrugged me away. I felt rejected, not because he shied away from my advances, which I understood, but because I realized I needed the comfort. I needed to share my loss with someone who was at least as close to Nick as I'd been. This was why Nick had wanted me to take care of Jamie: so Jamie would have someone to share his sorrow with. I knew I needed to give Jamie time, but my time in Spain was ending as well. I needed to return to work at some point.

The next morning when I got up, I found Jamie working in the garden. He looked rested after his first night in a decent bed in what felt like ages. I knew I had to have a difficult conversation with him, though.

"Morning."

Jamie looked me briefly and nodded. I supposed it was better than being ignored.

"Have you had breakfast yet?"

Jamie shrugged.

"You need to eat, J. Let me make you some toast and jam?"

He didn't respond, but I went into the kitchen anyway and took out the bread. By the time the toast popped up, Jamie was washing his hands. I wanted to hug him, more for my own benefit than his, I admit, but I wasn't ready for another round of rejection, so I didn't. I put jam on both pieces and handed one to Jamie. We sat in silence while I ate mine and he picked at his, eating mere morsels.

"Jamie, in a few days I'm going to have to go back to New York."

Jamie nodded.

"Nick wanted us to stay together. Will you come with me?"

Jamie waited so long to respond I was about ready to shake him into answering me. "Will you ever let me come back here?"

I closed my eyes, restraining myself. "Jamie, I'm not forcing you into doing anything. Of course we'll come back here. This is your home. You have so many memories here." To my surprise, I was the one less in control of his emotions than Jamie was. I ached to pull him into my arms and comfort him, but he looked as unaffected as always when faced with a dire situation. I suppose if he were really distressed he'd be upstairs scrubbing the bath.

Nevertheless, I could imagine him dreading leaving his safe little cocoon, the house and, most of all, the garden he loved so much. I automatically assumed that since I'd never seen Jamie leave it, he didn't want to. All of a sudden I started worrying about making him travel. How would he feel walking outside, driving to the airport, getting on a plane?

"Jamie, will you be okay flying to New York with me?"

"I've flown before, when we came here."

"I know, but that was a long time ago and Nick—" I almost choked on the name, but Jamie didn't react, "Nick never took you anywhere. Have you been anywhere in the past eight years?"

"I went to the hospital with you."

"Yes, you did." But that was a whole different ball game compared to flying across the Atlantic and moving from the peace and quiet of the villa to my apartment in the Garment District. I put my hand on his arm. "We'll come back here in a few weeks. I'll try to get some jobs in this part of Europe, and then we can come back and you can tend to your garden."

Jamie nodded, and he didn't look defeated or unhappy with the situation. Was I just projecting? Was I expecting him to act differently and since he wasn't, I was disappointed? I still felt like shaking him until he showed some sort of emotion. *That* I could deal with. We could fight about it, or I could comfort him if he cried, but this? This blank stare and unquestioning willingness to follow anything I suggested was grating on my nerves.

"I'll make a few calls and book us a flight. Can you be packed and ready to leave in three or four days?"

"Yes."

"You can take however much you like. We'll be flying first class so they don't count suitcases."

"Okay," Jamie answered as he remained seated at the breakfast table, staring at his crumbled toast.

THREE days later we closed up to leave. I'd asked the neighbor to water the plants and left him a phone number he could call in case anything happened to the house. Jamie had packed exactly one suitcase. I still had my garment bag and the one small suitcase I'd come with, since most of the clothes I'd worn around the house in the past month had been from Nick's extensive wardrobe of slacks and shirts that no longer fit him because he'd lost so much weight in the last months of his life.

It felt strange to leave. This last month had arguably been the most intense of my life, and these last few days had been a little strained but otherwise very calm and easygoing. When the taxi picked us up, Jamie didn't even look back at the house.

None of my fears came true. The flight home was uneventful and as I expected, Jamie didn't speak a word to anyone. I had to coax him through airport security and immigration, where we were met by strange looks because I answered for Jamie whenever he was asked a question. No drama unfolded, though. Jamie was an easy traveler.

Arriving at my apartment was strange too, since I'd left it expecting to be back in a few days and stayed away for an entire month. Masha, my housekeeper, had diligently cleaned the place so it was tidy and free of dust, but it was darker and gloomier than I remembered. Maybe I was so used to the whiteness and bright sunshine of Spain it was clouding my judgment?

I got Jamie settled in the guestroom and unpacked my stuff in my own bedroom, then gave Jamie the tour of the place. I knew he was going to be home alone quite a bit while I worked, and although I didn't like thinking of him as my housekeeper, I knew he'd do a much better job than Masha, however diligent she was, could ever do. I didn't want to take this for granted, though, so I focused on showing him how the TV worked and how to rent movies. To my surprise, the time difference got to me and I fell asleep on the couch.

SINCE I'd postponed leaving Barcelona until the last minute, I had to go into the office the very next day. Jamie was still asleep when I had to leave, so I left him a note and some money in case there was something he needed and it wasn't available in the house. I promised myself I'd call him before noon.

As it turned out, I'd missed quite a bit of commotion at the office.

"You look like you still weren't ready to start work again," a teasing voice said as I walked into my office. When I looked up, I stared right into the eyes of Lakiya, a gorgeous, curvy but petite African American woman who was the firecracker of the team. Before she started raising a family, she worked the international placements, just like me, and she was more than formidable competition. Now she preferred staying in New York, but she was still the highest earner of all the headhunters. I had always liked her. "We missed you," she said. "Norman got caught choosing with his dick rather than his expertise, and I've done two overseas jobs while you were gone." There was no malice in her words, but she made sure I knew just how glad she was to have me back. "Are you ready to fly again?"

She must have read my face. "So you really weren't ready to come back yet. Must have been one hell of a greener pasture."

I shrugged, then realized this was Lakiya, my partner in crime. I wasn't "out" at work, but Lakiya knew. She'd sussed me out during the first mission we undertook together and then broke protocol by introducing me to Peter, the right-hand man of the guy we were trying to sign for a larger corporation than he was running at the time. Peter and I had spent a passionate night together while Lakiya wined and dined the decidedly heterosexual CEO and got him to consider the position. He moved on to a few bigger and better things, always with the intervention of our company, and always taking Peter along with him. It was a win-win situation all around. Sometimes I really missed Lakiya out in the field. "Yeah, it was green all right," I told her. "But back to work."

She sighed, then handed me a data stick. "We need you in Latvia."

"Latvia? Why not the South Pole?"

She snorted, a very unladylike gesture for such a woman. "I'm sure we can arrange that too."

"How long?"

"If you leave tonight, five days."

I sank into my executive chair and contemplated telling her I couldn't. How could I leave Jamie in a strange apartment with nobody to keep him company for five days when he hadn't even started grieving Nick's death yet? Jamie was still in shock, but what if the bough broke while I wasn't there? The one hope I had was that Jamie was afraid to leave the safety of home when there was nobody to do the talking for him. At least that should keep him inside and safe from harm. And he was going to have to get used to me not being there all the time. He could cook, so if I got him groceries, he wouldn't starve.

"Okay, now you're starting to worry me."

I looked at Lakiya and saw the deep line above her eyebrows. "It's kind of hard for me to leave right now, Kee."

"It's what you do, honey. It's what you've done for fifteen years, and you revel in it."

"Yeah, I know," I said, not even convincing myself. "Okay." I lifted the data stick. "Everything I need to know is on here?"

"Did the research myself."

I smiled, knowing I couldn't lose then.

"I'll e-mail you your flight details. Knock 'em dead out there, soldier."

Chapter 16

ALL the way over to Latvia I kept doubting whether I'd made the right decision.

Should I have taken Jamie with me? Yes, he would be stuck in a hotel room in a city where neither of us spoke the language instead of a strange apartment where he did, but since he didn't talk to strangers, that would be a moot point. I could have easily made another airplane reservation for him and at least then I would have seen him every night, although I would have had to make sure he had his own bed, because he still didn't sleep in mine.

I admit I *wanted* to believe Jamie could fend for himself for a little while. After all, Nick's first suggestion was that I buy his villa and visit Jamie a few times a year to make sure everything was running smoothly. Didn't that mean Jamie could live on his own for a while?

I knew my reasons for not taking him with me were selfish. While I worked, I didn't want to think of anything else, and Jamie would have been a distraction. Too bad I only realized I would still be distracted by him not being there once I no longer could change anything about it.

BEFORE heading back to my apartment from the office, I'd stopped by the market for groceries, picking out lots of fresh produce, knowing Jamie would appreciate that. I'd also picked up some magazines and a Brita filter so Jamie could filter his water like he'd done in the villa. I'd arranged for the bakery to deliver fresh bread every day and hoped Jamie would let them actually bring it in.

When I arrived at the apartment, laden with shopping bags, Jamie was sitting on the couch, still in his pajamas although it was early afternoon. I dropped everything in my open-plan kitchen and ruffled his hair, which was growing longer than I had ever seen it. "I brought food and magazines for you to read." I sat down next to him on the couch and caressed his foot. "I need to go away on business, Jamie."

I braced for impact but it didn't come. "Where?"

"Latvia."

"Former Soviet Union."

"Yeah, but now a burgeoning capitalist market. I'll be back in five days."

Jamie seemed unaffected. "When do you leave?"

"I need to check my e-mail, but sometime tonight."

"Okay."

"Will you be okay?"

"Yeah."

I wasn't convinced, but there was nothing I could do except call Lakiya and tell her to find someone else. The only problem was that someone else would likely be her, so it wouldn't be fair, knowing how thinly stretched they'd been with me going AWOL for a month and Norman being fired for his unprofessional conduct. We were a small company with big revenue, but we didn't do the kind of job you could just hand over to anyone. I knew I'd have to bite the bullet, so I got on that plane and left Jamie to fend for himself.

Somewhere during the five very busy days I'd convinced myself everything would be okay. I'd sent Jamie an e-mail every day, talking about what I'd done and what I'd seen in the city and he'd e-mailed me back, simply telling me he was okay. Even over e-mail, he wasn't the most talkative, but it didn't matter. Silly as it was, I just wanted him to know I was coming back and that I hadn't forgotten him.

WHEN I arrived back in New York, it was the middle of the night, and I was yet again jetlagged. How could one month of downtime fuck with my body clock so much more than fifteen years of jetting around? I didn't care. All I wanted was a nice warm bed. As soon as I walked out of the elevator, I knew that wouldn't be waiting for me.

In front of my apartment door was at least three days' worth of bread delivery. I quickly unlocked the door and, taking the bags of bread with me, walked inside.

The apartment was clean and tidy, but there was a moldy orange in the fruit basket. I opened the fridge and found most of the produce I'd bought still there.

"Jamie?"

For some reason I knew he wouldn't be there.

"Jamie?" I walked into his bedroom and found the bed unmade and his clothes still in the wardrobe. That gave me a little bit of hope that he'd only walked out and would return soon, although the unmade bed was not the sort of thing I'd ever known Jamie to leave behind. To be safe I checked every room and under the bed, but Jamie was truly not there.

I called Masha, whose phone number I'd shown Jamie on speed dial, but she hadn't heard anything. The doorman downstairs hadn't seen Jamie leave. I didn't know what else to do, so I just waited. And fell asleep on the couch. When I woke again it was almost light.

"Jamie?" Of course he wasn't there. That meant he'd stayed out all night. Was this what it was like to have children? No. Jamie was hardly a child. Then again, there was a reason Nick had told me Jamie was no good on his own, and we'd never gotten around to the gritty details. Maybe this was my wake-up call.

I decided to call the police and report Jamie missing. I lied and told them he'd been gone for two days. It was a little white lie, which could have been true, but I had no way of knowing. They told me they'd send an officer to come by the apartment. They always did something extra in the more affluent neighborhoods, and for once I didn't mind being given preferential treatment.

I didn't want to leave in case Jamie returned. I almost wished he'd stumble in, still a little drunk from going clubbing. I knew the chance of that was virtually nil. While I waited for the cops, I called the hospitals and gave then Jamie's description. Nobody had seen him. Dread was creeping up on me.

The two uniformed policemen that came to my door didn't look like the empathetic kind, but I knew I'd have to go through the motions. They took my name and details and then started asking questions as if they'd memorized them at the police academy.

"And the missing person?"

"Jamie Kendrick," I repeated for the third or fourth time, since they couldn't seem to remember they were dealing with an actual person.

"Mr. Kendrick," the oldest one corrected himself. "Is he a relative?"

"He's my best friend's husband," I clarified.

"And where is she now? Your best friend?"

"My best friend passed away in Barcelona just over a week ago. *He* died of cancer." I couldn't help myself emphasizing the right pronoun.

"He?" the youngest one repeated.

I got really annoyed. "Yes, this *is* the 21st century. Even New York has gay marriage now. Yes, Jamie was married to Nick for three years, but they were together for eight. They *loved* each other very much." I could tell they were becoming uncomfortable, if not by my emotional account, then certainly by the content of what I was saying. "When Nick was dying, he asked me to take care of Jamie and I said I would, but I had to go to work. Now I'm worried that Jamie, in all his grief, did something... desperate." There. The word had fallen. Sort of. I was truly scared that Jamie had wandered off and jumped off a bridge somewhere. There were plenty of bridges within walking distance of my apartment. Did I really believe Jamie would do such a thing? I didn't know what to think anymore.

"So you have a picture?"

Did I? I remembered taking pictures of Jamie and Nick on one of Nick's last good days, but they felt too intimate to give to the cops. Also, I knew Nick would hate me for spreading around images of him looking as sick as he did. There were a few others from the first days I was at the villa. Nick still looked good in those, but they too were meant for Jamie to have something to remember Nick by. Then I remembered one Nick had taken of Jamie before I'd arrived. I recalled picking it up from the photo shop in town and seeing Nick's eyes light up when he saw the picture printed on really fancy paper. It showed Jamie sporting a shy smile as he looked into the lens, his hair still cropped really short and his aqua-blue eyes jumping out at you. He looked relaxed and happy. I knew exactly where the picture was because I'd taken it along with Nick's diary when I found out Jamie hadn't packed it. I'd hoped we'd be able to look through the diary when Jamie was ready for it.

I retrieved it from my room and gave it to the oldest cop. "I need it back. It's the only picture I have."

He eyed me with a mix of suspicion and pity. I couldn't hold his gaze. "We'll copy it and leave it at the front desk of the precinct. You can pick it up from there tomorrow. Who knows, you might want to come by to tell us he showed up anyway."

I decided to ignore the disdain in his statement, thinking it was probably more in my mind than it could ever be in his. I thanked them for coming and showed them out.

After sinking down to my couch and letting my mind wander for a while, I knew I couldn't just sit there and wait. Something had happened to Jamie, and I'd promised Nick I'd look after him so I had to find him. How the hell I was going to do that in a city of five million I didn't know, but I had to try. I'd always been a go-getter, had always achieved the impossible in my job, so why couldn't I apply that to this situation? My first task was to go through Nick's diary. I knew Nick had found Jamie here in New York, so Jamie was familiar with the city, although it had changed quite a bit in the last eight years. Maybe his diary would reveal where exactly Jamie could have gone to.

I'd always known Nick to be a man of many talents. He wasn't just a stupid, fickle porn star. He had a college degree, his villa was decorated with his own strange and wonderful paintings, and as I could tell from his diary, he should have become a writer too. It was very intimate, reading his diary. Nick wrote about feeling stuck in the shallow, superficial world of porn where drugs were freely handed out and men lived dangerously, all in pursuit of that elusive career of wealth and notoriety, if there was such a thing in that business. Nick was one of the few who'd succeeded in becoming a real international star. He wrote about many others ending up in the gutter, riddled with disease or emaciated by the drugs. I only skimmed over his entries about friends dying of AIDS and about how lucky he'd felt to have escaped that. I wanted to get to the part where he'd encountered Jamie.

IT WAS near the end of his career, when offers started drying up and he only got to play what he considered dirty old men. It had sent him on a downward spiral, leading him to try some of the drugs he'd always resisted. They made him feel better, at least for a while. Less filming meant Nick's libido was often shooting through the roof. So some of his entourage, mostly failed porn stars and their fans, would take him to the kind of clubs that had a back room or a shielded VIP area where public sex was available to anyone with a big enough dick. And Nick certainly had that. Soon enough his entourage grew and the clubs became more extreme. One day they'd taken him to a house in Brooklyn where men were screened before gaining entrance. They also had to pay a hefty entrance fee. Nick paid for all of them to go inside, lured there with promises of willing young men freely offering their services. Alcohol flowed copiously and cocaine, poppers, and Viagra were handed out on silver dishes. Nick felt like he'd died and gone to heaven. Soon after arriving he'd fucked a young man who'd recognized him from his movies, but fueled by the excess, Nick had gone in search of something more. He'd passed by a room where they were gangbanging another youngster, but the line of eager dicks was long and Nick hadn't paid it much attention. A little later, the drugs working their way out of his system, he'd fallen asleep on a plush couch amid two naked godlike creatures.

He woke up some time later with a raging hard-on and a full bladder. After an exhaustive search for a restroom, he'd found a young man inside of it. One of his eyes was swollen shut, there was blood running from his mouth, and his entire body was discolored with old and new bruises. He was huddled naked in a corner, and one look at his frightened face shocked Nick back to reality. That man was Jamie. The rest was history.

I SAT looking at the diary entry dated almost nine years ago. The description was very graphic and seemingly unemotional, as if Nick was taking a step back from it or it was written much later, after the fact. The following chapters were much more involved. Another explanation was that Nick hadn't fallen in love with Jamie until after he'd taken care of him those first few weeks when he was sick and unresponsive.

In any case, it was disconcerting that Jamie only knew the underbelly of the city. I didn't look forward to seeking out those dark corners again, but I now had a way to start my search for him. I unearthed my leathers from the back of my closet. The only good thing about it was finding out they still fit me.

Chapter 17

A WEEK went by with no sign of Jamie. I hated scouring the clubs night after night, but I knew I had no choice. Jamie couldn't have gone far, since he had no money to speak of. The fifty bucks I had left for him when I went away wouldn't have lasted him a few days on the streets, let alone the week and a half he'd been gone. So he'd have to either have found a sugar daddy or a seedy club manager who'd hire him. I couldn't stand the idea of all those strangers touching Jamie any more than Nick had. I clearly recalled the disgust on Nick's face as he told me how he'd found Jamie and then tasted bile myself rereading the description in Nick's diary.

New York is the city that never sleeps, and there are thousands of clubs all around the city, if you know where to look. This was the fifth club I'd entered that night. I was dressed as I always was for the kind of club I'd chosen: tight, black leather pants and a sleeveless jacket that showed off my buff chest and most of my tattoos. It gave me a dominant air and assured me that I would get cooperation even from the men who'd never seen me before. I shopped around the picture of Jamie I'd given to the cops and then had needed to argue to get it back at the precinct. I tried the bartenders and some of the men carting around subs or slaves, but caught nothing. I was only asked if I was a cop once.

Then as I walked outside, I was stopped by a guy who looked very much like I did: shaved head, leather gear, and tattoos.

"You're looking in the wrong places."

"I am?" I replied, purposely not sounding too enthusiastic. The man looked compassionate and willing to help, though.

"I think I saw your boy."

I wanted to protest the use of the term "boy," but figured it wouldn't help me any. "You think?"

"Lemme see the picture again."

I showed him the picture of Jamie. The man looked at it for a brief moment.

"His hair is longer now."

I nodded and tried desperately not to get my hopes up, although this was the first positive sign I'd gotten. "Tell me where you saw him."

"I'll do one better. I'll take you. It's not in a club. It's in a house where the owner throws parties. They'll never let you in by yourself."

"What kind of parties?" I asked, this time unable to hide the apprehension I felt. My heart was racing.

"I better show you." The man stepped outside and I followed. He hailed a cab at the corner and drove us across town to a row house that looked like all the other houses in the street. He let me pay for the cab. As I looked around the ordinary-looking street, I wondered if any of the decent families here knew they had an underground sex club next door, but then my nervousness started taking over again. I knew I shouldn't get my hopes up. For all I knew, the man had seen Jamie just once and Jamie didn't actually work there. The chances of finding him were next to none, I kept telling myself, but I had to follow every lead. I also had to keep a level head. As soon as that thought started calming me, another little voice told me to beware. I didn't know my guide from Adam. For all I knew, the man picked up affluent club customers with promises of an exclusive club experience and then sent them somewhere to be mugged, or worse. I didn't want to think about that. I may have looked butch, but underneath that thin veneer, I was just a businessman who knew how to use his body language to his best advantage.

The man who opened the door obviously knew the man who'd brought me with him. I was given a cursory look, but no more than that. I knew how these operations ran on trust and my guide was obviously trusted. There was no talk of payment. The man nodded at other men we passed in the dimly lit corridors and he whispered in the ear of a thin, pale-looking older man.

"Nicky? Yes, he's here," the thin man replied.

Nicky? Was Jamie using Nick's name?

The thin man looked me up and down. I could tell he didn't entirely trust the situation.

"Nicky's busy, I'm afraid. He'll have to wait," the man said to my guide without taking his eyes off me. "The boy can only take so many men, although I must say he enjoys every single one of them tremendously."

I could tell the thin man was telling the truth, or at least the version he thought was true. If anything, I was an excellent judge of body language and facial expressions, since this was an integral part of my success as a headhunter. This man meant what he said. Although I knew firsthand how much Jamie enjoyed sex, I also knew from Nick's account and my own experiences that Jamie needed to trust the person fucking him before he could actually enjoy it. They must have given him alcohol or drugged him up.

"Follow me," the thin man said, leading me, without my guide, into a room. "Can I get you anything to drink? Scotch? Bourbon?" He cocked his head in a peculiar way and narrowed his eyes. "You seem like a tequila man. Am I right?"

"Very rarely," I replied. "If anything, I'm a Rioja man." When the thin man threw me a questioning look, I elaborated. "Spanish red wine."

"I see," the thin man said with a nod. "I'm sure I can find you a nice glass of California red?"

I shook my head. "I'm fine, thank you. But I would like to see J... Nicky."

The man took a step toward the door. "I'll see when he could be free." He turned around and faced me again. "He's a popular boy around here. He's booked way in advance."

"I'm not here to.... I just need to talk to him."

The thin man sniggered. "Then you'll have a long wait. If you knew anything about Nicky, you'd know that Nicky doesn't talk."

I had a hard time controlling my breathing. This practically confirmed that Nicky was Jamie. I had to get to him. "I can make him talk. He'll talk to me," I said with as much conviction as I could master.

The thin man pursed his lips, and I wondered if it was amusement or strain. My own emotions at being so close to my target were clouding my intuition.

"Let me see him," I pleaded. "Just for a moment."

"Stay here," the thin man cautioned. "I'll be back to fetch you."

With that he left me alone. The room I'd been brought to was an elaborately decorated turn-of-the-century salon, with plush red velvet upholstery that showed appropriate wear near the seams but still looked immaculately maintained. Although I was tired, I couldn't sit down. After an exhaustive ten day search, I was finally close to Jamie, and I had to find a way to get him out of there. I had to figure out a plan, a way to get him past the thin man and past the goons in the hallway. Once outside, I was sure I could procure a cab and take him to my apartment.

What was taking the man so long? I paced to the door and opened it. The corridor was more deserted than it had been when I entered, and I decided to investigate on my own. I heard voices to the right, away from the door to the street. I tried hard to keep my bearings, knowing that if I needed to make a run for it, I wouldn't have time to think. I just hoped that if the time came to escape I'd have Jamie with me.

At the end of the corridor, droves of barely clothed men were standing in thick rows, stretching to look inside a doorway. From inside the room I heard cheering and men urging others on. Dread started forming in the pit of my stomach as I walked closer, trying to look like I belonged. I pushed through the first few rows and some men protested, but I didn't care. I needed to see inside for myself.

I was pushed against the doorjamb as I got my first look. A man was stretched over a table, totally naked, his hands taped together and pushed awkwardly behind his head. He had bruises on his sides and red marks in the shape of fingers and hands on his hips. Men were taking turns fucking him, from the back and from the front, laughing as they spit-roasted him. As one of the men pulled away, I saw Jamie's birthmark. There was no mistaking the lopsided star on his left ass cheek. I had to get Jamie out of there, but how could I do it with about fifty horny men surrounding me? What could I do? I thought of tripping the fire alarm, but the house was very much that, a house, and surely didn't adhere to fire regulations like a legit club would. I looked around at all the men who had one focus of attention: Jamie.

Then I looked at Jamie again. I didn't want to leave the room, but Jamie was facing away from the door, so he hadn't seen me yet. Behind Jamie, near the back wall, stood the thin man. He was leaning against the wall, talking to the man who'd brought me here. Both were fully clothed and clearly just spectators. I took a few steps back and then yelled: "Police! It's a raid!"

The men standing closest to me gave me a questioning look, but some of the other men started vacating the room, causing a ripple effect. The tension rose dramatically, and I pushed against the flow to get to Jamie. When I reached him and tried to pull him upright, I got a good look at Jamie's face. It was bruised and there was blood trickling out the side of his mouth. When Jamie looked me in the eye, he was confused and dazed. I was sure he was drugged.

"We need to leave."

Jamie didn't respond.

I tried to extricate Jamie's hands from the tape, but couldn't so I settled for pulling them over his head to a more comfortable position and making him sit on the side of the table. "Jamie?" Jamie didn't even let on he recognized me. I decided I'd deal with that later. "We need to leave. Now."

"I don't think so."

I looked up and saw the thin man standing there.

"I knew you were trouble the moment you walked in here. Nicky came here of his own volition. He wasn't forced to do anything. He's a natural. He likes the abuse. Gets off on it. And these men get off on his eagerness."

I pulled Jamie to face the men. "He's drugged out of his mind." I shook my head and murmured, "His own choice." Then I raised my voice. "Forgive me for not believing you. I'm taking him with me. Straight to the police station. End of story. End of business too." I didn't wait for an answer, but pulled Jamie to his feet and walked him out of there. As I expected, Jamie followed without a struggle.

The corridor was still full of men scrambling to find their clothes. It was chaos and I used it to my advantage. I grabbed a raincoat hanging over a chair and wrapped it around Jamie's naked body before making my way outside. There were men on the street as well, and I knew we'd have to walk at least a block to find a cab. I hoped Jamie would be able to handle the distance. Several cab drivers ignored us. I couldn't blame them. We made a strange pair, one man in leathers and another with naked legs sticking out from under a raincoat, but eventually one stopped to pick us up. I gave the man my address and then turned my attention to Jamie.

"You okay? Let me look at you."

Jamie didn't react. "It's me, Jamie. It's Jez, remember?"

"Jez?" Jamie croaked, as if he hadn't used his voice in a long time. I thought this was probably true.

"Yes, darling. I'm taking you home, where you'll be safe."

Chapter 18

I WAS glad it was a balmy evening, so there was little chance of Jamie catching a cold. It didn't stop me worrying, though, as Jamie sat next to me shivering violently while I tried to untangle the heavy duty silver tape wrapped around his wrists.

"Why did you let them do this to you, Jamie?" I asked, not really expecting an answer. "You had money for emergencies, and there was plenty of food in the house. There was no reason for you to do this of your own choosing. Did they force you?" I tried to establish eye contact while unsuccessfully struggling with Jamie's bonds. "I need scissors for this," I murmured, more to myself than to Jamie. "And I need to get you cleaned up so I can take a look at those." I pointed at the side of Jamie's mouth, which was split and had bloody goop sticking to it, and for the first time, Jamie reacted by pulling away as if I was trying to hit him. "Easy," I soothed. "Not gonna hurt you." It didn't take a lot of imagination for me to figure out how Jamie got that way, but I didn't want to think about it. I just remembered the look on Nick's face when he told me how he'd found Jamie. My expression couldn't have been that different. Maybe what Jamie was trying to avoid was the look of pity I knew I was sporting right now.

The cab stopped in front of my apartment, and I directed the cabbie to the service entrance in the alley at the back. The doorman would still need to come and open the door for us, but at least I could spare Jamie the embarrassment of walking through a heavily lit lobby where other people might see him.

The doorman was visibly concerned when he saw us. "Anything I can do for you, sir? Call a doctor?"

"No, thank you, Carlos," I said as I stood in front of Jamie to hide both his barely covered nakedness and his bound hands "I think we'll be okay for now. If I need anything, I'll give you a call."

"You do that, sir," Carlos replied while he pushed the button to open the elevator he'd obviously called down beforehand.

As the elevator doors closed and the cab started moving, I looked at Jamie and saw him waver. I turned to him and only just managed to keep him on his feet. "Hang on just a little longer. We're almost there." In the closed environment of the elevator cabin, the pungent smell surrounding Jamie became even more apparent. I just hoped Jamie could stay upright long enough to take a shower. When the elevator stopped at my floor, I wrapped my arm around him and led him into the apartment and straight through to the bathroom.

"Sit," I instructed, pointing at the closed toilet. As soon as I was assured Jamie wasn't going to fall over, I let go of him and opened a cupboard in search of a pair of scissors. The tape was wound tight and when I cut it away, red welts appeared underneath it. I tried to keep my face neutral and was silently happy that Jamie simply let everything wash over him, showing no expression or will of his own. I knew it wasn't a good sign overall, but for now, it made my task easier.

With a clean washcloth, wet with lukewarm water, I tried to be gentle as I wiped over Jamie's face. I frequently rinsed out the washcloth, but it slowly turned from pristine white to greyish pink as I continued washing the grime, blood, and spunk from Jamie's shoulders and arms. Jamie didn't wince until I tried to clean the area where the tape had been. "How long was it on for?" Jamie didn't even let on he'd heard the question, so I knew no answer would be forthcoming. "I'm going to have to disinfect it. It's going to sting." I got up and took what I needed from the medicine cabinet.

Jamie inhaled sharply as I used the disinfectant wipe on the welts, so I kissed his forehead in the hope it would soothe him. Instead, Jamie pulled away.

"'S okay," I said. "I won't do it again. You know I won't hurt you."

Jamie shook his head.

"You think I will? Hurt you?"

Again, Jamie shook his head "No."

I didn't know how to respond so I continued caring for Jamie, albeit keeping my distance.

"I'm dirty," Jamie eventually said.

"I washed you," I replied.

"Inside."

"You want to brush your teeth?"

Jamie sighed with an exasperated expression.

"They weren't using condoms, were they?" I said, realizing suddenly what Jamie had meant. I didn't wait for an answer. "We'll go to the clinic tomorrow and get you tested." When I looked at Jamie, he was staring at me, his face still unreadable, but two thick tears were rolling down each side of his face.

"Sssh," I said, wiping the tears away with my hands. "It'll work itself out in the end." This time Jamie didn't pull away as I pulled him into my arms, cradling his head and caressing his still crusty hair. "Let's get you in the shower and you'll feel better, okay?"

As usual, Jamie didn't respond, but he allowed himself to be led to the walk-in shower, where I turned on the spray and waited for the water to come to temperature. I figured Jamie wouldn't wash himself and contemplated getting in the shower with him fully clothed so not to startle him, but wondered if that wouldn't make it even more strange in Jamie's eyes. I decided to ask, realizing full well I probably wouldn't get an answer. "I'm going to take a shower with you, Jamie, so I can help you out. Is that okay?"

Jamie simply looked at me, his eyes a little sad, but the rest of his face just as impassive as always.

"Don't freak, okay? I'm going to take my clothes off so I can help you wash and so I can take a shower myself. Nothing's going to happen. I'm only going to wash you. No more, okay?"

Jamie nodded so slightly I wondered if I'd imagined it. He let himself be taken care of, though. I made sure the water was the right temperature before gently pushing Jamie under the spray. I washed Jamie's hair with shampoo and used a clean washcloth to wash the rest of his bruised body. I tried not to let the numerous fingerprints, welts, and scratches detract me from the fact that this was Jamie underneath them and Jamie who had undergone the torture, possibly partially willingly. There was no use questioning it. All I could do was to take care of Jamie as well as I could.

After Jamie was outwardly clean again, I made quick work of my own shower, simply using one kind of shower gel to wash my head and the rest of my body. As I emerged from under the spray that rinsed off the suds, I felt Jamie's arms enveloping me. "Hey, everything okay?"

As usual, Jamie didn't answer, but the tight grip he had on my chest prevented me from doing anything more than hug him back. We stood like that for a little while, not moving.

"Why don't we dry off? You look tired. You should go to bed and sleep."

Jamie let go and took a step out of the shower, where he waited patiently for me.

I wondered if Jamie would dry himself if I gave him a towel, but the answer to that was both expected and alarming. Although I was sure Jamie felt safe in my apartment, he simply stood there holding the towel while I dried myself off, as if he didn't know what to do with it. Not for the first time that evening, I wondered if Jamie had been drugged or if he was simply traumatized. I hoped a good night's sleep would help him come into his own again, so I simply took the towel from him and rubbed it over his body as I would do for a child. I was careful around the most bruised patches, but he didn't seem to be in any obvious pain. When I toweled off Jamie's hair, he gave me one of his clearest looks.

"Will you cut my hair?"

"Cut your hair?" I parroted.

"Nick always used to cut my hair. I like it better short."

I smiled. "Don't think I'll be as great a barber as Nick was, but I'll try. Wouldn't you prefer to get it cut by someone who knows what they're doing?"

"He just did it with the trimmer. Nothing fancy."

"Will you show me how he did it?"

Jamie nodded.

I left him in the bathroom while I went into my bedroom for a pair of boxer briefs and the trimmer Jamie had taken from Nick's things when we left Barcelona. I also brought some of Jamie's underwear from his room, thinking he would feel more comfortable if he was less naked. When I returned to the bathroom, Jamie was still waiting for me. The way he had his arms wrapped around himself betrayed that he was feeling cold, but otherwise, his expression was unreadable again.

"Here, put these on and I'll cut your hair." I handed Jamie his grey boxer briefs and left again to get a chair from the bedroom.

I loved Jamie's hair. Even as long as it was now, only just brushing over his eyebrows but not quite in his eyes yet, it was still silky smooth and lusciously thick; straight without being bristly. When it was short, like the very first time I'd ever touched it, it was like an incredibly soft brush. I was looking forward to caressing it again.

Jamie showed me how Nick always configured the trimmer, and I ran it through Jamie's hair with some trepidation as I tried to remember how my barber used to do it before I'd shaved it all off. When I was done, Jamie was smiling, though.

"You like it?"

Jamie ran his hands over and through it and nodded. I joined him, unable to contain myself. I concluded with hugging Jamie from behind. That was the first time Jamie looked at himself in the mirror he was sitting in front of. His smile waned.

"What's wrong?" I asked.

"I miss Nick."

"So do I."

Chapter 19

I TOOK Jamie to his bedroom and got him settled in. Once he was on his side, bedding tucked in all around him and my hand in his hair, his eyes closed and he drifted off. At least that's what I thought.

After sitting next to Jamie for a long time, I got up, but I'd barely reached the bedroom door when I heard his voice.

"Jez?"

"Yeah, Jamie?"

"Don't leave me alone."

"I'll be right across the hall in my room. Not going anywhere," I replied softly. As I walked out the door, Jamie didn't protest again. I got a drink of water and then went to my own bedroom to settle in with a book. I didn't read much, though. Barely half a chapter in, I caught myself falling asleep, so I put my book on the night stand and pulled the covers over my shoulder, expecting sleep to catch me soon.

I didn't think I'd slept at all when I heard my bedroom door open and close. I wasn't surprised to feel Jamie crawling into bed with me. "J?"

"I'll leave if you want."

"No, that's okay."

Jamie snaked his arms around my torso, and I had to admit the heat of his body felt nice against my back. I fell asleep almost immediately.

THE following morning I woke, like I always did, at the crack of dawn. Light was streaming through my white curtains and Jamie was still sleeping next to me, seemingly content and relaxed. The bruises on his face and the cut at the corner of his mouth already seemed to be healing and I figured the rest of his injuries, at least the physical ones, probably wouldn't take that long to fade either.

As long as Jamie was close to me, there didn't seem to be a problem, but I had to go into work today. I had several important meetings, and calling in sick when I wasn't sick at all was not in my book. That meant I had to leave Jamie alone for most of the day. There was nobody in the city Jamie trusted or who I trusted to stay with Jamie. For the first time in my life, I missed having a family.

I quietly slipped out of bed, managing not to wake Jamie, and walked into the bathroom for a leak. While brushing my teeth, I tried to remember everything Nick had told me about Jamie's comfort behaviors. At the time it seemed trite; now I wished I'd paid more attention. I simply had to find a way for Jamie to feel wanted and safe. I also had to make sure Jamie knew I was going to return later that day.

Walking into the living room, I decided to make Jamie a list. I remembered Nick making one for Jamie in his house in Barcelona just before he took me out for a day on the town. Maybe that was what Nick needed to do for Jamie so he could leave him alone for a few hours. I just hoped it would help Jamie, because I felt like I was writing a to-do list for an employee, not a friend. It wasn't easy coming up with things that needed to be done around the house, things for which Jamie didn't need to leave the apartment and for which everything he needed was readily available. Besides obvious chores, like watering the plants and Jamie's favorite, scrubbing the shower, I also added watching a movie, just to feel better about the whole list thing. I put a little star in front of the plants and the movie, indicating these needed to be done today. All the others were optional. I ended the list with "Love, Jez."

Content with what I'd arranged, I jumped in the shower and then walked into my bedroom to get dressed. As I got out my clothes, I turned around to see Jamie watching my every move.

"Sleep well?"

Jamie nodded. He was lying on his back, legs stretched out before him under the covers and propped up on his elbows. It gave his beautiful shoulders even more definition, and I had to look away or I'd get aroused.

"I need to go to work, Jamie," I said as I buttoned my shirt. As I feared, Jamie's face clouded over. "I'm not leaving on a plane. I just need to go to my office for the day. I'll be home for dinner. I promise. I'll bring take-away. Thai food okay for you?"

"I can cook," Jamie replied.

I moved to the bed and sat down, putting my hand on Jamie's arm. "I know. And you're a great cook, but there isn't much in the house besides a little cereal, some yogurt, and a few canned goods. I'll have a sandwich delivered to you for lunch, and tonight we can go grocery shopping. Then you can cook for me tomorrow."

"Will you have to work again tomorrow?"

"Yes," I said. I rubbed Jamie's arm. "I'm sorry I can't stay with you during the day. But I made you a list of things to do."

A shy smile broke on Jamie's face. Bingo. I had managed to find something familiar for him to hold onto. "And you'll be back tonight?"

I nodded. "Yes. Will you be okay here? No more wanderlust?"

"Wanderlust?"

I chuckled. "No more need to go outside and get into trouble," I explained. "I don't mind if you leave the apartment, that's why I left you a key, but I'd like you to be here when I get back." These were almost exactly the words Nick had used that one time he'd left Jamie behind to show me around. I hoped they'd do the trick.

"Okay," Jamie answered. "I'll be fine."

I leaned in to kiss him on the forehead, but Jamie was quicker as he pulled my head down and kissed me full on the mouth, tongue and all. I lingered, both because Jamie didn't let me go and because it felt so good to taste him again. Since my dress pants wouldn't hide the arousal Jamie had caused with his searing kiss, I stayed close, eyes closed for longer than I wanted to. When I finally got up, I saw Jamie's eyes wander to my crotch.

"Let me take care of that for you before you leave."

I smiled at Jamie. "Don't think so. I'm already late."

Jamie pouted, but I could tell it was his playful pout. He pointed his finger at me and narrowed his eyes.

"Don't give me that look."

Jamie giggled and I felt like I was soaring. I just had to remind myself of the Jamie I'd picked up the night before to let both my hard-on die down and my mood deflate. Jamie would need time to heal before we could engage in any sort of fun and games, and I figured it would take longer than the time for the welts to heal. I rubbed my hand through Jamie's short hair. "Have fun today and before you know it, I'll be back, okay?"

Jamie nodded and I got up, taking my jacket from the hanger and putting it on before making my way outside without looking back.

IT TOOK me longer than usual to get into working mode and all day long, in between meetings with business clients and my associates, my mind kept wandering to Jamie. I called him on the phone and even though he picked up the receiver, it was a one-way conversation as I asked him how he was doing and he couldn't answer me. I tried not to let it worry me too much and settled for getting Clark to buy Jamie an Oven Roasted Chicken sub and deliver it personally. When he came back, he reported that he'd had to leave the sandwich outside and walk away. Clark seemed disappointed, but I wasn't. I figured it was simply typically Jamie.

"You look all radiant," a teasing voice said, startling me out of my Jamie dream. It was Lakiya, and she was looking at me with an expression that said she was trying to get me to come clean about something.

"I suppose I should be flattered."

She rolled her eyes. "You were miles away. I'm not used to seeing you like that, Jez. You're always Mr. Focus-on-the-Target."

"I'm a little... distracted."

"Lemme guess." She narrowed her eyes. "She's twenty-seven and working on her PhD in International Relations."

"Hit it right out of the ballpark, Kee," I quipped.

"Thought so." She sent me a knowing smile and closed the door so we were alone in the office. "Okay, stud. Spill."

"I found Jamie last night."

"Oh, God." Her tough-as-nails expression softened in an instant as she pulled up a chair and sat next to me, taking my hand in a gesture I'd never seen her display.

I'd told her about Nick and Jamie and my month in Spain and then when Jamie disappeared, she'd covered for me occasionally so I could go look for him. She didn't know all the details and I wasn't about to give them to her now, but it felt good to have a confidante.

"How is he?"

"Bruised and battered. Abused."

Her forehead crunched up, and all of a sudden I could see in her something I'd only seen when she had her kids around. This was a mother, a woman who cared about what happened to other people and who could only think, "What if it had been my kid?"

"Did you report it to the cops?"

"No." I shook my head. "I couldn't let Jamie go through that. I'm taking him to the clinic tonight and that'll be bad enough."

"But these people who did that to him need to be punished!"

"Kee, please. In an ideal world, yes. But Jamie will never admit to—" I started to say "being raped" but decided to keep that little detail to myself for now. "—what they did to him. He might have gone there willingly."

"Nobody lets themselves be abused willingly, Jez. Unless they're some sort of... whatchamacallit... sadomasochist?"

I wondered how much I could confide in her. "He's not adverse to... a little pain."

"Uh oh."

"Don't uh-oh me, young lady," I teased.

"You saying he asked to be hurt?"

"I don't know, but the cops will give him a hard time about it, and he can't take that, Kee. You should have seen those officers who took my statement when I reported him missing. They were *this* far from asking me whether I'd *made* him run away. They think we're all a bunch of deviants anyway and if I tell them where I found him, the first question won't be where this place was, but how the hell I knew where to find places like that. The chance of me ending up in jail is infinitely bigger than them finding the people responsible."

There was a knock on my door and Clark's voice announced they were waiting for us. Lakiya got up and straightened her frighteningly figure-hugging skirt before pulling down the jacket she wore over it.

"Let's go see if we can nail this deal, stud," Lakiya said, donning her stern, I-may-be-petite-but-I'll-have-your-balls-for-breakfast look.

I laughed before composing myself and walking into the board meeting behind her.

Chapter 20

LIKE I had promised Jamie, I was home in time for dinner. I brought Thai food and some rudimentary groceries so Jamie could cook dinner the next day. When I walked into the apartment, it was so dark worry gripped me. "Jamie?"

A head popped up over the back of the couch, and a sad-looking Jamie looked back at me. "Hey, how was your day?"

Jamie didn't answer, but ducked back behind the cushions, forcing me to drop my groceries quickly before rounding the couch to sit next to him. Jamie was curled up, arms wrapped around his knees, still in the boxers and T-shirt he'd slept in. He'd clearly not shaved either.

I tried not to sound too worried. "So what did you do today?"

"I watered your plants, cleaned your bathroom—"

"Our plants and our bathroom," I interrupted. I so needed to get that into Jamie's head, because I couldn't bear the idea that Jamie saw it as simply a service to me.

"I was done by ten," Jamie continued.

"Did you watch a movie?"

"The list didn't say which movie I could watch."

"Oh, Jamie." I sighed. I didn't know how this was going to pan out. My plans of taking Jamie to see a doctor and get tested flew out the window. There were more pressing matters to attend to. Jamie was still too delicate right now to be poked and prodded by a man in a white coat. But there was no way I could instruct Jamie in everything. Besides, in Spain, Nick didn't either. I was sure of that. I let out an exasperated grunt. "How did Nick do this?"

"What?" Jamie asked innocently.

"Write up your lists. I know he didn't write up every single thing you had to do."

"We had agreements about some things."

I bit my lips and nodded. Maybe I could run this relationship as less of a dictatorship after all. "Why don't we agree that all the agreements you had with Nick are still valid?"

Jamie shook his head. "I had those agreements with Nick and Nick isn't here anymore, so they're invalid now."

"Okay." I took a deep breath. "Let's make our own agreements then. Can we do that?"

Jamie nodded.

"Can we agree that at all times, even when I'm not here, you'll get up in the morning and take a shower? You'll shave and get dressed and take a dump when you need to and have breakfast?"

Jamie was smiling and I couldn't help joining him.

"What clothes?"

"Anything you want."

"Anything?"

I chuckled. "All the time in Barcelona I never saw you in anything inappropriate, so anything you feel comfortable in."

"Even the red Speedos?"

I wondered if Jamie was having me on, but we were making headway and I didn't want to lose momentum. "You're going to hang around the apartment in a Speedo?"

"Okay, maybe not. But when we go to the house in Barcelona, I'll wear my Speedos for you."

I looked into Jamie's eyes and saw mischief there. God, how I'd missed that. "Deal." I also saw raw lust and it made me draw back. Not even twenty-four hours earlier I was washing blood and other men's cum off Jamie's body. Just the night before I was putting antiseptic ointment on his abrasions and soothing cream around his asshole. Surely I was interpreting Jamie's look all wrong?

"Have you eaten anything today?" I asked, purposely changing the subject.

"No," Jamie answered softly, the offending look wiped from his face and replaced by something I could interpret as shame if I wanted to. I didn't want to, though. My job was to take care of Jamie and I was not going to let my emotions, or my feelings of lust, come between me and my promise to Nick.

"Then it's time we eat before it's totally cold." I took out the cartons of take-away Thai and gave Jamie one set of chopsticks. Jamie was clearly starving and attacked the contents of every carton I handed to him. I realized I was hungry too and within no time, all the food was finished.

"You still hungry?" I asked Jamie as I got up to find something to drink.

Jamie stretched out on the couch as he followed me with his eyes. "Couldn't eat another morsel, but it was *so* good! Thank you."

"You're welcome," I replied, sitting down next to him with a glass of water for Jamie and a beer for me. "Do you want one of these?" I asked, although I'd never seen him drink anything else than water and the occasional glass of wine at dinner.

Jamie drank his water eagerly and shook his head at the same time. Sometimes he was such a child.

"More agreement time," I said, giving Jamie a serious look. "When I'm not here, you need to take care of yourself. Anything you do is fine with me. You don't need my permission. So you need to eat when you're hungry, drink when you're thirsty, wash when you're dirty, masturbate when you're horny." I smiled at Jamie and Jamie smiled back. I could see him blushing. "Seriously."

"Okay," Jamie agreed.

"I won't ever give you a hard time about your own decisions, unless you make one that puts you in danger. Going out and disappearing for two weeks and needing rescue was not one of your better decisions."

Jamie cringed and turned in on himself.

I felt guilty, but I knew we needed to get this out in the open. "I don't mind if you go for a walk. In fact I'd love it if you could pop down to the corner store for groceries on your own from time to time."

"I don't know these people," Jamie said, looking almost mortified. "I wouldn't be able to talk to them."

"I know," I said, putting my hand on Jamie's arm. "But you could look around for stuff and then give them a list for whatever you can't find."

Jamie hesitated. "I guess."

I figured that meant: "No, but get off my back," so I decided to leave that alone. "What I mean is, there's no doubt in my mind that you know the difference between actions that bring you in harm's way and actions that don't. As long as you stay safe, you can do whatever you want."

Jamie seemed to relax a bit as he lowered his feet off the couch.

"Now what movie do you want to watch?"

Jamie shrugged, and I figured that was an unfair question to ask of someone who didn't even dare to put on clothes because it wasn't on his to-do list. So I chose a *Die Hard* movie and let Jamie snuggle close to me to watch. I'd seen the movie a few times, but Jamie was enthralled by it, so I just relished watching him enjoy it. His attention didn't stay on the movie the whole time, though. After yet another car chase, I felt his hand wander over my leg to my thigh, where it lingered along the sensitive skin of my inner thigh. Somehow the delicate touch was enhanced by the stretched fabric of my jeans and it tickled and aroused at the same time. I shifted to accommodate the growing tightness higher up my leg and moved a pillow to obscure it from Jamie's view. This only invited Jamie to slide his hand underneath it. Eventually I pushed him away. He sat up and moved to the other side of the sofa.

"Jamie." I sighed.

He looked at me with his damned blank expression and I'd suddenly had enough.

"Talk to me. Shout at me. I don't care, but don't sit there as if you don't give a damn."

He did just that.

"You need more instruction? Fine. If I hurt your feelings, you need to tell me. If you like something, you need to tell me. If you want something, you also need to tell me."

For the first time in what felt like weeks, I saw Jamie warring with his feelings. Gone was the blank expression, replaced by thin, strained lips and a clenched jaw.

"Spit it out."

"I can't." His voice jumped from holding back.

"Why not? There's nothing you can say that can hurt me. There's nothing you can say or do that can make me turn away from you. I love you, Jamie." I was surprised at my own words, but I couldn't show him that.

"How about…." Jamie stopped, his breathing labored and heavy.

"What?"

"How about if I say I want you to fuck me, hard, until I bleed."

I swallowed to keep myself under control. "You know I won't do that, Jamie."

"Why not? You said I just had to tell you what I wanted and you wouldn't turn away from me. So I wanna get fucked so hard I won't be able to sit."

"You can barely sit now," I said slowly.

"But I want it!"

"I won't turn away from you, but I won't fuck you, Jamie."

"You fuck anything in pants. That's what Nick always said. Even the occasional woman." Jamie looked defiant.

"I haven't fucked a woman in a long time," I replied, glad for the change of subject.

"So why won't you fuck me then? I said I wanted it. It's not like you're raping me if I ask for it, right?"

I decided to return his insolent stare and moved to sit in front of him, my hands on his knees as I stared him down. "I don't do pain. When I go out to leather clubs, I may dominate another guy, fuck him in front of others, but I won't hurt him. I don't want hurt done to me and I refuse to inflict it on others."

"That's not what Nick told me."

"Leave Nick out of it."

The pained expression returned to Jamie's face. "But I want the pain."

"You're sick."

"And here I thought you said you wouldn't turn against me."

"I won't. I'll help you in any way I can, but I won't hurt you."

"I want you to hurt me."

We were going around in circles and I didn't like it. Jamie was trying to make me hate him and I simply refused to. He was trying to make me do what he expected of me and tell him I was disgusted by him and never wanted to see him again, but I could never do that. "Why would you want me to hurt you when you're already hurting so badly?"

"Because… because I want it to hurt."

"No, you don't. You want the pain to go away, and it will, but you need to give it time."

"Because I want to know the hurt comes from you." Tears were filling Jamie's eyes. "Because I can take it if you did it, but I can't if I don't know who hurt me!"

I pulled Jamie into my arms and he started sobbing. It felt so cathartic to see him surrender to his pain. I just rocked him back and forth gently, slowly coaxing him to lie down on the couch. Despite his almost six-foot frame, he was a little boy again, clamoring for comfort. While I hugged and soothed him, I thought about the dichotomy that was Jamie. From the neck down, he looked like a guy you didn't mess with, with a square, muscled frame of more than average height. He was physically strong too and could hold me down, despite the fact I was far from a wimp. His face gave him away, though. Round, soft, with small, aqua-blue eyes and a thin, curvy mouth. He didn't exactly have a baby-face, but it revealed his naiveté. In public he always kept his face neutral, but in private, I could read him like a book. Once he'd started trusting me, he could keep very little secret from me. And he knew it.

Our positions were a little awkward so I pushed him back and joined him on the sofa, cradling him between my body and the backrest. Little by little the shaking stopped as I kept caressing his hair. "Better?" I asked after a long time of silence.

He nodded. "Kind of."

"'Kind of' is a start. Give it time, Jamie."

"I meant it when I said I wanted you to fuck me so I'll remember you inside me instead of them."

"I will once you're healed. Right now I couldn't get it up if I wanted to."

Jamie pushed his groin against mine. "I bet I can make you hard."

"And you'll win that bet, but every time I think of the hurt you'll feel if I actually go through with it, I'll lose it again. Stop asking me, Jamie."

Jamie nuzzled me until his head was lodged under my chin. "But you won't turn away from me?"

"Never."

"Okay."

Chapter 21

I TOOK the next day off to take Jamie to see Sem Garner, my doctor. I knew the guy well since he always gave me my sexual health checks, and I could trust him to be gentle but thorough. He was a few years younger than me, but he had a comforting yet casual air about him and I trusted him implicitly. We had history together, thanks to a few shared interests that involved leather and rope bondage, but he seemed as casual about them as I was. Jamie, as usual, went along with everything without a muscle of his face twitching or a single sign of tension creeping into his shoulders. Even the most intimate of examinations, the swabs and samples taken from his rectum and urethra, were done without drama, as long as I stayed in the room. I kept wondering how Jamie had let all those men gangbang him, but he couldn't see a doctor without someone there he trusted.

I did the talking, something I was getting used to, since Jamie barely nodded or shook his head. While Jamie dressed, Sem took me aside.

"Does he talk, usually?"

I shrugged. "Not to strangers. Long story."

"Where did you find him, Jez?"

"Let's say I inherited him."

Sem looked at me with concern. "I may be out of line here, but does he enjoy pain?"

"Is it that obvious?"

"Is he your slave boy?"

I chuckled. "No, trust me, between us it's entirely consensual."

"Most slaves consent to being treated like a slave," Sem lectured me.

"You know I hate inflicting pain. He's my ward, Sem. I was asked to take care of him."

"Well, he's got a lot of bruises, caused at different intervals. This isn't about him being abused once, Jez. If I didn't know you better, I'd suggest counseling for spousal abuse."

"I didn't do this!" I'd inadvertently raised my voice and looked at the curtain in the corner of the room to see whether Jamie had heard me.

"I know you, remember?" Sem replied, keeping his voice subdued. "I trusted you more than once not to lose your temper. So what's his story?" Sem too looked at the curtain.

"A long one," I said dismissively. "He's the husband of one of my best friends, and the best friend died three weeks ago."

"He seems close to you."

I saw Sem's curious look and knew what he was thinking. "He trusts me."

"Have you slept with him?"

"Sem," I hissed.

"Well, have you?"

I didn't want to answer him. What could I say? Yes, I fucked Jamie while his husband was dying? With the husband's permission and with the husband present sometimes? So I just nodded.

"I hope it was safe, because he looks like he might show up positive for a few nasties," Sem said, not without compassion. "Whoever did this to him doesn't sound like someone who'd bother with condoms."

I nodded again, taking a deep breath, but didn't say anything more to Sem because Jamie appeared from behind the curtain.

"You okay?" I asked him. Jamie smiled at me, but only with his eyes. I grabbed his shoulder and gave it a squeeze.

"I'll call you if anything shows up that needs immediate attention," Sem said. "If everything is fine, I'll send you the results through the mail."

IN THE cab on the way home, Jamie leaned against me and I put my arm around his shoulders. "That wasn't so bad, was it?"

"Sem's nice," Jamie admitted. "Thanks for taking me to see him."

"He's worried about what happened."

Jamie shrugged.

"Don't shrug it away, J."

"What happened, happened," Jamie said. He pushed away from me and sat upright, his arm leaning on the door as he looked out the cab window.

I took his hand. "I'm not turning away from you, no matter why you did it, Jamie," I repeated. "I just want to understand."

Jamie remained silent, impassive. I knew pushing him would be futile. I could only hope he'd tell me in his own good time.

Not asking was hard, though, so I dove into work with the excuse that my not going into the office didn't mean I had the day off. Not that I got a lot of work done. I kept thinking about the kind of relationship I had with Jamie. Did I really love him? Or was I still just looking out for him, albeit not as well as Nick would have liked? I listened to the soft noises in the apartment, evidence that I wasn't alone, and realized I actually liked it. For some reason I didn't understand, I enjoyed thinking that if I emerged from my office, dinner would be ready, and although Jamie still wasn't very talkative, it was nice not to have to eat alone. How did I survive all these years without a companion?

The only thing that still bothered me was the fact that I was usually not home more than two weekends a month and occasionally a few days during the week. Taking Jamie with me was not an option either, because he needed stability and I needed as little distraction as possible when I was working. How could I ever leave Jamie again, knowing he'd barely lasted four days the first time I left him alone? I needed to know what had happened to make him run away, otherwise I'd never be able to fix it. But how was I going to coax it out of him without him shutting down?

I walked out of my home office to be greeted by the fragrant aroma of mushroom risotto. It brought me back to the villa in Spain and the first time I'd really heard Jamie speak. I remembered how surprised I was by hearing that sexy, low voice of his. I wanted to hear it again.

Jamie was standing with his back to me, stirring the pan. I put my hand on his shoulder and he jumped, then looked over his shoulder and smiled. I moved my hand to the back of his neck and enjoyed how he leaned into the touch before I enveloped him in my arms. It felt so good to hold him. "This smells great."

"You know it's good. I've made it for you before."

"You burned it last time," I recalled.

Jamie went silent. I could feel him tense up under my hands, and I rubbed his arms to soothe him. "It's okay to miss him, Jamie. I miss him too."

For a while all Jamie did was stir the risotto. Then out of the blue he said, "You must miss him more because you knew him so much longer."

"Oh no," I replied as I put my chin on his shoulder. "He was your husband. I was just a friend."

"That's not true," Jamie said without any sort of hurt in his voice. "He loved you. When I first met him, and I couldn't talk to him yet, he sat with me for hours every day. He'd read to me sometimes, but more often he'd tell me about you and how you'd shown him around New York and educated him about living in the Big Apple." Jamie pushed me aside a bit as he took out two plates and divided the risotto between them. "Look, I managed not to burn it this time."

I looked him in the eye and felt my center go soft. "You were distracted last time. And you made up for it by starting again."

He took out two forks and handed me my plate. "Can we eat in the living room?"

"Sure."

We settled on the sofa, Jamie with his legs over my knees. I put my plate on his legs and he smiled.

"I better stay still."

"Yes," I said with a mock stern smile. "Otherwise we'll be picking grains of rice out of the upholstery for weeks."

He chuckled and then turned serious. "How did you meet Nick?"

I took a bite of the risotto to stall for time. Why, I don't know, since it was no big secret. "I was a fan," I simply stated.

"Just like that?"

I swallowed another bite. "I was working my way through college and, in a way, out of the closet. Back in the days when you couldn't just get any old porn off the Internet, you had to get it in movie houses or behind the counter of certain video rental stores in the Village. I was too shy for either."

Jamie gave me a look like he didn't believe me.

"My dad threw me out when I told him I was gay. My mother never knew. She'd died when I was younger, so it was just me and Dad. He was the first one I'd told, although I think the girl in high school who had her eyes on me caught on eventually. So I was pretty much in the closet, but like any youngster, always horny. I didn't dare buy a ticket to a movie house and sit with the other patrons watching porn, but I did get a job cleaning up in one."

"That must have been disgusting. All those old men jacking off to twinks."

"It kind of was, yeah, but they paid me cash every day so I got by. One day they showed *Thoroughbred*, and the theater was packed. I came in just before it ended, and I was enthralled. I got the projectionist to run it again for me while I cleaned. Can't say I worked very hard that evening. I had to stay late to finish up."

"You saw *Thoroughbred*? That's like his breakthrough movie, but it was never released on video because the company went bankrupt."

"I know." I nodded. "And I remember it well. It was pretty crude, but Nick looked amazing. Buff body, light brown hair, gorgeous face, chest hair, none of those shaved pubes like they do now."

"Nick said he started trimming his body hair when it turned grey and it was obvious that he was dying his hair. He always claimed he started a trend."

I chuckled. "He probably did."

"You shave your chest?"

"I wax."

"Why?"

I shrugged. "Habit, I suppose. It shows off my tattoos better. Besides, if I let it grow, I'll be a bear, and I always thought I was more of a muscle man."

"I always thought you were more of a bear. Big and cuddly," Jamie said, looking at the contents of his plate and moving it around.

I squeezed his knee. "You think I'm cuddly?" I gave him my best steely stare, but all he did was chuckle.

"I don't just think, I know." He wiggled his toes and I needed to rescue my plate.

"Watch out. We'll make a mess."

"You know I'll clean it up."

I squeezed his knee again and this time he didn't move. "You don't have to, Jamie. You're not my servant."

"You know I do a better job than Masha," he said without even a hint of arrogance or pride. He simply meant it.

"You do, but I don't want you here just to clean."

"Please don't take it off my list," Jamie said softly, his eyes pinned to the contents of his plate.

I put my plate aside and rubbed his legs. "I know you like to clean, but you don't have to."

"I want to. I want to feel useful."

Since Jamie wasn't eating from his plate, I took it from him and put it aside before scooting a little closer. "You are useful to me."

"I'm a burden. I was a burden to Nick and now I'm a burden to you." Jamie kept staring at our hands and how mine enveloped his, but he didn't move them.

"Nick loved you so much, Jamie. He never saw you as a burden. He was devastated when he learned he was going to die, not so much because his life was ending, but because he didn't know what was going to happen to you. He was desperate when he asked me to take care of you."

"And now I'm your burden."

"No, you're not."

"You don't love me like Nick did, so I'm a burden." He didn't wait for my reaction and got up from the couch, taking the plates and bringing them to the kitchen. Although I knew he was right, it also hurt to hear him say it. How could I ever live up to the lover Nick was? Even if I did love him—and I was pretty sure that what I felt for Jamie was love of a sort—Nick and I were different in so many ways. For one, I wasn't about to give up everything to hide away with Jamie in some gorgeous villa in Spain. I had a life outside of the relationship. On the other hand, I knew keeping Jamie in an apartment in New York wasn't fair either. He couldn't go for a swim or work in his garden, both things he loved immensely. There was only so much cleaning he could do, since it wasn't a huge place. I came to the startling conclusion I didn't know what he liked to do besides those things.

I followed Jamie to the kitchen where he was doing the dishes by hand, although I have a dishwasher. I took a dish towel to dry and he took it from me.

"I'll do it."

"Jamie, I...."

He threw me a stern look as if he just wanted me to leave him alone, but I couldn't. It wasn't in my character to bow out of a challenge, and I certainly wasn't the type to run away from responsibility. So I grabbed the towel back and dried the dishes in silence. When everything was put away, I placed my hand on Jamie's shoulder. "I want to talk to you. Will you come back to the living room with me?

Chapter 22

I sat down on the couch, but Jamie didn't follow. I tried to quell my nerves and resisted going back to the kitchen to see what was keeping him, but the minutes ticked away on the living room clock and it was silent in the apartment.

Eventually I noticed Jamie standing at the door to the kitchen.

"Come sit down," I said, patting the sofa next to me and trying to make it sound more like an invitation than a command.

A little hesitantly, Jamie sat next to me, with sufficient distance between us to make sure we didn't touch.

I had no idea how to start. How could I convey to him that I didn't know what to do about our situation, but that I didn't want to lose him? How could I make him see that he'd changed my life for the better, although, technically he *was* a bit of a burden, since I always had to take him into account. Not something I was used to.

"Jamie, we need to talk about us."

Jamie didn't react, not that I expected him to.

"I love having you around. I like that I can come home to you at night." I didn't tell him it was with some apprehension I opened the door every time, hoping he'd still be there. "But I want you to be happy." I saw his face soften. He wasn't smiling, but he seemed a little less tense. "I still have to work, Jamie, and while I can just work at the office for a few days, I need to travel as well." The tension was back as Jamie sat more upright, bracing himself for what I was going to say. "I'd like to ask Lakiya and her husband to dinner so you can get to know them." Although Jamie wasn't looking at me directly, I could see his eyes turn toward me. "That way, if I need to go away for a few days, you can call Lakiya if you need anything." Jamie's silence told me he still didn't trust my suggestion. "She's like a sister to me. I trust her, and I'd like you to meet her so you can see whether you could possibly trust her too."

"Do I need to go to her house?"

"No," I said, unable to hide my smile. I felt I'd won some small victory. "I just want you to have someone to turn to when you need help or advice. Or just someone to talk to. Kee is pretty special to me."

"Is she one of your women?"

"My women?"

"The women you sleep with."

I chuckled. "I told you I haven't slept with a woman in a long time. No, Kee is a colleague. She's married to a nice man and has two children with him. I've never slept with her. Don't think she ever wanted to either."

"But you wanted to?"

"As pretty as she is, no, I've never wanted to sleep with her. She wants a guy she can boss around, and she knows that doesn't work with me."

"Nick managed to boss you around."

"Nick being the possible exception to that rule," I was quick to answer. "And if you wanted to, you probably could as well."

"Me?" Jamie asked.

I realized this conversation was so not going where I'd expected it to go, but at least Jamie was talking to me. "Yes, you. If you wanted to."

"I wouldn't know what to ask. Besides, you don't want to sleep with me anymore."

I sighed. "I want you to heal a bit more first, Jamie." In more ways than just physical, I wanted to add, but didn't.

"You want to make sure I don't have AIDS."

I swallowed, hearing him say it. I couldn't pretend it hadn't crossed my mind. "I'm sure you wouldn't be my first HIV-positive man, if that is the case. Or do you already know?"

Jamie hesitated. I don't scare easily, but the idea that Jamie knew something he wouldn't divulge to me, something as important as his HIV status, made me feel uneasy. I'm a stickler for safe sex, and I knew whenever Jamie and I had fucked it was always safe, but I couldn't put it out of my mind that what I'd seen at that club was in no way safe. If he was HIV-positive, he could have infected a whole house full of men.

"Nick could have given it to me."

I looked at Jamie and grabbed his arm, trying to make him look directly at me, but although he turned, he stared at his knees instead of me. "Nick was positive?"

"You didn't think he quit porn for me, did you?"

"I did, actually."

Jamie shook his head. "He'd tested positive, and nobody would hire him anymore. He couldn't understand it and went on a binge. Too much booze, drugs, and men. And then he was offered me. He saw it as a way out. He'd rescue me and save himself. We didn't start out safe, so we never bothered afterward."

"Fuck." I just couldn't put together any more eloquent response. If Jamie and Nick had been having unsafe sex for eight years, the chance that Jamie was still negative was almost non-existent. And then he spread it across the gay community of New York during his two week stint at Fuck'm'all. "Have you ever been tested before?"

Jamie shook his head.

"You didn't even bat an eyelid when Sem asked you if you wanted to be tested and I said yes."

"Maybe it's time I found out."

Jamie was slumped against the side of the sofa and for the first time since our tiff, he was looking at me. There was a vulnerability in his eyes that struck me, and I pulled him into my arms. Feeling him fold into them was amazing. I knew right there and then that even if he was positive, which was likely, I wouldn't leave him. This went beyond my promise to Nick.

"When will we know?" Jamie asked.

"The HIV results usually take a few days, but Sem said he'd call me if anything needed attention. He tested for more than just HIV."

"I know. I was listening."

"Good." I rubbed his short hair and caressed it, reveling in the soft, bristly feel. He felt relaxed in my arms. After a while, he sighed. "Want to watch a movie or something?"

I flicked through the pay-per-view and settled for *The Fast and the Furious*, hoping the mindless action would distract me. Instead, not having to try too hard to keep up with the story meant I had too much time to think. In the past I'd always been afraid of HIV, often wondering if my one-night stands were infected. On more than one occasion I asked, although I'm sure I rarely got a truthful answer. When one of my gay friends settled down with his HIV-positive boyfriend, I tried to talk him out of it. I just didn't see myself doing something like that.

Now, as I lay there on the couch, legs stretched out, Jamie draped half over me with his head just underneath my chin and my hand slowly rubbing his hair, I suddenly understood my friend.

"You're not paying attention."

"Uh?"

Jamie looked up at me and smiled. "You're not paying attention to the movie," he repeated. "You'll miss the best action."

I shrugged. "Doesn't matter."

"You're thinking about what Sem's going to tell us." It wasn't a question. Jamie said it like he simply knew what I was thinking.

"Doesn't it scare you?"

Jamie shrugged it off.

"I suppose it's not a death sentence anymore, at least not like it used to be," I said. Was I just saying this to soothe myself, or did I want to put Jamie at ease as well?

"The HIV didn't kill Nick. Cancer did," Jamie said a lot more sternly than I was used to from him. "Nick was never sick until he got cancer."

"I know." I also knew enough about HIV to know that on average, HIV-positive people got more cancer than HIV-negative people, because cancer is sometimes caused by problems with the immune system. We'd never know if this was the case with Nick, of course, so I let Jamie believe what he believed.

After the movie was over, Jamie went to his room and I went to mine. It took forever for me to fall asleep, and when I did, I dreamed about Sem calling me frantically to get Jamie to the hospital because his T-cell count was nonexistent. After a quick trip to the bathroom, I entered Jamie's room and crawled into bed with him. He didn't wake, but simply rolled into my embrace. I slept much more soundly then, dreaming of Nick and how gorgeous he looked when I first laid eyes on him after our long separation, just before his cancer took a turn for the worst.

That morning I woke up to Jamie's voice. "You called me Nick."

I kissed his neck, simply because it was the closest thing to me. "I was dreaming of him. Of how beautiful I thought his grey hair and beard looked on him."

"I know," Jamie murmured. "I always thought it was a good look on him. I hope I get to grow old like that."

I pulled him tighter to me. "So do I."

Chapter 23

THE longer Sem took to call us, the more I was confident everything would be okay, and the more I realized I was at a loss about what to do with Jamie. New York was like every big city, cold and impersonal, and I couldn't babysit him all the time. I'd taken some time to work at home, nursing Jamie back to health while doing research on prospective customers, but with one man short at work, I couldn't hide forever. At some point, I was going to have to leave Jamie for longer than an afternoon.

We'd found some sort of routine. I'd go out for groceries in the morning while Jamie tidied up around the apartment, we'd have lunch together, and then Jamie would cook dinner while I went to the gym to work out. Sometimes I went to the office or met an out-of-town client, sometimes I'd just walk around the park. I wanted to get Jamie used to being alone for a little while, but I knew the real test would come if I went away for another trip. I was going to have to introduce Jamie to someone he could turn to in case of an emergency.

"Jamie, remember when I told you about Lakiya?"

Jamie looked up at me from his position on the sofa where he'd been reading, his head on my lap while I surfed the TV channels. "It's your house; you can invite whomever you want."

"I know, but I want you to join us." I knew from when we first met how hard this was for Jamie, but I couldn't let him keep living on an island.

Jamie sat up and shook his head. "I'll cook for you and your guests."

"And eat with us. Please?" Jamie looked tense, but he didn't answer. "I know it's hard for you, J, but this is a very good friend of mine and I'd like you to meet her. You don't need to talk. Just sit with us so you can see whether you like her and maybe, after a while, you can learn to trust her."

"Why?"

"So you'll have someone to call when I'm not home."

"Why would I need to call anyone?"

I had to bite the bullet. "Remember when I went away last time?"

Although Jamie had looked at me all through our conversation, now he turned his head and his gaze drifted to the carpet in front of the couch. "Yes."

"Next time I go away for a few days, I want you to know there's someone you can call in case something happens."

"Nothing happened last time."

"Jamie, you ran away."

"Having someone to call wouldn't have changed that."

I took his hand, but he pulled it away. I knew this was hard for him, and we'd never really talked about why he'd done those things, so I left my hand on the couch between us as a silent invitation. Then he sat up and his expression turned cold.

"I had some wine and then I wanted sex, so I went out."

"Jamie, you made some decisions that got you into trouble. I'm fine with you going out for sex, but I want you to be safe. I want you to come home at night." He still wasn't looking at me, but I wasn't too worried about that. Every time the topic of conversation was difficult for him, he withdrew, and I didn't really expect that to change overnight. Or ever. At least we were still talking.

"Those men... they don't want you there for just one time."

I swallowed away a hard lump when Jamie said that. He seemed unaffected, and I had to resist grabbing his shoulders and shaking him. Instead I tried to grasp his hand, and again he pulled away in such an unassuming way I couldn't even take offense. "You know I try to keep you safe, J, but I'm not always here. There's no doubt in my mind that you can make your own decisions regarding your safety, but those men.... You can't trust them with your life, Jamie."

Jamie nodded almost imperceptibly.

"You knew those men from before, didn't you?"

Again, Jamie nodded. "They remembered me."

"Are they the men Nick rescued you from?"

"Yes."

"Then why did you go back to them, Jamie?" I turned away from him when I realized I'd raised my voice. A little calmer, I continued, "They broke your ribs and your jaw last time. Why did you give them the chance to do it again?"

Suddenly Jamie turned to me, his eyes watery and his usual disconnected, unemotional manner totally gone. "Because I wanted to get laid. Because I wanted to get fucked to within an inch of my life, so I'd hurt and wouldn't be able to sit for a week. I wanted a guy with a big dick who didn't give a fuck about the ass he was fucking as long as the other end moaned and pretended to be really into it."

"But you said yourself you knew it wouldn't be just one dick. You knew they'd let other guys abuse you."

"Maybe that's what I wanted. Maybe I wanted it rough and impersonal, not that lovey-dovey thing that you call sex."

"We haven't...." I wanted to remind him we hadn't had sex since Nick had been taken to the hospital in Spain, but he knew that better than I did, so I didn't finish my sentence.

"I'm only human, Jez. I'm a man who likes men." The sudden change to utter calmness in Jamie's voice surprised me. "I needed the sex, but I don't think I can take the tenderness that comes with it when it's you."

I thought briefly of all the nameless men I'd fucked over the years who would never believe I'd be tender in bed, but Jamie brought it out in me. Had I neglected the side of him that wanted to be manhandled? Had I forgotten how Nick had told me that Jamie had a kinky side, and that Jamie's imaginative appetites were the only reason Nick had given up all those other men? Jamie's hand brushed against mine and it didn't feel accidental, so with a quick move I grabbed his wrist. The flicker in his eye made it clear to me he was both surprised and not entirely adverse to it. I yanked at his arm and got him up out of the couch and down the corridor. For a moment I wanted to take Jamie into his bedroom, but then I thought it would make a better statement if I took him into my room. I pulled at his arm hard enough to turn him around and then pushed him back so he fell to the bed. As I let go of his hand, he raised his arms to break his fall and my eyes fell on his groin. He was rock hard in his loose fitting pants. This was actually turning him on.

I had to forget for a moment that I had more than a few tender feelings for Jamie and that my first instinct was always to protect him from harm. I had to view him as an object of desire again, and seeing how turned on he was helped in that respect. I gave him my best leather Dom stare and a faint smile appeared on his face.

"Strip," I commanded. Jamie only hesitated for a moment and then yanked down his jogging pants, letting his cock spring free. I could see his muscles ripple as he pulled up his legs to free them from the fabric and then as he pulled his T-shirt over his head. It had taken him mere moments to lie there on my bed in his full glory, and it barely took me longer to see Jamie differently. After all, this is what he wanted, and if I could give him what he needed, he wouldn't need to go outside the house to find it. When had I become so monogamous? It only entered my mind for a moment that I hadn't had sex with anyone else than Jamie in the last months, that I hadn't even given it any thought. When Jamie ran his hand casually over his washboard stomach, I knew I had to get a handle on the situation again.

"Touch yourself," I said in a voice that was definitely a few notches below my usual commanding one. He complied teasingly, smiling slightly as he used as few fingers as possible to move the skin over his erection, like he was trying not to obscure my view. He was so hard I could barely tell he was uncut. "Does it feel good?"

Jamie nodded and licked his lips. I couldn't resist leaning over him and kissing him. I remembered just in time to make it a relentless, hard kiss and Jamie surrendered to me. I grabbed his hands, which he'd considerately returned to the space above his head, and kept them pinned there with my left hand while I pushed my right hand between our bodies. By now I was hard too and I was sure Jamie could feel it, but I wanted to give him pleasure since he'd so articulately conveyed to me how he wanted it. I was still fully clothed and had no intention of changing that fact anytime soon. My clothes were the barrier I needed to keep this from turning into the tenderness Jamie didn't want.

"Don't come until I tell you to," I commanded. Jamie nodded as I took his erection in my hand and fisted him roughly. I could tell it wasn't going to take him long to lose it, no matter how hard he tried to stave off his orgasm. He'd asked for it and I was giving him what he wanted, but in a safe environment. "How close are you?"

Jamie opened his mouth and closed his eyes.

"Look at me! How close are you?" I continued roughly pumping him. He was leaking so much I could spread it around and use it to smooth my ministrations. I carefully avoided rubbing over the head, since I knew how sensitive it was and would send him over instantly. "Look. At. Me," I repeated sternly. This time Jamie opened his eyes, but control was failing him, so I slowed down. "How close are you?"

Jamie grunted.

"How close?"

Jamie's pained expression spoke volumes. "Please."

"Please what?" I shook his hands, still pinned over his head, to bring him back to the present. "Please stop?"

"No!" Jamie was panting hard. "Please, can I come?"

"Of course you can, but you may not. Not yet," I added quickly.

Jamie groaned with exasperation. "Please, sir, may I come?"

I waited for a moment, my hand the only thing moving, until I thought Jamie was literally going to burst. I leaned forward a bit and whispered: "Come now." My groin had been rubbing along Jamie's leg and when he lost it, he lifted it ever so slightly. Together with the look on his face at finally being allowed to let go, the pressure sent me over as well. I came in my pants while Jamie creamed his chest in ribbon after ribbon of white, milky release. He was still convulsing when I sagged down next to him on the bed, letting go of his hands.

Jamie slowly turned toward me and when our eyes met, he threw himself at me and buried his face against my neck. "I'm sorry."

"Why?" I asked softly, totally letting go of my dominant persona.

"For telling you I didn't like the tenderness you gave me. I lied, I do like it, but it reminds me too much of Nick. You're so much like him, it hurts."

I wrapped my arms around Jamie's body and rocked him. "Then I'm the one who should be sorry."

Jamie raised his head and shook it. "Don't be. Nick loved me very much. So much that he indulged me whenever I wanted it rough when he really didn't like it. Just like you."

"It's not that I don't like it, but…." I sighed as I tried to explain to Jamie. "I've never been a relationship guy, and finding one-night stands you don't need to pay for is just easier in leather clubs. They're in every big city if you know where to look. And I just happen to have the right look to be a leather daddy."

"I still think you're a big teddy bear," Jamie replied.

"Let's get cleaned up, okay?"

As we got up off the bed, the phone rang, and while Jamie went into the bathroom, I jogged into the living room to answer it.

"Hello."

"Jez, it's Sem. You need to bring Jamie in to see me."

Chapter 24

A SHOWER and a shave each later, we were on our way to Sem's downtown practice. Jamie seemed unfazed, but I was pulling out all my coping techniques to keep myself from going crazy. I knew it wouldn't be something that required immediate attention, because five days had passed between the tests and Sem's worried-sounding phone call, but I knew that if everything had been fine, Sem would have put me out of my misery on the phone. My worst-case scenario was coming, and I would have given my left nut to change what I knew to be inevitable.

I was glad to see Sem's waiting room was empty. He came out to greet us as soon as we walked in.

"Jamie, Jez, come right on in."

I could tell Sem was nervous, and while I wanted to practically shake it out of him right there and then, I had to remind myself this was Jamie's news, not mine. While we sat down on the two chairs in front of Sem's cluttered desk, Sem sat down on the corner of it.

"I have your results, Jamie. Do you want to hear them?"

Jamie nodded before looking at me. I did my best to give him a compassionate smile.

"The good news is that your tests for hepatitis B and C came back negative."

Jamie nodded again and I wanted to urge Sem to tell us the final news, but at the same time, I didn't want to hear it either. "I'm afraid...."

I closed my eyes and somehow missed the rest of the sentence. I was sure Sem was going to drop the bomb on Jamie, but when I opened them again, he was holding out a prescription to Jamie and Jamie was taking it.

"I'm going to give you a shot of penicillin, and you need to take these pills for ten days. I suggest Jez take them too, as a preventative measure. After that we'll test both of you, but I'm sure things will have cleared up by then."

"What?" I asked as if I'd just been shaken awake.

Sem gave me one of his perfect-bedside-manner smiles. "I was explaining to Jamie that he has early stage syphilis, and he also tested positive for chlamydia, and that you need to be treated for that as well. Both will clear up just fine with the right medication."

When I turned to Jamie, he was looking at me as if I was the patient.

"And his HIV test?" I asked Sem, feeling like I was still surrounded by an emotional fog.

Sem bit his lower lip and I knew what was coming; this time I wanted to hear him say it, though. He looked Jamie in the eye. "You know you're positive, don't you?"

As clear as I'd ever heard Jamie speak, he said, "Yes, I suppose I do."

"Are you taking medication for it?"

"No," Jamie replied softly. "Nick and I were never safe, and Nick was positive for eight years. I never got tested because I figured he'd given it to me, but I didn't care."

"Well, the good news is your T-cell count is excellent, and you seem to be in amazing condition. Also, you have antibodies against HIV, but no detectable viral load. That doesn't mean it can't change, but it's pretty good news, all things considered. I would suggest safe sex from now on, though."

Jamie looked at me and I lost it. I got up from my seat and walked out. I only just heard Jamie say casually: "Jez is a safe sex guy. We've always used condoms."

By the time I reached the small bathroom adjacent to Sem's consultation room, I was about ready to explode. I raised my hand and only just managed to avoid banging the mirror hanging over the washbasin. Instead I hit the pristine white tiles around it and cracked one, hurting my hand. I shook it to alleviate the sting and saw myself in the mirror. I was crying. Crying over Jamie's test and crying because Nick had neglected to tell me this one detail.

No matter how much I'd prepared myself beforehand, I wasn't prepared for the one feeling I had no recourse against. Betrayal. Nick had handed Jamie over to me, knowing he had to stay quiet about the HIV, knowing that if he'd told me what I knew now, I would never have let Jamie get under my skin. I would have put up my scaly armor, protected myself so fiercely I wouldn't have given it a second thought, and I would have walked away.

Now I knew I couldn't. No matter how hard my head told me to run, to get as far away from Jamie as I could, I wouldn't be able to live with myself if I did. I was angry at Nick and mad at myself for not digging deeper or asking Nick the serious questions, but it was clear to me that we'd been so intent on making the last weeks of Nick's life worthwhile that I'd barely bothered with what would happen afterward.

I looked at my bloodshot eyes in the mirror and knew I had to make myself presentable before going back inside to see if Jamie was okay. Opening the faucet and letting the water run until it was ice-cold, I started to calm down. Once I'd let the water cool my face, I realized Nick had done the right thing. His goal had been to find someone for Jamie, knowing Jamie would need someone to take care of him. I was their last hope. Nick knew me well, even after eight years apart. He'd known that I would have said no and never looked back if he'd told me. He must have known Jamie would worm his way into my heart somehow, and then it wouldn't matter if he was positive.

When I looked at myself again, I saw something that hadn't been there just moments before. Determination. I dried my face and hands with a towel and discarded it in the hamper before pacing out. When I reached the door and peered inside, I saw Sem sitting in the chair I'd vacated, talking to Jamie. He was explaining Jamie's options to him, telling him he didn't need medication yet, but he would need to be monitored at regular intervals. He would also need to take care of himself, and that included not exposing himself needlessly to all sorts of opportunistic infections.

My biggest surprise was that Jamie was talking back. He was asking questions. And he was looking Sem in the eye. I almost didn't want to interrupt them, but I knew, after storming out of the room right after hearing the verdict, I had to show Jamie that I was still there for him.

When Jamie spotted me, he stopped midsentence and got up from his chair. "Jez?"

I took a step inside and saw Sem look at me as well. "Sorry I ran out like that. I had to… gather my thoughts for a moment."

Jamie smiled at me as if he hadn't just received his death sentence, and maybe he hadn't. I suddenly remembered that Sem had said he was in excellent health, and that medication would clear up the two infections he'd sustained from his little excursion into New York City's underbelly.

"Come and sit down, Jez," Sem said, inviting me to sit in the chair he vacated. "I was telling Jamie I should take a few samples from you as well. Better to be safe than sorry. It's always possible you've been exposed to a few things, and we might as well check. Also, I'd like to be sure you need the antibiotics. Since you're all about safety, chances are you're all clear."

I nodded and let Sem draw blood from me. He was quick and thorough with the swabs, but I wasn't really too worried. Technically, since I gave blowjobs without a condom, I could be carrying chlamydia or syphilis, but they'd clear up with a simple prescription, and it was better to be safe than sorry. Other than that, like Sem had said, being careful was second nature to me, and I was used to Sem's calming hands.

In the cab on the way home, Jamie was quiet, as usual, but he wasn't as touchy-feely as he usually was when we were out of the apartment. He simply sat next to me and stared out of the window at the hustle and bustle of Manhattan.

"If you want to talk about it, I'm here," I told Jamie, just to break the silence.

"Life goes on, Jez," Jamie replied calmly. "The only difference is that now I know."

I couldn't argue with that. When we arrived at the apartment, Jamie followed me inside and hung up his coat.

"Are you going to call your friend?" Jamie asked, out of nowhere. "If we wait too long, she might have other plans."

"Lakiya?"

Jamie nodded. "I'd feel better if she came alone. Without her husband. It will be easier for me if I can just focus on getting to know her."

I smiled and nodded, picking up the phone to give Lakiya a call. I'd asked her to pencil in the dinner invitation, but had warned her I'd need to square it with Jamie first. Now all I needed to do was tell her the invitation was only for her. I knew she'd understand.

Chapter 25

WHEN Lakiya arrived, she looked every bit the little firecracker I knew she was, minus the flaming red lipstick she favored for board meetings. In fact, she looked relaxed, her petite frame enveloped in a very feminine, flowery dress I knew she'd never wear to the office. I had given her precise instructions on how to handle Jamie, most notably that Jamie would initiate contact if he felt comfortable. That was also what I'd asked Jamie to do.

"I heard you two missed the Spanish Rioja," she said, handing me the bottle she'd brought. "Not easy to find, even in New York. Guess the Californians think they can do better than the Spanish." Her eyes scanned the room, but Jamie was in the kitchen.

"He'll appear when he's ready," I told her. "The upside is that you'll be spoiled by the food he cooks. Too bad I had to say no seafood. He makes a mean paella."

"I bet he does," she said with a smirk. She took two steps in the direction of the living room, and it dawned on me that she'd never been to my apartment. "Do you want the grand tour? It'll take at least three minutes."

Lakiya looked uncharacteristically unsure of herself. "Just tell me where I can find Jamie in case you're not around and he needs rescuing."

I gestured in the direction of the small hallway. "This is the bathroom." I didn't let her in, although I knew it would be spotless, since Jamie had spent at least two hours cleaning it. "Across from it is my bedroom, and this is Jamie's."

She gave me a rather surprised look.

"So he can choose where to sleep. Sometimes he sleeps in his own room and sometimes in mine."

"I see." She took one step into Jamie's room, which was minimalistic and spotless, as if I ever needed to worry about that, and then turned around and walked into mine, which was just as minimalistic, but not quite as spotless.

"Can I get you a drink now?" I offered as we walked back to the living room.

"Sure you can," she said, "but I want to find out what that delicious smell is." She was quick on her feet and in the doorway to the kitchen by the time I could call her name. She didn't react, but entered. "Jamie, darling, whatever you're cooking smells divine." By the time I'd followed her into the kitchen, she had her hand on Jamie's back and was peering into his cooking pots.

Jamie didn't say anything, but he didn't retreat either. He didn't even pull away from her touch like I'd predicted.

"Anything I can do to help, Jamie?"

I wasn't surprised when Jamie didn't respond.

"Come help me cut the bread," I told Lakiya. "Jamie will be done in about five… ten minutes?" Jamie nodded without turning around. "I'll get you a glass of wine, Kee. You took a cab, right? You can have a glass then."

I was glad Lakiya followed me out of the kitchen. I could almost hear Jamie's sigh of relief. He'd been a bundle of nervous energy from the moment I confirmed Lakiya was coming, and I knew her entering the apartment would have only added to that. I could have kicked her—if I were that kind of man—for entering the kitchen and breaking the promise I'd made to Jamie, but all I could do now was try to rescue what was left of the evening.

Lakiya walked into the living room holding her wine and sauntered around the various pieces of art I'd collected over the years. She stopped at a small lithograph.

"It's an early Luc Tuymans," I said, trying my best to do the Flemish name justice.

"He's beautiful, Jez," Lakiya replied. I knew she wasn't talking about the angel in the painting, although she kept looking at it. "And he cooks too. Are you sure you want to give up the bachelor life for him, though?"

"Kee," I warned her.

"I know. Love is blind."

I sighed. "Please get to know him first."

She looked at me. "Okay, but only if I can worry about you."

I chuckled. "Why would you need to do that?"

"We'll see," she said. She turned around and then nodded at me. It made me turn around too. Jamie was standing behind me and the food was on the table. He'd been unusually quiet and looked immensely uncomfortable.

"Looks good, Jamie," I said, putting my arm around him as I directed him to the table. "Sit."

Jamie sat in his usual chair, but I knew he was warring with himself to make a dash for the kitchen. I decided to direct attention to the food. "Jamie made us osso bucco. Why don't I serve you some?" I squeezed Jamie's knee under the table before getting up to take Lakiya's plate and the bowl of veal shanks in tomato and vegetable sauce. I served all of us, and Lakiya dug in like a pro.

"This is amazing, Jamie," she said after inhaling half her plate in a very unladylike manner. "You should work in a restaurant."

I looked at Jamie but he didn't respond, although there was no doubt he'd heard her compliment. "For now, he works in my restaurant and that will have to do," I said, brushing my knuckles over his thigh. "Don't know if I'm ready to share him yet." Jamie didn't smile when I said it, but he looked at me and as usual, I could read his thoughts.

In line with the Italian theme of the evening, Jamie had made tiramisu for desert. I could tell Lakiya was close to loosening her belt a notch. "I'm not coming here again," she said with a sigh after putting her spoon down. "I won't be able to fit through the door if I do."

I helped Jamie clear the table and got a moment alone with him in the kitchen. "You okay, J?"

Jamie nodded. "She's nice."

"So talk to her. Just a bit. She's a little crass and in your face sometimes, but she means well. She cares, Jamie."

"I know. But you know I can't." He stopped wiping the counter and looked at the wall he was facing.

I put my arms around him and felt him relax a little. "Will you be able to call her if you need her? When I'm not around."

"I don't know."

I sighed and Jamie tensed up again. I knew it was useless trying to push him, but it didn't exactly leave me confident he'd do okay when I left, and I needed to go away for three days in the coming week. "Just promise me one thing, okay? Don't run away again. Even if you need to call me in the middle of the night in Albuquerque, I'll pick up the phone."

"Okay," Jamie conceded.

"Now I need to get back to our guest. Will you be okay in here?"

Jamie turned around, nodded, and smiled. "Go be with her. I'm a lousy host. I'll be fine here in the kitchen."

I squeezed him tight and kissed his neck. "Okay, Cinderella. I'll make it up to you."

When I returned to the living room, Lakiya was still standing. "I better leave."

"No, Kee, stay. We've barely had the chance to talk."

Lakiya shook her head. "He's seen me now. Tell him he can call me anytime. Give him my private phone, the one I keep for George and the kids."

She gave me such a compassionate look it made me feel uncomfortable.

"He'll get used to you traveling."

I nodded, although I wasn't sure about that. "Thanks for coming by, Kee. At least I can hope that he'll be able to text you or something."

"I'll keep an eye on him for you."

I let Lakiya out and returned to the kitchen, which by now was spotless. Jamie was sitting on the counter drinking what was left of the Rioja. He looked sad.

"Does the wine bring back too many memories?"

He looked up and smiled just a little. "No, but I just realized I shouldn't have drunk it."

"Why not?"

"Because it makes me horny, and I can't do anything about it."

I moved to stand between Jamie's spread legs and needed to look up at him to meet his eyes. "We have condoms and lube. What more do you need?"

"Will you still fuck me, Jez?"

"I'll even make love to you. Hard or soft. Whatever you want."

For the first time all evening, I saw Jamie's full-on smile. "Take me to bed or lose me forever!" he crooned in his best Meg Ryan imitation.

JAMIE beat me to the bedroom. My bedroom. And he was stark naked by the time he got there. He barely gave me a chance to shed my own clothes before he dragged me down to the bed and practically had me for dinner. It was frantic and fast and he put the condom on me as soon as he'd fisted me to full readiness. It was no secret who was in charge here, and for a moment I thought, *If only Kee could see us now.*

Jamie lubed himself up and then me and started sinking down over me. I knew it would be fast and furious, but then I felt resistance. I also saw Jamie's pained expression. Jamie, who opened like a flower and barely needed preparation of any sort if he was this horny, was tight and unwavering. He grabbed the lube again and added another big dollop, reaching behind to open himself up. I could see his confidence wane by the second, and then he finally got up and ran to the bathroom.

When I followed him there, he was washing his hands. "It won't work. I'm sorry."

I wanted to put my arms around him, but he turned away. "Jamie, it'll work if we take it a little slower. You were rushing it, that's all."

"I wanted you to fuck me. Hard. Not *make love to me*. I wanted a good fucking."

"You can still get a good fucking, after we take our time to relax."

"I want it now."

"J, you know that's the alcohol talking."

"But I want it," he repeated, with a lot less conviction, I noted.

"I know," I said. This time he let me put my arms around him and eventually I led him back to the bed. This time Jamie was completely passive and remained so for as long as I took it slow. I massaged his back and legs and took my time with his buttocks. Little by little, and with a lot of lube, I tried to make him open up, but he was so tight I gave up. When he turned around, he wasn't even hard.

I lay down next to him.

After what felt like hours, he finally spoke again. "I thought it wouldn't make a difference, knowing I was positive. But you're so scared of it. What if the condom breaks? You tell me it makes no difference, but I don't want to be like Nick, Jez. I don't want to not care if I infect you."

I shook my head. "Nick loved you, Jamie. He probably thought you'd be positive already after what you'd been through."

Jamie bit his lip but didn't answer. He seemed to relax, though, and turned his head in my direction.

I leaned over him and kissed him. What started soft became more passionate when he finally kissed me back. When I came up for air, Jamie looked flushed, and I knew I'd managed to persuade him. "I've fucked you a number of times, J. Nothing ever happened. All this diagnosis means to me is that we'll always have to use condoms. That's fine by me. I haven't had unsafe sex in more than ten years."

"It makes a difference to me, Jez. I'm scared too."

I pulled him into my arms and held him. "What are you scared of?"

"I don't know."

"Dying?"

"Yes."

"Infecting me?"

"Yes."

"You won't infect me. We'll be careful. Safe sex is second nature to me, and it will soon be second nature to you too. You'll get used to the idea."

"I'm scared of getting sick and becoming dependent on someone else."

"We'll cross that bridge when we get to it. Who knows, you might end up having to take care of me in our old age instead of the other way around."

"Don't say that, it's not funny."

I squeezed him again. "Neither of us have a crystal ball. But not knowing what will happen makes it interesting. And you can't live your life avoiding everything that scares you, Jamie."

"I know."

We settled in for the night, all ideas of having sex abandoned. Jamie let me hold him and I slowly felt him relax until I thought he was asleep. I knew I had to follow my own advice of not fretting over what could happen and probably never would, but it was easier said than done, so sleep evaded me for the longest time. It wasn't until I'd gone over my own words again, and realized that Jamie did live his life avoiding everything he feared, that I decided I needed to somehow make Jamie more self-sufficient, for both our sanity. Then I could sleep too.

Chapter 26

TWO days later I left for Albuquerque in the morning, but not before going over his lists with Jamie. I'd prepared three of them, one for each of the three days I'd be gone, and I'd done an extended grocery run so he'd have enough food to last three times as long as he needed. At first I'd contemplated not making any lists at all, hoping to wean Jamie off them, but then I figured it would be like making him quit cold turkey, so I made lists where nothing was compulsory. He seemed happy with them, and I knew I couldn't quite take his safety blanket from him yet.

I didn't stretch the good-byes out and Jamie was his usual unemotional self, which meant he was trying very hard not to cry.

In the end he didn't, but I shed a few silent tears in the cab to LaGuardia. I was worried about leaving Jamie, and I didn't think he'd call Lakiya if he was in trouble, so all I could hope for was that he was still in the apartment when I returned.

On the second day of my trip, I had Lakiya on the phone to discuss business, but I couldn't resist asking her about Jamie.

"He's fine, Jez. Stop fretting. I called the house and he answered."

"He did?"

She laughed. "Well, he picked up the phone and then didn't say anything, but I told him I hoped he was okay and reminded him he could always call me. Then I hung up."

"Well, at least I'll be home tomorrow night."

"You're going to kill yourself worrying, stud."

I knew she was right. I just didn't want to come home to an empty apartment again.

My plane back was late and I could feel the sweat stains forming under my armpits. Luckily, I was on my way home and could take a shower before bed to wash the proof of my anxiety down the drain. It didn't help that I called home from the airport and nobody answered.

In my building, the elevator took its time getting to the first floor, and I actually ran up eight flights of stairs before the lack of oxygen made me call the elevator for the rest of the way up. I barely managed to open my door and burst in.

"Jamie?"

Jamie walked in from the bathroom. He was drying his hands on a towel.

"Oh, God." Relief flooded me and I wrapped my arms around him.

"I guess you missed me, hey?"

I took his face in my hands and kissed him. "More than I'm willing to admit."

Jamie smiled into the kiss. "I'm okay, Jez. A little lonely, but that's over now that you're back."

"I'm only home until Sunday evening."

"I know." Jamie didn't seem to mind all of a sudden.

"You did okay this week?"

"I was fine," Jamie replied casually. "Just missed you."

"Good." I smiled at him and then hugged him to me before realizing I was still sweaty, so I let go of him again. "I better jump in the shower before you think I haven't seen any soap in days."

"You smell all manly," Jamie replied. "I like it."

"So join me in the shower?"

To my surprise, Jamie paused to think about it. "Do you need to go to work tomorrow?"

"'Fraid so. But I'm home all weekend."

"Show me how much you missed me then." Jamie dragged me to the bathroom and we watched each other get naked. "Those stains are going to be a bitch to get out," Jamie said with a broad smile as he took my shirt from me and threw it in the hamper. He moved closer and inhaled my scent as if he really liked it. "Enough pheromones. Let's get you cleaned up."

We didn't take long and Jamie was quite playful, soaping me up and rinsing me off. By the time he stepped out of the shower, I was relaxed and happy to be home. When I walked into my bedroom, still drying off, Jamie was under the covers of my bed, but threw them off when I approached. He was stark naked and aroused. I joined him on the bed and half covered him with my body. "You look good enough to eat."

"You look tired," he replied. "Turn over?"

We rolled around until Jamie was on top. He straddled me and started massaging my pecs, shoulders, and arms with his strong hands. Our groins rubbed together, and it didn't take me long to become as turned on as Jamie clearly was too. In between it all, he kissed me without holding back, and it reminded me of the beginning of our relationship, back in Spain, before Nick got so sick we all forgot there was such a thing as an innocent sexual fling among friends.

Jamie grabbed the lube and a condom and started preparing himself. I wanted to help, but he swatted my hand away. All I could think of was how before I went away Jamie was so tense we didn't even manage to make love. Jamie seemed a lot more relaxed now, and I remained the passive one, even when he grabbed a condom and put it on me. When he sank over me, it was without show, but it still felt glorious. With it, he dispelled all my worries: about whether we'd ever manage sex again; about whether I could dispel my fears of his HIV; and about whether or not we'd make it as a couple.

Jamie rode me like a cowboy, seemingly only occupied by his own pleasure, and I reveled in his abandon. He was beautiful and passionate as he occasionally bent down to kiss me, reminding me that he knew I was there and that I was a living, breathing person. I didn't deny him his pleasure. Between Nick's impotence and our bumpy push-and-pull, he deserved a healthy man in his bed. In return, he made it good for me too.

"I'm so close, Jez," he murmured against my mouth while he fisted himself between our bodies. "Come too?"

I nodded. He was tight and hot, but I figured he'd beat me to the post. Nevertheless I grabbed his buttocks and urged him on. In the middle of a kiss, he came, convulsing on top of me, and to my surprise, feeling him shoot his load all over my belly sent me over as well. We lay there panting for a while and then cuddled some. Jamie finally got up, getting rid of the condom and grabbing a washcloth to clean us both up before crawling back into bed with me. It almost felt like this was an everyday occurrence, the way he slipped into my arms without talking. It felt familiar though it really wasn't.

"I'm glad you're home again," Jamie mumbled. "Makes the being apart worth it."

I agreed with him, but as he slipped away into slumber, I couldn't sleep. What kept me awake this time was the feeling that I couldn't live like this forever. I didn't want to be jetting around the world, working more hours than anyone should. Not when I had a lover waiting for me at home.

I SPENT the next few months trying to keep our company afloat, which meant a lot of work and more travel than I wanted to do. Every time I left, it became a little easier, but every now and then fear crept in, and I wondered how long I could keep Jamie like a bird in a gilded cage. Every time I returned home, Jamie was over the moon to see me, but while he seemed happy and content, I wondered what he did all day. The apartment was spotless and he made me delicious food, but other than that, he didn't seem to have a hobby or anything else to keep himself busy during the long weeks I was gone.

When a trip to Spain came up on the books, I decided to let Jamie tag along.

"How does a little time in Spain sound, J?"

"Spain? Barcelona?" he asked, peering out from the kitchen where he was making dinner.

"Madrid, actually. I need to work."

"Oh."

"We could spend a few extra days and fly to Barcelona to see if the villa is still standing."

Jamie's disappointed look turned a little brighter and he smiled. "I'd love to."

"In two weeks. Shall I book the flights?"

Jamie nodded and I could tell I'd made him happy.

"You have to go away again before Spain, right?" Jamie asked me while we were eating fried rice with clams.

"One more trip," I said, nodding at him. "And then I'm taking you with me."

Jamie didn't seem too worried, and I let the feeling slide that there was something he wasn't happy about. I decided to focus on planning our trip to Spain. We didn't have a lot of time there, but I knew that if I got the timing right, it would still mean a great deal to Jamie.

I couldn't wait to leave.

Chapter 27

AS SOON as my plane from San Francisco touched down at JFK, I started to smile. Three more days and then Jamie and I would be flying to Madrid and then on to Barcelona. I switched my cell phone on to receive calls as soon as I was allowed, but the flurry of messages made me feel more than a little uneasy.

Most of them were from Lakiya, which could be business, but the three messages from Sem made me worry a lot more. We hadn't had any tests done recently, and I hadn't even spoken to him since the follow-up to our last visit, so these surprised me. The fact they were all under ten minutes old told me he urgently needed to get a hold of me.

While I waited for a cab, I tried to call him, but his phone went to voice mail immediately so I sent him a text message. I'd barely gotten into my cab and relayed my address to the driver when my phone rang.

"Jez?"

"Sem? What's up?"

"Get home ASAP."

"I'm on my way. Is Jamie okay?"

"You're in New York?"

"I just landed. I'll be in Midtown in less than an hour, I suppose. Sem, what's happened to Jamie?"

"I'm with him. Just get here, okay?"

"Sem! Fucking tell me what's wrong!" The cab driver looked into his rearview mirror, and I realized I'd shouted loud enough for him to hear me over the music blasting into his ears from his iPod.

"Just get here. We're in your apartment. I'll explain everything then."

I knocked on the partition of the cab. "How quick can you get me to my address?"

"About an hour," the man said lazily.

"If you get me there in under 40 minutes, you get a hundred dollar tip."

The ride was the longest of my life, but the guy earned his tip. As I got out of the cab and collected my bags, I saw ambulances and police cars with flashing light parked at the corner. For a moment I worried that this could be related to Sem's messages, but that would mean Jamie had left the apartment, which didn't seem very likely.

I would know soon enough. Luckily the elevator was right there, and I was at my front door in minutes. When I stuck my key in the door it was opened, and to my surprise, it was Lakiya.

"Kee, what are you doing here?"

"Jamie called me and I called Sem." She took a step back to let me in and took my garment bag from me.

Once inside, I saw Sem sitting next to the couch and Jamie on it. There was dried blood on Jamie's face and he was clutching a towel, which I presumed had ice in it. I rushed to go to him and Sem vacated his seat.

"What happened, J?"

It was no surprise to me that Jamie didn't answer. He was obviously still in shock, and he shut down for less stress than being hit over the head. I took his hands and they were cold, so I took the ice bag from him and tried to warm them.

"What happened?" I repeated, this time asking Sem and Lakiya.

"Where do you want us to start?" Sem replied.

"I don't care! Just tell me what happened to Jamie!" From the corner of my eye I saw Jamie cringe at me raising my voice, so I pulled him into my embrace. "It's okay, J. I'm here now."

"The corner shop was raided by a guy wielding a gun. Jamie came to Mrs. Wu's rescue and was held hostage there for about two hours before the guy became desperate for drugs and tried to get out. Of course, by then the cops were waiting for him outside."

"What was Jamie doing in the corner shop? I do the grocery shopping, and I made sure he had plenty of food in the house and everything else he might need."

Jamie pushed me away, and I let him so I could take a good look at him. "Jamie?"

"I go there sometimes," Jamie said in a soft, raspy voice.

"He's been helping out Mrs. Wu since her son's back surgery," Lakiya added.

"And you knew about this?"

"Jez, calm down," Lakiya said, nodding at Jamie.

"I don't want to calm down. I turn my back for a week, and I find out you and Jamie have both been lying to me?"

Lakiya raised herself to her full five foot two and gave me her best stern look. "Jeremy, get your head on straight. If you don't calm down, you'll make it even harder than it already is." She looked at Jamie as if she was asking permission, and he nodded almost imperceptibly.

"Jamie's been going to the corner shop since the first weekend you left. He's gotten to know Mrs. Wu quite well, and they get along although she doesn't speak a lot of English. Her husband used to run the shop, but he died last year. Her son took over, but he's had back trouble and needed surgery. That shop is their only means of support. When Jamie found out, he volunteered to help with stacking the shelves, and he's been teaching Mrs. Wu English."

I looked at Jamie to see if all this was true, but he didn't let on. "Why didn't you tell me, J? I told you it was okay to go out, as long as you were home at night and stayed safe. I think this qualifies. Why didn't you tell me?"

From the corner of my eye I saw Lakiya gesture at Sem, and they both left the living room.

"Jamie?"

Jamie looked up at me. "I wanted to surprise you."

"Well, you certainly did." I ran my hand over his face, stopping short of the bruises. "You could have just told me, J."

Jamie nodded, his face full of remorse, and I couldn't stay mad at him. Not that I was angry at him as such. I was more angry at the fact that I was uncomfortable not being in full control of the situation. I took him into my arms and hugged him close. Then it dawned on me that Jamie must have felt pretty secure if he'd not just left the apartment, but had gone to the corner shop and struck up a conversation with the petite but frantic Chinese owner. I smiled as I remembered her always shouting at her husband and her son, both men of infinite patience and capacity to endure her wrath. Jamie and she had communicated enough for him to conclude she needed help, and to persuade her to accept his help as well. Not to mention the fact that, because of her limited English, patrons of the shop would have often turned to Jamie to ask for help instead of her.

I let go of him and caressed his hair again. "You did a good thing, Jamie. I'm proud of you."

Jamie smiled as he fell back against the pillow of the couch. I looked at the clock and realized it was way past midnight, so there was a good reason he was tired.

"You ready to go to bed?"

AFTER making sure Jamie was comfortable, I returned to the kitchen.

"I was just about to leave," Sem announced.

"So he'll be all right?"

Sem nodded, pursing his lips. "Physically he's just got a few bruises. The ambulance guys checked him over and didn't want to take him in, and I concurred. He's been through an ordeal, though. No telling how he'll react. Expect a few nightmares, at least."

"What about the blood? Did you have to tell them?"

"The ambulance guys? No. They wear gloves as standard procedure. Any blood is suspect to them, so no, I didn't tell them. And you know what to do. Just wash your hands when you touch any of his torn skin. Unless you have bruises of your own?"

I showed him my hands and turned them over. "All clear."

"See, no problem. He'll heal. He's in good condition."

"Thanks, Sem."

"You're welcome. Now I better leave. I have a full schedule in the morning." He patted my arm, saluted Lakiya, and let himself out.

Lakiya handed me a cup of steaming hot coffee.

"Thanks for coming, Kee."

"Don't mention it," she said with such a tone that I expected a flood of recrimination from her about leaving Jamie alone. Instead, she gave me a concerned look.

"What's wrong?"

She bit the inside of her lip. "I'm a little worried about your relationship with Jamie."

"In what way?"

She inhaled deeply. "I realize this is your first taste of what it's like to be in a long-term relationship, Jez, but a true partnership is between equals."

I was used to being lectured by Lakiya. She had more experience than anyone else at the office and she'd been my mentor for more years than I cared to mention. I'd never expected her to give me a piece of her mind about Jamie, though. "We're good, Kee," I said dismissively.

"I realize he's done a few things on his own now, but in essence, he's still a child. At least emotionally. I thought he was going to cry when you walked in. He was afraid of your reaction. That's what worries me."

"Listen," I said, trying not to give *her* a piece of *my* mind. "I don't hurt him. Ever. If that's what you're asking me."

"I know *that*. I'm just saying—" She hesitated before continuing. "—what do you get out of it? What do the two of you talk about? Does he even understand what you do for a living?"

"He's not stupid, Kee. And he's a grown man, despite the fact he needs someone to help him make decisions. Just believe me when I say we're good for each other."

Lakiya wasn't convinced. I didn't need a big flashing light bulb to tell me that.

"Fine, you want to know?"

She raised an eyebrow and nodded.

"I've always just wanted casual hookups. No commitment, no nagging afterward, no responsibility. I always felt like I didn't have it in me to love another person. When I saw Nick again, I realized he was the only man I'd ever given a damn about, but when we were casually seeing each other years ago, he was a one-night stand guy too. When I saw his commitment to Jamie, I didn't get it. I didn't understand what had changed. It wasn't until I took over caring for Jamie that I realized he wasn't as big a burden as I always thought. Because he takes care of me as much as I take care of him. And it isn't tit for tat. He gives regardless of how much time I have to spend with him. Even when I'm up to my eyeballs in work and jetting from left to right, Jamie is always there for me. He'll fix me dinner and do my laundry and keep my apartment clean."

"A housekeeper with benefits."

"Don't!" I lashed out, pointing my finger at her, and immediately I realized how loud my voice was. "Don't be like that," I spit at her, taking it down a few notches. "He's *not* my housekeeper. I offered to keep Masha so he wouldn't need to do the housework, but he wants to do it."

At that moment, Jamie walked into the kitchen and I wondered how much he'd overheard. He looked afraid, like Lakiya had talked about before.

"Everything okay, J?" I asked, reaching out to touch him while trying to sound soothing and calm, although my heart was racing inside my chest.

"Just wanted to get a drink," Jamie said, taking a glass out of the cupboard and filling it up with water from the Brita filter. I put my hand on his shoulder and squeezed it. "I'll be right with you. As soon as Kee leaves."

Jamie nodded and smiled at Lakiya before leaving.

She was still smiling when she trained her eyes on me. I wasn't sure how much of it was mockery and how much was satisfaction at being proven right.

"He showed me what love is, Kee. And because of it, I can't wait to come home after a trip, and I love every minute I get to spend with him."

"All right, all right," she conceded. "I guess I only saw one side of the equation."

After pausing to drink our now lukewarm coffee, Lakiya seemed more relaxed and so was I. "I'm taking Jamie back to Spain, Kee."

"I know," she replied with a smile. "He'll love seeing his villa again."

"I mean permanently."

"Have you told him yet?"

I sighed. "You said yourself he doesn't make decisions, Kee. When we came here I simply told him and he followed."

Lakiya shook her head the way she always did when she thought I was saying stupid things. Usually they didn't pertain to my private life, though.

"Kee, he needs lists to get through the day. If I don't tell him what to eat, he doesn't eat. He literally can't make a decision to save his life."

She smiled and I felt patronized. If any other person looked at me that way I'd be offended, but this was Lakiya, my confidante and biggest treasure. She could patronize me all she wanted. "I don't recall helping out at the corner shop as being on his list. Or defending a Chinese lady from being robbed at gunpoint."

"I'll admit that surprised me too, but that doesn't mean I can ask him to make a decision like where we're going to live."

She leaned a little closer, although there was nobody within earshot. "You'll still be making the decision, darling. As if anyone would ever stop the unstoppable force," she mumbled under her breath. "Just talk to him about it beforehand. Test the waters. New York might have grown on him by now."

I felt my thoughts drift to the villa in Spain, the white corner tiles, the seemingly haphazardly built additions, the eternal vistas from every corner. "He has his garden there, his swimming pool. A whole house to take care of instead of a few rooms. In New York he's a bird in a golden cage. In Spain he's free."

"How poetic." Lakiya's voice sounded stone cold but her smile was teasing, telling me she approved of this side of me I so rarely showed to anyone.

"It's him I'm thinking of, Kee."

"And the little fact that our company is on the brink and you're running for the hills before it all blows up in our faces has nothing whatsoever to do with this." It wasn't even a question.

"I have a business proposition for you. That's got to be better than running for the hills, right?"

Lakiya narrowed her eyes at me.

"It requires absolute trust. From both of us."

"So it's illegal then?"

I laughed nervously. Why was I nervous? "Oh no, not at all. It's perfectly on the straight and narrow. The trust between you and me means we'll need to travel less. You take care of the US side of things while I cover Europe."

"Doing what?"

"What we're so damn good at. Headhunting. I find European CEOs who want a taste of the US, and you find American managers who want a European company on their résumé."

Lakiya's smile told me she wasn't averse to the idea.

Chapter 28

WHEN I returned to my bedroom, Jamie was still awake. I undressed and slipped under the covers next to him. He grabbed hold of me and snuggled into my arms. I figured Lakiya was right and I would have to ask Jamie how he felt about making our trip to Spain a little longer than we'd originally planned.

"Jamie?"

"I'm glad you're home."

"I'm glad to be home. Can we have a serious talk?"

Jamie looked up at me, and even in the faint light of the bedroom I could see the worried expression on his face.

"If it were up to you, would you rather live in New York or in Spain?"

Jamie relaxed, lying down inside my embrace. "I don't care, as long as I'm with you."

"What if I told you I'd follow you anywhere?"

"Then I'd still want to be where you are."

"What if I told you we were going to be spending about as much time together in Spain as we would in New York? Would you rather be alone in the villa in Spain or this place?"

"It doesn't matter," Jamie answered matter-of-factly, and I was starting to get annoyed. Then I reminded myself that I was asking too much of Jamie. Making decisions for himself when it didn't concern anyone else was easier than deciding something that we would both need to brave the consequences for. I decided to try another avenue.

"What if you had to live alone, if I wasn't with you?"

Jamie jerked his head in my direction. "Please don't leave, Jez. I'll never do it again."

"You didn't do anything wrong, J. And I'm not leaving you. I just want to know you'll be happy, no matter what decision we make."

Knowing I'd never get Jamie to commit to either New York or Barcelona, I decided to ask him something else. "How much did you hear of what was said in the kitchen?"

"Lakiya thinks I use you."

"What?" I asked, sure that no such thing had been discussed.

"She doesn't understand what I see in you. She figures you use me for sex and I use you so I don't need to work for a living. Oh, and she's jealous of my housekeeping skills."

I couldn't stifle a chuckle. "Seriously?"

"That's what I think. I might be wrong. You know her a lot better than I do."

I couldn't deny Jamie had read Lakiya pretty well. But there was something else I'd touched on that I was sure Jamie hadn't heard, unless he'd waited outside the kitchen door after he'd gotten his drink. "I told her I thought you loved me. Do you love me, Jamie?" While I thought the question would make him uncomfortable, he simply turned around and nudged me to embrace him so we were spooning.

"I don't know what love is, Jez," Jamie answered, as if he was just telling me what he was making for dinner tomorrow. "If it means that I want to be with you and I'm sad when you leave, then I suppose so."

"Did you love Nick?" I asked, although to me, the answer was apparent. I just wanted Jamie to think about it and possibly voice it.

"Nick took good care of me. He saved me and took me away from the men who abused me. He took me to Spain and bought me a house. We were very happy there."

"I saw that. The two of you made me believe in love for the first time in my life."

"We did?"

I nodded and kissed Jamie's neck. "You two were so beautiful together."

Jamie turned around again, forcing me to let go of him, but as soon as he buried his face against my neck, I pulled him closer again.

"I think Nick loved me."

"I know he did," I replied, running my hand over his hair.

"I think I loved Nick too."

"I never had a doubt." Jamie shook once and my shoulder became wet. I knew he was crying, and I didn't stop him. I just caressed his hair and his back while I held him. He hadn't really cried about Nick's death, at least not in my presence, and I knew he needed to mourn the loss of his husband. I found myself being patient and caring, not something I would have ever described myself as, but Jamie had changed that. If he ever got around to asking me whether I loved him, the answer would be "yes" without hesitation.

Although he cried for a while, he was calm, and I must have dozed off when I suddenly felt him stir. I glanced at the bedside clock to see an hour had passed.

"I think I'm starting to love you too, Jez."

I kissed his wet lips and lingered, tasting the salt and avoiding the side where his lip had been split and was painfully swollen. The alarm clock told me it was past 3:00 a.m. "You think you can sleep now?"

"Yeah. I think I can."

I turned to my back and let Jamie rest his head on my chest.

"Nick always let me sleep like that. I could hear his heartbeat. It made me feel safe."

"You're safe now too," I said, in the hope of reassuring him.

That night Jamie didn't have any nightmares, and I was glad for the uninterrupted sleep.

THE next morning I picked up the moving to Spain discussion again and decided we would take our trip as planned and see how it felt to be back in the Barcelona villa. Jamie liked my suggestion, but I told my boss I was likely moving to Spain anyway. Unless Jamie decided he couldn't live in the house he'd shared with Nick for eight years, I knew the change of pace would do us good. My boss wasn't happy, but he sensed I had nothing to lose, so he grumbled something about me having to come by the office at least once a month.

The nightmares started that night, and by the time we were ready to leave for Madrid, Jamie and I both looked like we hadn't slept for days. It felt like that too. Every time Jamie fell asleep, he'd wake up thirty to forty-five minutes later, shouting "No!" or "Leave her alone!" If he didn't wake up, he fought against an invisible enemy and dealt me some blows until I shook him awake.

Sem wrote him a prescription for sleeping pills and I had it filled, but Jamie was reluctant to take them. I kept hoping the trip would take care of the nightmares.

IN MADRID, the sleepless nights were not making my work any easier. Jamie seemed depressed, and I wondered if the trip was a good idea. I kept hanging onto the hope that in Barcelona everything would work itself out.

The day we were going to fly to Barcelona, Jamie stayed in bed.

"We need to leave for the airport in two hours, J. Can you be ready to leave the room when I get back from the office?"

Jamie rolled himself into a ball, taking most of the bedding with him, so I sat down on his side of the bed and put my hand on his back. "Just think, we have four lovely days to relax by the pool in the villa. And maybe even more. There might be another assignment for me in Rome, and then you can stay in the villa while I do that. How does that sound?" Jamie pushed my hand away, and I decided not to push it. "An hour and then you need to get up, take a shower, and pack your bag, darling."

When I arrived back at the hotel just over an hour later, Jamie was sound asleep in exactly the position I'd left him. We had to leave if we wanted to catch our plane, so I shook him awake. "Come on, J. Get up and get ready. We need to go."

Jamie groaned and turned to his back. When he opened his eyes and saw me, his expression went blank and I knew what to expect. He'd come with me without a fuss, although he really didn't want to. All the way to Barcelona he didn't speak, and I wondered if he was afraid to go back to the villa. I'd called ahead to the neighbor who was supposed to take care of the place to make sure it was aired out and clean enough to look hospitable. I wasn't disappointed when we arrived. The villa looked like we'd simply left that morning to go grocery shopping.

Jamie hesitated when he crossed the threshold, so I took his bag from him and dropped it in the hallway next to mine. Right across from the entrance door was the small downstairs bedroom where Nick had spent the last of his days. I decided to give Jamie some time and leave him to get reacquainted with the house on his own. I walked straight through to the garden and the swimming pool.

The garden was a little overgrown in places and barren in others due to the sun and lack of watering. I figured Jamie would have his work cut out for him. The swimming pool, like I'd asked, had been cleaned and refilled, so it looked good enough to jump right in. I took off my shoes and dipped my toe in. Perfect. I couldn't wait to see Jamie in his Speedo again.

"J? Come out here. The water's perfect. How about a dip in the pool?"

Jamie didn't answer, so I walked inside, through the kitchen to the hallway. Our suitcases were still there, but Jamie wasn't. He wasn't in the downstairs bedroom either, so I ran upstairs, wanting to take two steps at a time, but being painfully reminded of how awkward the stone steps were.

"Jamie?"

The door to Nick's bedroom was open and the bed was barren with just a mattress and no sheets or blankets. I looked inside and was ready to continue to Jamie's favorite bathroom when I heard a quiet sob. Jamie was sitting with his back against the near wall, facing the empty bed. His knees were drawn up and his head was resting in his hands. When I crouched down next to him, he looked up at me and all I could do was wrap my arms around him before he started crying in earnest.

We sat on the hardwood floor for a long time and I just let Jamie weep, rocking him back and forth from time to time. Eventually he was exhausted and stopped shaking.

"I miss him, Jez."

"Yeah, I miss him too. Even more so than in New York," I added, trying to voice what Jamie was feeling.

"I didn't want to be here without him."

I swallowed. "Why didn't you tell me?"

"Because I also wanted to come and remember the garden and the swimming pool and the feeling I got when I'd see you watch me from your terrace while I took a swim and flaunted it a bit."

"You flaunted it?" I said, although I wasn't really surprised.

Jamie punched me and I pulled him closer, trying to make it feel playful. Jamie turned so he was leaning with his back to me and then draped my arm over his shoulder.

"It's strange to be here without Nick," Jamie said.

"I keep thinking he'll call for you or stroll in here in that swoosh he called a walk."

"Now *he* knew how to flaunt it," Jamie replied.

"He certainly did. Must have had something to do with the size of his dick."

Jamie chuckled. "Even when it didn't work anymore, he still knew how to swing it."

"Years of practice, I'm sure."

Jamie nodded and then grew quiet. After a while he took a deep breath. "Will it ever go away, Jez?"

"What? Missing Nick? Probably not. You were together for eight years. That's a long time. He meant a lot to you and you to him."

Jamie sighed. "I guess it's nice that we both miss him."

Chapter 29

ALMOST from our first night in the villa, Jamie's nightmares got better. He'd only wake up once, maybe twice, and I'd be there to soothe him and he'd fall back asleep. He started looking less haggard now his bruises had faded, and he was working out in the attic again. He returned to being the calm and content Jamie I first got to know here in Spain.

After a week, I had to leave for a short job in Rome and when I returned, the house was spotless. It didn't take a genius to figure out Jamie had done nothing but spring cleaning during the three days I'd been gone.

I found him in the garden, weeding. A head with a large straw hat popped up between the plume grasses as I called his name. He got up immediately. "Jez!" I was welcomed with a full body hug and a lovely, intense, but rather chaste kiss. I was used to it by now. Sex was non-existent in the villa.

"I made you paella, but there's no more wine in the cellar."

"We took what was left with us to New York, remember?"

Jamie nodded, but his elated mood from earlier had disappeared.

"What's wrong, J?"

Jamie couldn't have looked more guilty if he had killed my dog and my best friend on the same day.

"I called the winery. The one where Nick used to get that delicious Rioja?"

I nodded, hoping Jamie's guilty look would wane once he realized I was perfectly fine with his actions. I had more problems hiding my surprise that he'd taken the initiative, without the least bit of prompting from anyone, to call the winery. I was touched by Jamie doing this to please me, but this was definitely a leap into the dark for him. Jamie still barely spoke to strangers. Calling one on the phone seemed almost insurmountable. I decided to pretend it was just business as usual.

"So did you order us some more wine?"

"It sounded like there wasn't going to be more wine."

"What? Is Pablo retiring?"

Jamie seemed to lighten up. "I can't be sure, of course. His English isn't that great and my Spanish is non-existent, so I could have misunderstood, but he said he was sick and didn't know whether he could get the grapes in this year."

"Now that would be a pity," I replied, a plan growing in my brain instantly. "Would you come with me to see him?"

"Jez… I can't. You know that!"

"No, I don't. You took that phone and called Pablo. You talked to him. Can't be harder to come with me to see him. I'll do the talking, don't worry."

Jamie opened his mouth to speak and then closed it again. I smiled at him and he thawed, smiling back at me, so I pulled him into a hug and he looked at me and kissed me quite unexpectedly.

"I'll come with you. I can always go back to the car if it gets too much."

I nodded. "You'll do fine. You're not the same guy who left here."

"No, I'm not," Jamie said as if he was contemplating my words. "Nick never pushed me to go anywhere. Like he wanted to keep me hidden."

"No, Jamie. Nick never wanted to hide you. Protect you, yes. Hide you? No, I don't believe that for a minute. He loved you so much. He knew you were uncomfortable around strangers—"

"I still am, Jez."

"I know."

"I still can't talk to strangers."

"You called Pablo. If I recall, Nick told me he'd never come to the house, so he's a stranger."

Jamie nodded, a mischievous smile on his face. He leaned closer, putting his arm around my shoulder and whispering in my ear. "I wanted to have wine with the paella tonight. I wanted us to have a little fun."

"We can have fun without the wine too," I suggested, knowing full well what he was hinting at. Whenever Jamie and I'd had sex, Jamie had drunk some alcohol. In fact it had dawned on me a while ago that Jamie needed it, since we slept together almost every night, but we hadn't gotten very far in a long time.

"It's hard for me," Jamie said softly, pulling back his arm. "I can't relax when I don't feel at least a little lightheaded."

I smiled, trying to keep it casual. "So you're saying I should feel flattered?"

Jamie threw me a questioning look.

"You overcame your shyness of strangers to get laid."

Jamie bit his lips. "I suppose."

"Don't you trust me?"

"I do. But I just think too much when I'm in bed with someone and I'm stone cold sober."

I decided not to push my luck. My options were either drive into town to get a bottle of wine from the supermercado, or have a quiet night in and no sex for yet another night. Not that I was counting.

Jamie looked sad again. "I'm just scared that you're going to go looking for it elsewhere soon if I don't put out."

Now it was my time to pull Jamie closer to me. "J, I'm not with you for the sex."

Jamie snorted. "Obviously."

"The last time I slept with anyone other than you was the day before I first met you."

Jamie's eyes grew to the size of saucers. "You and Nick?"

"Only when you were there and you know exactly what we did."

"He got you off."

"So yes, the last time I slept with anyone other than you *and Nick* was the day before I first met you."

"Are you serious?"

I nodded. "I told Lakiya and it only really dawned on me then, I must admit."

"Wow."

"Well, she was as surprised as you are."

"Why did you tell her that in the first place?"

Anticipating a serious conversation, I led Jamie to the lounge chair, which three days ago had still been covered with leaves but now looked pristine, and I pulled him to sit down next to me.

"You overheard her being worried about me and my relationship with you. She doesn't understand our relationship, because she doesn't see us as equals."

"Because I need you to take care of me."

"But you see, that isn't true. You take care of me too."

"I do?"

I pulled him closer. "When I need to go away, I can never wait to get home again. I count the days, hours even, until I can see you again."

"I miss you too when you're not here."

"So I guess Kee was wrong then."

"About what?"

"I think we were meant to be together."

Chapter 30

THE next morning I managed to persuade Jamie to take a drive with me. We took Nick's Volkswagen Beetle, a car that was probably older than Jamie, and I could tell Jamie was nervous. I tried not to notice, asking him about things we saw along the way. It became even clearer that Nick had never taken him anywhere, because it seemed he saw a lot of the sights for the first time. When we passed a large man-made Virgin Mary grotto, Jamie asked me to stop, and to my surprise, he got out of the car and walked over to the bench in front of it. An old lady was sitting there praying a rosary and Jamie sat down next to her. He didn't speak to her, but mimicked her stance, entwining his hands and holding them in front of his mouth. He murmured something as if in prayer, then looked up at the beautifully maintained statue. The old lady put her hand on Jamie's knee and then smiled at him.

When Jamie returned to the car, he was smiling too.

"I didn't know you were Catholic?" I asked when we drove off.

"I'm not," Jamie replied matter-of-factly.

"But you were praying?"

"I suppose. I did ask the Lady if she could keep you safe and healthy."

"Me?"

Jamie nodded at me. "Yes. The Virgin can do that, you know."

"If you believe that sort of thing."

"It doesn't matter if I believe it. I don't want to run the risk that she can do this sort of thing but wouldn't know about having to keep you safe. So I asked. Just in case."

I tried not to laugh at his naive way of thinking, and I realized I found it quiet endearing and very typically Jamie. "You didn't ask for her to keep you safe as well?"

Jamie shrugged. "I have you for that."

For a moment I took my eyes off the road to look at Jamie. He was sitting next to me looking quite content and happy as his gaze rested on something outside the car and over the low stone border around the road. "You should have asked for her to keep you safe too, Jamie."

"I'm not sick," he answered resolutely.

"No, but neither am I."

"I could make you sick, but I'm not sick."

I couldn't disagree with that. Jamie was as healthy as I was—his little scare after his excursion notwithstanding. "You won't make me sick," I assured him. "We can take precautions." *If we ever have sex again*, I caught myself thinking. Did I miss it? Of course I did, but nameless sex didn't appeal to me anymore. Even before I met Jamie, I'd go without sex in times I was working hard and traveling so much that every hour of sleep I could get was treasured. But as soon as work let up just a little, no matter where I was in the world, I'd find myself a gay club and work off some of the tension. Now, taking care of Jamie, I hadn't had the urge to go looking for a club. Jamie would cuddle up to me on the couch sometimes, and he slept in my bed most nights these days. We'd never get past the cuddles and occasional kiss, but I had to admit it felt good to be touched.

Reaching the driveway up to the winery, I left the paved road and started driving between the grapevines toward the one-story house. It looked very different from what I remembered when Nick drove me up there just under a year ago. Then there was a hustle of activity going on, now it seemed dead to the world.

"I don't think I misheard," Jamie said quietly. "The house looks like it's about to fall down. Did it look like this when Nick brought you here?"

"No," I said equally solemnly. I thought back to the evening we'd spent sampling the many wines Pablo had in his bodega, and how he'd called his neighbor and his neighbor's son to drive us and our car home, since neither of us were in any fit state to drive. "Let's go see if Pablo is here."

I parked the car near the bodega, but as we exited, we walked toward the main house. It took the occupant of the house a while to answer the door after I knocked, and when it finally opened, I saw a much aged version of the Pablo I remembered. "¿Señor Quintana?"

"Sí?"

"Me llamo Jeremy. Soy un amigo de Nick," I tried in my best Spanish. "Visitamos el año pasado."

It took him a few seconds to remember, but then he smiled. "Sí, claro, Nick. ¿Qué tal está?"

Having reached the end of my Spanish, I answered in English. "Nick passed away a few months ago. Jamie and I just returned to the villa." I put my hand behind Jamie's arm to pull him into the conversation, but I felt Jamie resist, so I let go of him. "Jamie called you and told me you were sick?"

"Sí, sí. Cancér," he answered, coughing as if to prove a point. "My… uvas… grapes?"

I nodded that I understood.

"They die on the field. I cannot bring them in." He gestured for us to come inside his home, which looked very much in disarray. He cleared a sofa so we could sit.

"You have helpers?" I asked. "People you can hire to harvest? Your neighbors, maybe?"

He shook his head. "No tengo dinero. I have no money to pay them." He got up from his chair with some difficulty. "I will get you some wine."

As he left, I looked at Jamie. I could practically see him thinking. And he was thinking the same as me. "Jez, I have Nick's money. We can hire some people to help Pablo get the grapes harvested."

I smiled. "I agree, but hold onto your inheritance, Jamie. We're using my money to invest in the vineyard." For once I was glad Jamie had little notion of money so he didn't fight me over my suggestion.

"You like the Rioja, yes?" Pablo said, holding up a bottle with a simple label, like the ones Nick always had at the house. "I am not allowed to use the name Rioja, even if I use grapes from the Rioja wine region but Señor Nick, he likes my version of Rioja so much, he buy all the bottles every year."

"I can understand that. It's the best Rioja I've ever tasted, Pablo. Maybe we can strike a deal? I pay for workers to harvest your grapes and you tell me the secret of *your* Rioja."

His tired old face lit up. "You want my secret? You want to learn to make wine?"

I nodded. "And Jamie too. He's an excellent cook. I'm sure you can make a winemaker out of him too." As my gaze traveled to Jamie, I saw him smile, which was something he very rarely did among people he didn't know.

Pablo got up and put his arm around me. "You make an old man without children very happy." When he moved away, I saw tears glistening in Pablo's eyes, and I felt I'd done the right thing.

The three of us finished the bottle of wine and by the time dinner rolled around, Eduardo, the neighbor's son, was calling some friends to help out in the vineyard for a few days. This would give us time to recruit a field manager and some seasonal workers to bring in the harvest. I suggested I drive into town to get some paella, but the neighbor's wife insisted on cooking for us. Pablo didn't seem pleased, but I was forthright enough to accept without consulting him. We had a lovely meal of pata negra, Russian Salad, Spanish omelet, olives, and an assortment of local cheeses with bread, very much like the food Jamie had prepared for me on my first night at the villa.

By dusk Pablo took us into the vineyard to show off his grapes. I'm no expert, but I could tell the vines needed weeding and were a little short on maintenance, but they bore plenty of fruit, and Pablo let Jamie taste some of them.

Jamie didn't speak, like I'd expected, but his facial expressions showed me the different tastes he was offered. Pablo didn't seem to mind his silent pupil. He talked enough for all three of us. By the time the sun had set, the tiredness returned to Pablo's eyes and we said our good-byes, but not before I assured Pablo we'd be back the following day to learn more about the business. He sent us off home with two bottles of his prized but unofficial Rioja.

On the way home, I couldn't help but notice that Jamie was still smiling.

"You enjoyed the vineyard?"

"I did. It's so interesting. I never knew that's how they made wine. Well, I sort of knew, from what I'd read on the internet, but I never knew the details. And now Pablo is going to teach me!"

"I think he's glad to have someone show interest in what is pretty much his life's work."

"Will he give it to us after he dies? So we can make our own wine?"

I put my hand on Jamie's knee to calm him down while I tried to navigate the narrow, meandering streets in the dark. "He barely knows us, J. I'm sure he has some family somewhere that will inherit the vineyard, but we can help him out this season and maybe the next as well, if he lives long enough. That way we can learn what it takes, and maybe we can buy a vineyard of our own one day."

"Oh, stop at the Virgin!" Jamie cried out.

I'd almost missed the grotto and had to swerve to park in front of it. I'd barely killed the engine before Jamie was out of the car and practically ran toward her. I didn't have a flashlight, so I had to tread more carefully than Jamie had, but I saw him feel underneath the blue-and-white figure until he'd clearly found what he was looking for. He fumbled a little and then struck a match, lighting one of the candles in front of her.

"Please, Santa Maria. Keep Pablo healthy enough for him to teach us to take care of his grapes. And keep Jez happy so he will continue to love me."

I was surprised by the emotions Jamie's innocent words invoked in me and had to swallow away a lump in my throat. Jamie stopped talking, looking up at the statue and illuminating it with his candle. "And please keep me healthy, because Jez needs me to love him too." Jamie stayed still, looking up at her, and my vision clouded over, so I wiped my face. I stopped telling myself I didn't cry.

When Jamie looked over his shoulder I almost lost it again. There wasn't a lot that was delicate about him. He was a healthy looking young man with broad shoulders, a wholesome, round face, and sparkling eyes, but in the light of the single candle and with the Virgin Mary as a backdrop, he looked positively angelic. When he held out his hand, I grabbed it and pulled him into a tight hug.

"What's wrong, Jez?"

"I love you," I whispered against his soft, bristly hair. "Let me take you home."

Chapter 31

JAMIE barely let go of my hand, which was pretty inconvenient since the car was a stick shift, but I didn't fight him over it. His touch felt needy and soothing at the same time. I felt needy too, and I wondered if things were really as different between us now as they felt to me. I decided to let him take the lead, something he barely ever did, but tonight he seemed to want to. I figured I could always invite him to my room if he left me to go to his.

As it turned out, I didn't need to. After walking in through the front door, he led me straight up the stairs, where he stopped halfway up to kiss me.

"Will you come to my room tonight?"

I knew the reason for Jamie's invitation was the effect the wine had on him, but I wanted to make love to him tonight, so I nodded, even though Jamie's room was the one he used to share with Nick. He walked backward up the stairs and by the time we reached the landing, my shirt and the top button of my jeans were unbuttoned. When I tried to reciprocate, Jamie swatted my hand away. I didn't get an explanation until we were inside his room and he'd pushed me to sit on his bed, my back against the headboard.

"Nick always asked for a show," Jamie said without a single hint of sadness in his voice. "He'd always ask me to take it slow." Jamie raised the hem of his T-shirt. "Ask me."

"To take it slow?"

Jamie nodded.

"Take your clothes off. Slowly. Please, Jamie."

Jamie smiled, just a hint of coyness on his face. At these times he didn't look his age at all, and I was reminded I didn't generally like younger men, but Jamie was different. He was a grown man, bulky enough not to be a twink, yet he had an innocence and openness about him I'd never fallen for in any other man. Now I couldn't keep my eyes off him. He was slowly stripping for me, touching himself in the process, telegraphing to me the areas he wanted me to touch him later. His almost-washboard stomach and the area around his belly button as he lifted his shirt. His muscled shoulders as he drew it over his head. The incline toward his hipbones as he pulled his jeans down and exposed his pubic hair.

I moved around on the bed until I was on all fours, but he pushed me back until I was sitting on my knees and I was left to passively watch him. My hands ached to touch his skin, though. When he slipped his jeans farther down, taking his briefs with them, he turned around to give me a full view of his perfectly round ass.

"Jamie," I groaned.

He looked over his shoulder. "So take your clothes off then!"

I got up from the bed so fast I almost knocked over the bedside lamp. It took some scrambling to save it and put it back in its place, albeit a little farther from the edge than before. When I stood at my full height again, Jamie wrapped his arms around me from behind.

"On second thought, let me."

He pulled my shirt apart and off my shoulders, throwing it in the corner as soon as my hands were free. His mouth latched onto my nape and I couldn't help a moan escaping from my throat. I knew he was marking me, but I didn't care. His hard-on grinding against my ass and his hands brushing across my nipples as he moved them south didn't help abate my arousal. Maybe I was wrong earlier when I thought I hadn't missed the sex.

I wanted to turn around, but Jamie wouldn't let me. He continued to caress my skin, sometimes soft and teasing, sometimes hard and direct. All I could do was reach back in an attempt to grasp at some skin as well.

"What are you gonna do, Jamie?"

Jamie didn't hesitate for a moment. "Drive you crazy."

"Won't take much." I chuckled.

He kissed my neck again as he slipped his hand into my boxers and took hold of my half-hard cock.

"I clearly haven't tried hard enough."

Jamie started slowly rubbing me to full mast and there was nothing I could do. I tried to breathe slowly. Submitting to another's touch was something I did so rarely, yet it didn't feel strange. The only other man who had ever done this to me was Nick, and Jamie had clearly taken a page out of his late lover's book. As I was trying to distract myself from his expert handling, it dawned on me that, in fact, it was strange to have Jamie in control of my pleasure. Sweet, innocent Jamie, who couldn't even make it through the day on his own without a to-do list, was now in complete command of me. Jamie, who'd made love to me the first time without speaking a single word, was now whispering in my ear, telling me how good he was going to make me feel and how much I needed him for my pleasure.

I could do nothing more than give in, and I did so willingly. The part of my brain that was still capable of conscious thought knew this was the surefire way to prevent two things I wanted to avoid. With Jamie in control, he couldn't make me roughhouse him, and he couldn't make me fuck him so hard it would hurt him. Anything that would happen, he'd do to himself.

For now, Jamie's movements were slow and deliberate, but I was becoming impatient. Then he suddenly turned me around and kissed me hard. I wasn't used to Jamie being so aggressive, but it turned me on and he knew it. Most of my casual encounters were far from lovey-dovey and if kissing was involved, it was to arouse, not to entice. Jamie clearly knew he didn't need to seduce me, and since I'd told him, he knew the kind of sex I was used to. Was this our compromise?

Jamie moved his hands over my back and down to my buttocks. He squeezed them and then let go to roughly pull my pants down. There was nothing sweet about his expression when he sank down to his knees to help me step out of them. I was still wearing my boxers and they were tented because of Jamie's earlier actions, but Jamie inserted his hand and freed my cock. When he also took my balls out and sucked them into his mouth, I moaned. I reached out my hand to rest it on his head when the images of our first time flooded my brain. Jamie liked to have his mouth fucked. Was that what he was aiming for again?

I had feelings for him now and didn't know whether I could do what I'd done that first time, despite the fact that I knew he liked it. I tensed up and Jamie noticed. He got up from his crouching position.

"For a big, butch, leather dude you scare easily," Jamie said without compassion. He pushed me down onto the bed and I gladly let myself fall. When he crawled on top of me, he looked predatory, and he grabbed me by the throat. "What, no fight? You disappoint me."

I knew I couldn't. If I fought Jamie, he'd crawl back in his shell and ask me to hurt him, and that was the last thing I wanted. I'd made up my mind a long time ago that I'd rather take care of him without the sex than to arrive at the point again where he begged me to inflict bodily harm. I tried to keep my face neutral instead of defiant, and he loosened his grip on my windpipe. His face softened, and this time when he leaned down to kiss me, it was a tender, noninvasive kiss. I hesitated to touch him, although my hands ached to, until he was lying fully on top of me. Only then did I kiss Jamie back and let my hands roam over his tight swimmer's physique.

Jamie's kisses became more desperate as he ground his erection against the coarse hairs on my belly. My arousal, which had abated a bit after the earlier tension, was back to full height as our kisses became more passionate and our combined movements more efficient. My need for Jamie was immediate, and for a moment I wondered if I'd deluded myself all those weeks I didn't lust after him. Suddenly my boxers were a hindrance, but we were so close together, getting a hand between our bodies was impossible. I tried to pull them down, but I couldn't, not even with Jamie's hand between the fabric and my skin.

Jamie was making delicious noises, which became louder as he pulled his mouth away from mine to catch his breath. We were rutting against each other, desperate to get off, but there was something missing. Jamie's grunts were becoming frustrated, desperate, and I managed to worm my hand between our bodies because Jamie had moved a little to the side. He started riding against my hand until he looked up at me and lost it. He buried his head against the side of my neck as he came hard across my belly.

I wasn't nearly as close, and as Jamie made a half-assed attempt at touching me, I put my hand over his and rubbed them both over my cloth-covered crotch until I too came hard.

When I opened my eyes, Jamie was looking at me. "I missed you."

I wiped my hand on my already soiled boxers and grabbed his head to pull him into a kiss. "Did we know how much we needed this?" I asked as we broke the kiss.

"I missed this more," Jamie answered.

"Which this?"

"You holding me."

"I hold you all the time," I was quick to reply. "On the couch in front of the TV and when you slide into my bed in the middle of the night."

"I usually hold *you* at night."

"You do," I agreed.

"And I missed you holding me after the sex."

"But you don't miss the sex." I looked down at him with one raised eyebrow.

"You didn't want to have sex with me anymore."

I purposely ignored the accusatory tone. "I wanted something we shared, not what you wanted. Which was for me to hurt you."

"I don't need to hurt all the time," Jamie said as he settled his cheek against my chest.

"I'll make love to you if I can do it without pain, J."

Jamie was growing heavy in my arms, and I knew the conversation was over.

Chapter 32

I WOKE up a few hours later, still some time before daybreak. Jamie was still in my arms, but my bladder was complaining about all the wine we'd drunk the night before, so I slipped from underneath him and went to relieve myself and have a cursory wash, since we hadn't bothered wiping ourselves the night before. When I returned, Jamie was lying on his side and his eyes were open.

"I didn't mean to wake you."

Jamie shrugged. "You didn't. I felt you move, but I didn't feel like opening my eyes."

I sat down on the chair opposite the bed and Jamie followed me with his gaze. Then he held out his hand and beckoned me with his finger. "Come back to bed. I need a warm, bulky pillow."

Jamie knew I couldn't resist him so I walked slowly over to my side of the bed, enjoying Jamie's scrutiny. I was naked now, and because of my earlier full bladder, sporting some morning wood. Despite Jamie's lustful looks, he simply cuddled against me as I got into bed.

We lay there for a while and then suddenly Jamie took a deep breath. "Do you still miss Nick?"

"Yeah," I replied honestly. "He was one of those friends I thought would be around forever. We didn't need to stay in touch all that much, but we were there for each other and we knew it."

"He told me you were the first man he ever fell in love with."

"Did he tell you that?" I asked.

Jamie nodded.

"Nick fell in love all the time, Jamie. Every new guy who walked on the set that was remotely his type, he fell for like a ton of bricks.

He'd seduce him with cakes and wine and outings to exclusive clubs." Jamie looked at me as if he didn't believe me. "I know, J, because I was the guy who had to go out to buy all that stuff, *and* the guy Nick would come lament to about how much of a psycho the guy had turned into after all the wining and dining ended. Nick would lose interest pretty soon. I always thought Nick liked falling in love, but didn't understand that it was always a passing phase. He loved the rush, the butterflies, but didn't like the reality of living with someone else."

"He lived with me."

I kissed Jamie's hair. "You can imagine my surprise when I heard you were together for eight years, right?"

"He loved me, Jez, and despite appearances, I'm not all that easy to live with. He left everything behind for me and took me here, just like you left everything to bring me back to Spain."

"I had a lot more selfish reasons than you think, and I'm sure it was the same for Nick."

Jamie looked up at me. "What do you mean?"

"You told me before that Nick knew he was positive and that nobody would hire him. Performing in front of a camera was all he had, J. He was Mr. Porn. It's how he got into clubs, got free champagne, and how he got laid. The moment the Biz dropped him, he became a has-been, and there's nothing worse in the shallow world of porn than a guy who can no longer perform."

"Nick could perform. At least in the beginning he could," Jamie said in Nick's defense.

"Not in front of a camera. Because everyone was afraid of the scandal. So Nick lost his identity."

"And what about you? You weren't in porn. You're a businessman. What did you do to have to run away?"

I bit my lip to stall for time. "The company I've worked for all my life was built on hot air. I've known that for a long time. We work on trust and discretion. Multinationals trust us with secrets that could potentially gain or lose them billions of dollars because we place the right people at the top of their corporate ladder. All it would take was one man or woman to break that trust, and someone did. Now they shun us, and we're not getting the contracts we need to stay afloat. Lakiya and I are cutting our losses, but we need to keep our heads down, otherwise we'd burn ourselves as well. Kee can't leave New York because of her kids, but I could, so I did. We're going to try to start our own small company with her taking care of the US side of things and me covering Europe."

Jamie turned around and sat up, his hands resting on his bent knees. "So you're still going to be working. Are all the plans for the winery just hot air too?"

I sat up as well and tried to touch his arm, but he shrugged me away. "No, J. I meant what I said. We'll help Pablo out to harvest his wines, but neither of us are used to much manual labor, so we'll do what we do best: I'll find capable people to do the work, and you'll gobble up Pablo's advice and learn from him how to make the wine. It's like cooking, and since you do that exceptionally well, I'm sure you'll get the hang of winemaking soon enough."

"I wanted us to do this together, Jez. You and me."

I scooted up the bed to sit next to Jamie, not trying my luck touching him for the time being. "I'm doing this for you, J."

"Well, don't. Nick doted on me so much he practically locked me in this place."

"I don't lock you up, J. You know that."

"You found me a minder in New York."

"Kee? She's a friend. I wanted you to have someone to call in case of an emergency. And after your little excursion—"

"Please stop digging that up, Jez. What do you want me to say? That I'm a stupid kid who doesn't know right from wrong?"

"Knowing it won't happen again is more than enough for me."

"So lock me up, like Nick did."

"Nick didn't lock you up. He took care of you. He loved you."

"Yeah, he did." Jamie was sitting slumped over, elbow resting on his knees, and I couldn't help feeling there was more to the story. This conversation was going nowhere, though. The perfect image I had of Nick and Jamie's relationship was starting to show cracks, and so was everything Nick stood for in my mind. I wanted to know more, but Jamie didn't seem eager to share. The defeat in his demeanor was so evident, I just wanted him to feel comforted, safe, loved. So I touched his arm again. This time he let me, and he even turned into the touch.

"Come back to bed. Everything looks different in the light of a new day."

Jamie rolled his eyes. "You're so over the top sometimes."

"That may be, but I just want what's best for you. And I'm sure Nick wanted that too."

Jamie pushed me to lie down on the bed and snuggled into my arms. It was easy to find a comfortable position, since we did this almost every night. I could only hope it would stay that way.

A while later I woke up from Jamie shaking me. "We need to go to Pablo's!"

I smiled at Jamie's enthusiasm and how his midnight anger was totally forgotten. Maybe he was right. Maybe this was what was meant for us. The transatlantic business idea wasn't floating right now anyway, so I figured I could focus on the winery for a while. And like Jamie asked, the added bonus would be that this was something we could do together. At least his dark mood had disappeared.

We stopped at the Virgin along the way, where Jamie said a quick prayer and I decided not to look for a meaning behind Jamie's suddenly found religion. Maybe it gave him comfort and courage to face the big bad world, and he'd be able to talk to Pablo so they could start building a working relationship. Maybe he was just trying to exert his new freedom by testing how far I'd let him make his own decisions. I'd decided a long time ago that as long as he didn't put himself in danger, I'd support any decision he made, and this was my way of showing him that.

It was full-on summer in Spain, and the dry heat was fine as long as you stayed outside. When we arrived at Pablo's, the inside of his spartan cabin soon became oppressive. The heat was sweltering, and I wanted to open a few windows and leave the door open as well, but

Pablo didn't look ready to face the day yet. He smiled when he saw Jamie, though, patting him on the arm before Jamie silently offered it as support.

Before I knew it, Pablo was in his kitchen, sitting behind his sink to wash, and Jamie was opening windows. I just managed to ask Pablo whether he objected to everything being thrown wide open, but he gestured good-naturedly at Jamie and smiled as if to say he was powerless to resist him. I knew the feeling all too well.

It didn't dawn on me until we were eating breakfast, while sitting in the shade of a large olive tree just outside Pablo's house, that Jamie was doing everything totally unscripted. He was the one who decided Pablo needed fresh air and who had cleaned up all around the bed Pablo spent most of his time in these days, it seemed, without even discussing it with me or Pablo. Jamie had simply taken things in hand, and neither Pablo nor I had thought of resisting. He'd ordered me to go to the bakery in town to get rolls and told me exactly what to bring to put on them. And even then it hadn't occurred to me to protest.

I was still the only one Jamie talked to directly. Obviously, including Pablo in the conversation was one bridge too far, so here we were, sitting in the shade, munching on our bread and salami and cheese in total silence, if you didn't count the birds and occasional cicada. Pablo didn't seem to mind. He looked content and quite happy, actually. Jamie kept looking at him and then smiling at me as if he was saying: "See, Pablo doesn't mind us swooping in here and taking over the place."

I, on the other hand, wasn't so happy with the silence, so I struck up a conversation, trying to figure out how many men I had to try to find to work the vineyard. Pablo was a little vague on that, though, telling me one or two workhands were enough until the grapes were ready for picking. When I asked him how many he needed for harvesting, he shrugged as if he didn't know.

We were still at the breakfast table when Eduardo arrived with a friend in tow he introduced as Fabian. Both young men were not bad looking and scantily dressed in cut-off jeans, but they felt like jailbait to me. I couldn't *not* look at them, but they were a little young for my taste. As soon as they walked onto the courtyard, Jamie's happy-go-lucky attitude changed, although he didn't say anything. He disappeared into the house, and I had a pretty good idea what he was going to do. The boys looked bored, so I asked Pablo to show us what needed to be done. He took us to the vineyard and showed us how to pull weeds and generally maintain the vines. The young men went to work while I took a tired Pablo back to the house. I settled him back under the olive tree and went inside to get him some water to drink. I found Jamie in the kitchen, scrubbing the sink.

"The boys are working and Pablo needs a drink," I told him. Jamie didn't react. When I put my hand on his shoulder, he shrugged it off and continued scrubbing. I knew Jamie was upset about something, but I didn't know what.

"J, what's wrong?"

"Your boys," he mumbled under his breath.

"*My* boys?"

"The neighbors' sons," Jamie said, his voice flipping. He was still scrubbing, his back to me.

"Pablo asked them to come and help with the vineyard. They grew up around grapes, so they know what to do, and Pablo didn't need to explain much to them."

"I saw you looking at them," Jamie said, turning around to face me. His face was tense, and I thought he looked sad. Then it dawned on me.

"They're good-looking kids, but they're kids, Jamie. You didn't think…."

I raised one arm in defeat and Jamie threw himself at me. "I'd never make a move toward them, you know that. They're jailbait. I don't go for kids. In fact, you're probably the youngest guy I've ever had. I usually go for the mature men."

"Like Nick?" Jamie asked from where he had his face buried against my neck.

I chuckled. "Yeah, he became even more my type when I saw him again last year."

Jamie looked at me, and I realized he was still sad. "I miss him too, Jamie."

"But if Nick was your type, then what am I to you?"

I smiled at him and hugged him tighter. "My partner. My lover, sometimes, when you feel like it."

"I'm your partner?"

"Yes, my silly man, you are."

Jamie looked at me again. "But I'm not your type."

I chuckled. "Type is great for checking out guys when you're cruising. For finding a partner, you look at different things."

"Like what?"

"Like how compatible you are."

"And we're compatible?"

I thought about it for a moment. On the surface, I had to admit we didn't have all that much in common, but I knew what I felt. Jamie had changed my life, and it was for the better. No doubt about that.

"J, are you happy with me?"

Jamie nodded, although he didn't seem entirely convinced.

"Well, *I'm* happy with *you*. You've given me a home, and someone to come home to. You made me see there was something essential missing in my life and that was… consistency and… love." I hesitated using that last word. I'd never told anyone I loved them, at least not out loud. But it wasn't the first time I'd told Jamie, and I meant it more every time I said it. I just wanted to remind Jamie that this had gone way past my promise to Nick.

"So you wouldn't take one of the boys up on it if they made a pass at you?"

I shook my head, looking Jamie in the eye in the hope the doubts would leave him. "So can you stop scrubbing that sink?"

Jamie smiled ever so slightly. "It needs a good scrub, like the rest of the house. I don't know how that man can live this way."

"Tut, tut. We're in a stranger's house here. We shouldn't judge him too harshly. He's sick, remember?"

Jamie pursed his lips and looked around. "So he needs help keeping it clean. I'm sure he'll feel better once it's all neat and tidy."

"You mean you'll feel better?"

Jamie smiled more widely, clearly feeling caught.

"Ask Pablo if you can help him clean his house."

"Aww, Jez, can you ask him? Please? I don't speak Spanish."

I shook my head. "I don't speak Spanish either. Pablo understands enough English." I let go of Jamie and filled a glass with water to take out to Pablo. Jamie picked up his scrub brush again. "I'm going to ask Pablo for a tour of the winery so he can show me the equipment for turning the grapes into wine. Want to come take a look at it with us?"

Chapter 33

OUR trips to Pablo's winery became an everyday occurrence. We'd bring food for the day for us, Pablo, and Eduardo and Fabian, and share that in between the work. It had taken a few days, but Jamie had conquered his shyness enough to talk directly to Pablo, and Pablo acted like he hadn't noticed that Jamie had never talked to him before. They cultivated a quiet understanding where Pablo taught him about the winemaking process, and when he grew tired and needed a rest, Jamie would retreat inside to muck out the small house.

In the meanwhile, I did things I wasn't used to at all. Things like driving a tractor and telling the boys off for fooling around too much. It wasn't until Pablo gave me access to his accounts that I started to feel like I was in my comfort zone again. It was disconcerting to see that Pablo barely had the means to make ends meet and no room for investment. His equipment was in dire need of maintenance, and when I called a man to come and do that, Pablo protested that nobody knew how to maintain his equipment like he did. When I suggested I invest in some new fermentation vats, I got a lecture on how Pablo made traditional wines by traditional methods and how his vats were the reason for the distinctive taste. I didn't even dare mention the irrigation methods I'd found information about on the Internet. I somehow felt that would be crossing the line.

The winemaking business had sparked my interest, though. While Jamie was busy learning the hands-on aspects, I spent my afternoons, and sometimes evenings, searching the Internet for ways to increase the yield of the vineyard. It all came down to the same thing: traditional Spanish winemaking methods had widely spaced vines because of the sparse soil, and relied heavily on manual labor. It traditionally produced excellent, but expensive wine. More modern methods, with soil irrigation, made it possible for vines to be planted closer together, like in the Bordeaux and Bourgogne regions of France. Making this change, even if Pablo wanted it, would take years, because young vines needed time to mature before growing grapes of any sort of decent quality. I therefore understood Pablo's reluctance to change, since he probably wouldn't be around to see the increased yield. That didn't mean I couldn't dream, and as I did my grocery run, I found myself checking barren fields to see if they had the right orientation to be turned into vineyards. Maybe once we got the hang of the winemaking business, Jamie and I could buy ourselves some land and start for ourselves.

I didn't tell Jamie about my plans, not even after I'd visited the local estate agent to ask whether he had any vineyards or appropriate land for sale.

Every night after dinner we'd return to the villa to sleep. We barely spent any time there these days, and I sort of felt it was a waste of a perfect house, but I knew our work at Pablo's would be short-lived. Once the harvest was in and the grapes crushed, there'd be little more to do than wait. I knew Jamie would still want to take care of Pablo, but we both knew his time was limited, although, just like with Nick, Jamie avoided any conversation about it.

Jamie slept in my bed most nights. Although we worked hard all day and I was tired by the time we returned, Jamie was usually still full of life and never stopped being excited about what he'd learned or done that day. I loved seeing him so happy and contented myself with the thought that me bringing him to Pablo's made him smile. Sometimes I'd stop and remember the quiet, brooding man I first met, and how he would barely talk to me. Now I couldn't shut him up.

One evening he seemed more contemplative, though.

"What's wrong?" I asked him when I came into the bedroom freshly showered and he was sitting on the bed in his night clothes.

"Is Pablo going to die like Nick?"

"I don't know," I answered truthfully. "He told me he had cancer, but I don't know how advanced it is, or even where it is. If it's lung cancer then it's like Nick's, and some things might start looking familiar to us."

"He's already losing weight, and it's not like he doesn't eat. Nick would sometimes not eat."

"Nick ate your cooking," I said, sitting down next to Jamie and bumping him with my shoulder in the hope he'd smile. Of course, he didn't.

"That's why I cooked all the time."

"And why you're cooking for Pablo."

"I don't want him to die, Jez."

I pulled Jamie into my embrace and rested my cheek on his hair, which, I noticed, was getting long again. "I don't want him to die either, but there isn't a lot we can do about it, J."

"Do you think if I pray to the Virgin she'll make him better?"

I shook my head, letting my cheek brush over Jamie's hair. Sometimes I was reminded of how delightfully naive Jamie was. "It doesn't work that way, Jamie."

"But it won't hurt, right?"

"No, I don't suppose it will," I said with a smile. I didn't want him to pin his hopes on his prayers, though. I also didn't want Jamie to lose another person he trusted. But should I be the one to dash his hopes and tell him it was probably inevitable? I was too much of a coward for that, so I just smiled at him, wrapped him in my arms, and lay down on the bed with him. He seemed to settle just fine and it was nice to fall asleep like that.

When I woke up a few hours later, Jamie wasn't there. I'd slept like the dead and had a hard time getting my mind to kick into gear. When I tried to get up, my chest felt heavy and I could barely breathe. When I opened my mouth to call Jamie's name, the sound was barely audible, even to me, and I couldn't figure out what was wrong. I tried to shout again and this time no sound came out at all. I started to panic and then everything turned black. I vaguely remembered my name being called but I couldn't respond. I figured I should fight this feeling, but somehow couldn't muster the strength. All I could think of was that someone needed to take care of Jamie, and I hadn't bothered putting my affairs in order.

Chapter 34

THE first thing I remembered was slow, steady beeping somewhere behind my head. I was in desperate need of a drink of water and when I tried to wipe my mouth, I found I couldn't. When I tried again, a blaring alarm went off and someone told me to stay calm. It wasn't a voice I recognized.

The next voice made me smile, since it brought clear pictures to my mind of a petite African American woman who could bust anyone's balls in a ten miles radius. Lakiya. When I opened my eyes, I saw it was true. She was standing next to me, one eyebrow raised, a stern look on her face like she wanted to reprimand me for something, and one hand firmly planted on her hip.

"What did you go and do to yourself, Jeremy?" she asked me, in the same way she would ask a client why he'd pass up a golden opportunity she'd personally selected him for.

"I didn't do anything," I replied with a voice that sounded—and felt—like it was made of sandpaper. "What happened?"

"You had a 'cardiac episode'," Lakiya replied as if she was quoting a doctor. "You didn't even have the decency to have a real heart attack, but you've been out cold for five days to fix you up anyway."

"Heart attack?" I parroted.

"Well, enough of one to give you arrhythmia so severe you arrested every time they tried to wake you up. They tell me you'll make a full recovery once you're all healed, but they're also pretty flabbergasted you actually made it to the hospital still alive. Lucky for you Jamie's learned to talk to strangers by now."

Jamie. I suddenly remembered we were in Spain and Jamie must have been alone with me in the villa. But what was Lakiya doing in Spain? "Where's Jamie?"

This time Lakiya's stern look was replaced by one with a lot more concern in it. Somehow it made me more worried.

"He's curled up on the couch in your bedroom at the villa. He won't talk or eat. I don't think he believes you're still alive, although I tell him every time I see him."

Suddenly I needed to see Jamie, so I sat up, making more alarms go off.

"Lie down, man!" Lakiya shouted in her slightly nasal voice. "You're in no fit state to walk out of here yet. I'll try to get Jamie to come here so he can see for himself that you're good."

It was as if it had taken until now for facts to seep into my brain. I was in a hospital in Spain, having barely survived something gone wrong with my heart. Jamie must have seen it happen, called an ambulance, and then Lakiya. How else would she have found out?

"I need to see Jamie."

Lakiya smiled as if all of a sudden everything was right with the universe. "Not as much as he needs to see you, trust me."

"So go get him."

"Yes, sir!" Lakiya saluted me, then spun on her heels and walked to the end of the room before turning around. "I can see why he needs you, Jez. He's a mess without you. I'm glad you survived, because otherwise I would have had to bury both of you." She started to walk out and then hesitated. When she turned to face me again, her face was serious. "I can't pretend to know what you get out of it, Jezzie, except for a piece of ass, of course, but I get you're in over your head."

"I love him, Kee," I replied in Jamie's defense. If I looked at it from a distance, I got why nobody else understood, including my well-meaning best friend. We were far from a traditional couple. Jamie's dependence on me would make it seem to an outsider like the balance of power was firmly in my camp, but I knew better. I'd had this conversation with Jamie, about how he felt like he was a burden, and we'd resolved it, but that didn't mean the outside world had.

I was still lost in thought when the nurse came in to check up on me. I hadn't really come to terms yet with the fact I was in the hospital and utterly at other people's mercy, but even after what little Lakiya had told me, I knew the last thing I should do was get worked up about it.

The nurse, whose name tag read "Maria," wasn't really looking at me, but at the screen behind me. I looked up, but all I saw were some colored dancing lines, and I had no idea whether they were doing the right kind of dances. "So will I live?" I asked her.

"We worried you would not for a long time," she replied with a heavy Spanish accent, but a neutral face, after jotting down some things on a sheet of paper. "But your heart muscle still seems strong. It was only your rhythm that was bad. They fixed that."

"How long was I out for?"

"Four days," she replied without checking it in my file. "Every time we tried to wake you up, we had to start your heart again."

"Yes, Lakiya told me."

"She is your friend," Maria said. It wasn't a question, but I nodded anyway.

"I hope she's bringing my partner this afternoon."

"You were here on business?"

I chuckled, then remembered that would probably set off an alarm, so I stopped. "No, I live here with him. He's my life partner."

"Ah, your… esposo. Your husband."

"We're not married, but yes, in spirit, he is my esposo."

Maria smiled at my confession. It was the first crack in her armor. "I hope your friend brings him. It would be good for you to see him. And I would like to meet him."

"He's very shy. He doesn't speak Spanish."

At that moment I saw Lakiya standing in the doorway. I didn't see Jamie behind her, though, which worried me.

"Kee, where's Jamie?"

Lakiya ignored me and looked at Maria instead.

"I am done here. You can come in," Maria told Lakiya. "He's doing well, but keep him calm, especially when he sees his husband, yes?"

Lakiya nodded, but waited for Maria to leave before sticking her hand out and pulling Jamie into the room. It was amazing to see him, although his hair was sticking out all over the place and he clearly hadn't shaved in at least four days. Lakiya directed him to a chair next to my bed and pushed him down on it. To an outsider it would have looked like she was manhandling him, but I knew from experience, and from the blank look on Jamie's face, that if she didn't do it, Jamie would stay where he was and not move. I reached out my hand to touch him, but he just stared at it.

"Jamie, will you hold my hand?" I shook it to draw his attention, and he put his hand into mine as if this was a slow motion movie. He didn't look me in the eye, and I knew better than to push him. I simply squeezed and enjoyed what little contact he allowed me.

When I looked up, I saw Lakiya's concerned face. She ran her hand through Jamie's hair in a motherly gesture that made me want to do the same, knowing how bristly soft it always was. "He's been like this since I arrived. It took some mighty persuasion for him to open the door for me. He won't eat, although I make him food. Fortunately he does drink water, but only when I'm not looking."

I recognized the pattern from the days after Nick's death, only nobody had died. I was still alive, although it had been a close call.

"He called you?"

"Yes and no. Let's say he dialed my number and I recognized it from when you call me. When I called him back he picked up, but didn't speak. I asked him to put you on the phone, but nothing happened. I figured something was very wrong so I jumped on the first plane."

"Thanks, Kee, I owe you one."

"No, you don't," she replied in her usual no-nonsense manner. "He's the one who called an ambulance. I guess he only fell silent after they took you away. The nurse told me he wouldn't come with them."

That made me look at Jamie again, who was still sitting there with his hand in mine and that blank expression on his face. "I'm okay, Jamie. The nurse said I was going to live. And they already fixed what was wrong with my heart, so in a couple of days I'll be allowed to go home, and then we can finish helping Pablo with his grapes." Then it dawned on me. "Did anything happen to Pablo? Jamie?" Jamie didn't reply. "Kee?"

"Who's Pablo?"

"He's the man who used to make wine for Nick. We've been helping him at his vineyard since we found out he has cancer. Jamie and he really get along well."

Lakiya shook her head. "First thing I heard about it."

"Could you call him to be sure? His number is in the phone at the villa. He speaks passable English, so just ask him if he's okay and tell him what happened. He must be worried since we didn't show up for work."

"All right, hon," she drawled. She nodded in Jamie's direction. "I'm going to get me some coffee, and I'll bring water for Jamie."

I knew she hoped that her leaving would make Jamie talk, but I knew better. I had to try to get through to him, though. "J? Look at me, please?" He didn't. "I need you to eat something tonight when you go home with Kee. I want you to be healthy and strong for when I come home, okay? Jamie, please don't shut me out like this."

Somehow this seemed to resonate with him. For the first time he looked up at me, and I could see a little hint of sadness in his eyes.

"Get up and come here," I said, letting go of his hand and gesturing him to come closer. To my surprise he got up from his seat and simply crawled into the narrow bed with me, pushing his back against my side. I put my arms around him and winced at hearing alarms go off. Within seconds, two nurses and what I presumed was a doctor ran into my room.

"I'm fine," I said, holding up my hand and hoping they wouldn't scare Jamie away. "He needs this. Please don't make him get up."

Maria nodded at her colleagues, who reluctantly left the room.

I couldn't see Jamie's face, since it was turned away from me, but he stayed put and that was all that mattered. I could feel his breath against my arm and it was calm, which also helped me.

"This is your husband?" Maria asked while the alarms suddenly stopped.

"This is Jamie," I acknowledged. "I told you he was shy. Well, that was an understatement."

"I need to attach the wires again for the monitors."

"Can't it wait? They're off now anyway."

Maria shook her head. "They put the alarms on hold, but if I don't fix, then they will go off again."

"Okay," I conceded. "But please try not to scare him."

She smiled at Jamie as she approached the bed. "His eyes are closed. He looks happy." With efficient gestures she reattached the clips that connected the wires to stickers on my chest and adjusted some of the alarms. "If you keep getting better, we won't need these in a few days." With that statement she left Jamie and me alone, or at least as alone as we could be in a bed in Intensive Care.

It felt good to have Jamie in my arms, even though he was asleep by the time Lakiya returned. She stopped in the doorway and smiled. "It's about time he slept. I think he's been awake for the last four days."

"I wish he could stay here, but he can't," I whispered so not to wake Jamie.

"I know. I'll take him home with me, and we'll come back tomorrow and however long it takes until I can take you home too."

Chapter 35

LIKE Lakiya said, she brought Jamie to the hospital until I could return to the villa with them. Jamie hadn't spoken in all that time, and although I knew this was his strange way of coping with everything that had happened, I still worried. It resembled Nick's homecoming, although the doctor had assured me that I wasn't going home to die.

On my final check-up, the cardiologist told me I'd had a potentially fatal coronary blockage, but since Jamie had practically seen it happen and had called an ambulance immediately, and the ambulance had been close by because of an earlier false alarm, I had been given the best possible care. My heart was in near perfect condition, despite the arrhythmia I'd developed in the first few days. The doctor had assured me that because they'd been able to unblock my arteries before any major damage was done, this was unlikely to happen again in the near future.

I knew my less than healthy lifestyle, with stressful meetings and lots of jetting all over the place, resulting in near-permanent jetlag, were to blame for this, and I knew the life we were living now was much healthier, so I wasn't all that worried.

I couldn't convince Jamie, though. Once Lakiya had gone home to her kids and Jamie and I were alone, he cooked for me and cleaned the house, but wouldn't let me lift a finger. He slept in my bed, but wouldn't let me touch him. During the day I'd sit on the bench in the shade of the vines and he'd weed his garden, but he barely spoke unless it was to ask me if I needed something. I, in turn, was trying to walk the fine line between coaxing him out of his shell and leaving him to grieve on his own. It hadn't escaped my attention he didn't let me out of his sight for a moment.

One evening, it all became too much.

"Jamie, leave the dishes for a moment and come sit here with me."

Jamie shook his head and cleared the table anyway. I followed him into the kitchen with the empty salad bowl, and he grabbed it from me as soon as he put down the plates he was holding.

"Jamie, stop and look at me."

Jamie didn't even acknowledge my statement, so I grabbed his hands and pulled them until he was facing me. He avoided eye-contact by looking at our hands

"I'm not dying, J. I'm right here and I'm very much alive. You didn't grieve for Nick until he was dead, and I don't want you to grieve for me now. I may outlive you for all you know, so don't shut me out!" I knew I was shouting, but Jamie's lack of response was the most frustrating thing in the world, and I'd had my fill.

Jamie fought the hold I had on his wrists, but it only made me squeeze him harder. He was strong, though, and I knew he had more stamina than me, since I was still recovering, so I pushed him against the counter with my hips. That made him look at me and I saw he was close to tears. It broke something in me and I let go of him. "Jamie!" I shouted after him, but he was gone. I heard his footsteps stomping up the stairs and knew where I'd find him: scrubbing the tub in the upstairs bathroom. I decided to give him some time to cool off, so I put the dishes in the dishwasher, in exactly the place my anal-retentive boyfriend liked them to be. It also gave me some time to calm down before I went upstairs in search of him.

As I predicted, Jamie was on his knees, wearing his purple rubber gloves and scrubbing as if the bath hadn't been cleaned in ten years. I couldn't help smiling as I sat down on the closed lid of the toilet. For once I decided not saying anything would probably be my best bet.

Again, he had more stamina than me. I eventually got up and walked out, leaving him to stew some more. I went back to my seat under the vines, and I tried to read but couldn't. After what felt like forever, Jamie came down in his red Speedos and gracefully dove into the pool. I was standing by the side with his towel as he got out after swimming several lengths. There was still no emotion in his face, but he let me put the towel around his shoulders. When I tried to rub him dry, he walked away.

"Jamie, I want to talk to you." As soon as the words left my mouth I realized how condescending I sounded. "Jamie, please talk to me," I said in a much softer voice. He didn't come out of the kitchen until ten minutes later. He was dressed in jeans and a T-shirt and carrying plates of boquerones and olives and pata negra, just like the first meal I'd had in the villa. He started cutting the bread and poured some olive oil in a small dish so we could dip the bread in. All in all it was a very Spanish meal.

"This is nice," I said, as sweetly as I could manage.

Jamie nodded and continued ripping tiny morsels off his bread and slowly eating them. He was sitting as far from me as he could manage around the square six-person table, so I scooted a little closer.

"I love you, Jamie, more than I could have ever imagined back when Nick asked me to take care of you." I paused to gather my thoughts and decide what I had to say to win Jamie over. I knew he wouldn't give me a lot of chances. "I can't do this when you give me the cold shoulder, though. I can't take this tension, J. I want my chatty boyfriend back."

Jamie looked up at me with that same sad look he gave me earlier. I hated to see him like that, but it was better than the blank stare.

"What can I do to make you talk to me again, Jamie?"

Jamie didn't answer me for what felt like long minutes, so I occupied myself eating bread and ham.

"Can you take me to see the Virgin?"

I tried not to smile at hearing his low, careful voice again. "Of course I can."

He didn't speak again as we finished eating, cleared the table, and got into the old VW beetle that miraculously still started every time we took it out. I stopped the car at the turn in the road where the man-made grotto housed the statue of the Virgin Mary and watched Jamie get out. He sat on the bench in front of the statue and looked up at her. I waited patiently in the car, which was heating up at an alarming rate to the point where open windows didn't cut it anymore and I needed to get out. Jamie was still looking up at the statue when a little old lady in black widow's attire sat next to him. Just like the first time, I saw her taking Jamie's hand, and he let her. I sat down on the back bench so as not to disturb them, but I noticed they were talking. I couldn't make out what was said or in what language—Jamie didn't speak Spanish and as experience had taught me, little old Spanish ladies generally didn't understand much English—but both seemed to enjoy the interaction. To my surprise, Jamie got up and walked over to me, took my hand, and led me to the front bench.

"This is Jez," he introduced me.

She smiled at me, took my hand between both of hers and shook vigorously. Then Jamie waved at her and took my arm, leading me back to the car.

"Do you feel better now you've talked to the Virgin?"

Jamie looked at me as if I was clueless, and maybe I was. "It's just a statue, Jez."

"I know, but you like coming here, and you've told me you asked her to keep me safe and to help Pablo get better."

"She can't help me."

I could hear the defeat in Jamie's words and that worried me. "But you still wanted to come here?"

"Like you said, it won't do any harm."

I wanted to point out she made him talk to me again, but I decided to leave it be for now. "So now we're out, what else do you want to do?"

"We should go back so you can rest."

"I don't need to rest. I've been resting for weeks."

"Ten days," Jamie corrected me.

"Fine, ten days. But I can drive the car. Want to go see how Pablo is doing?"

Jamie looked at me as if he needed to assess how much of a risk that would be.

"Have you talked to him since I was in hospital?"

"Kee called him on the phone like you asked, and he was fine then. I think she went out and got him some groceries."

Jamie's unaffected words surprised me. I knew how close he felt to Pablo and how much he trusted the man. I also knew how much he enjoyed learning from him. "Do you *want* to go see him?"

Jamie shrugged. I grabbed him by the shoulders and shook him, which startled him. "He's your friend, Jamie. You know he's sick. Maybe he needs our help?"

"You're more important than he is, and I know you. If we go over there, you'll start working morning to night again and you can't do that."

"Hey, wait a minute." Well, this was quite a leap from the Jamie who couldn't even get dressed or eat unless I put it on his to-do list to the Jamie who was telling me what I could and couldn't do. Although I'd seen the gradual change and part of me was happy with it, what I was seeing now was of an entirely different caliber, and it fed my commitment phobia. Who was he to decide what was good or bad for me? "You have no idea how I feel and even less idea whether I can work or not." My armor was up, so I didn't bother smoothing over my tone. I knew I was pointing at him, but only because I didn't want to get physical with him. I wanted to shove him, show him rather than tell him that I wouldn't stand for being told what I could and couldn't do, but despite my physical appearance, I'd rather run away than attack him.

"Jez, what if it happens again?"

"It won't happen again!" I fully realized I was shouting. "They fixed me so it wouldn't happen again!" Just when I saw Jamie's reaction to my loss of control, I felt a cold hand touch mine. When I looked down, I saw it was the old woman Jamie had been talking to. She took my hand and Jamie's and put them together, then tied her rosary around them. Was this her way of telling us we belonged together? Or that we should kiss and make up? Not wanting to shock her, I simply looked at Jamie, who seemed to be as puzzled as me, so I simply gave him a compassionate smile.

"We should go see Pablo," Jamie said softly.

"Yeah, we should."

I looked at the old girl, but she smiled her nearly toothless smile at me and wouldn't let go of our hands. "We're okay," I told her. "I'm sorry we were fighting." I didn't really expect her to understand me, but I realized this was directed at Jamie as much as her. She finally let go and left her rosary behind. "Don't forget this," I said raising my voice again, because she'd already turned her back to me. She simply waved her hand without turning around and continued walking off.

Jamie looked down at our entwined hands and the simple but beautiful rosary twisted around them.

"You know how to do this?" I asked him.

"Pray a rosary? I so hoped I'd never have to do that again."

"Your mother?"

Jamie nodded. "All night, every night. Some nights were worse and she'd keep me up as well."

That was the most Jamie had ever told me about his mother. Everything else I knew had come from Nick. "Well, just because we have one now doesn't mean we need to use it. We can hang it somewhere in the villa. Might score us some Brownie points with the neighbors."

Jamie pulled his hand away from mine and then took the rosary, folded it, and put it in the pocket of his cargo shorts.

Chapter 36

BACK at the vineyard, everything seemed to be going okay. Without Jamie's care, Pablo looked his scruffy self again, and his house was a mess. At least he seemed to be eating. Judging from the leftovers, the neighbors were bringing him food, which was just as well.

Jamie ran me out of the house, leaving me to check out the wine storehouse. The door was ajar and I figured the guys were inside cleaning out vats. At least, that's what Pablo told me. The noises coming from inside the storage shed sounded a lot more intimate than scrubbing, though. For a moment I hesitated to walk in, figuring I'd give them their privacy, but I was starting to get turned on. I figured I had to admonish them—it wasn't like it was the first time I had to give them a hard time for fooling around when they were being paid to work—but I thought it could wait until they were done. So I tried to be as quiet as possible, sneaking in around the side, and there they were. I was surprised at the tenderness between them. When I was their age, all I wanted to do was get off, but these two were kissing, groping, their shirts open, hanging off their shoulders. Neither of them were particularly hung, but that didn't make them less enticing, despite their young age. What I was witness to was two guys slowly grinding against each other. There was none of the clumsiness I expected; these guys had done this before, and they knew exactly how to make it good for the other. I didn't wait around for their climax. I didn't need to. Yes, I was turned on, but the guy I wanted was inside the house, and nobody was more surprised than me. I'd never had a problem separating love and sex. I didn't need to love the man I fucked, and I generally didn't fuck the man I loved. Not anymore, it seemed.

I walked outside the storage barn and made my way to the house. Yes, Jamie had turned me down more than once in the last weeks, and I knew which reason he was going to give me now, but I wasn't about to give up trying.

I found Jamie where I expected him, elbow-deep in soap suds standing over the kitchen sink. Pablo was outside, under his tree, so we had privacy. I wrapped my arms around him and he didn't jump. In fact, he pushed against me, moving into the touch. I couldn't resist sliding my hand underneath his shirt to touch his skin. He let me for a few seconds and then pushed me away.

"We can't, Jezzie."

"I know, but it's getting late. We could go home and come back in the morning. It's not like we'll get it all done today."

To my surprise, Jamie nodded. "Just let me finish this. Can you check whether there's food for Pablo?"

So Jamie was taking care of Pablo again. I didn't mind as long as he was coming home with me.

ON THE way home, Jamie was silent next to me. I was too preoccupied figuring out how I was going to persuade him to do more than just sleep beside me. I knew he'd be worried about my heart, and although my cardiologist had given me the green light for any "normal activity," I had to admit I had some apprehensions as well. Then again, I wasn't planning on a full-out fucking session. I only wanted some reassurance that our bond was still there. I wanted some nice, tender one-on-one make-out time. Who knew I had it in me? I certainly didn't.

I was fairly sure Jamie would turn me down, so I didn't wait until we got to the bedroom. I cornered him in the kitchen, where he was unloading the dishwasher. He stopped moving when I put my arms around him from behind and kissed his neck. He didn't just lean into the touch, he actually moaned. How long had it been?

"We can't, Jez."

"I know," I answered, and clearly that surprised him, as he turned around in my embrace and looked me in the eye. "I think we need to talk first."

"About…?"

"About us. Our relationship."

Jamie nodded, although he didn't look convinced.

"Let's go sit down in the living room," I suggested. Jamie followed me, although this was a seldom used room. I figured we'd both feel equally out of place.

I didn't know where to start, so I simply sat down next to him. I wanted to make sure he understood the purpose of this talk was to bring us closer to one another. The problem was that I wasn't good at this. This was my first serious relationship and with my more fleeting ones, I'd never gotten close to having "the talk." Even with Jamie, I wished I could just forgo it, but if Jamie's need for to-do lists taught me anything, it was that he needed structure, and although he'd progressed to being a lot more self-sufficient, I wanted both of us to know where we stood. And the one thing my near-death experience taught me was that there was a certain urgency to "the talk." Not that I was planning on dropping dead anytime soon, but I was at a point in my recovery where I had to start taking into account that I could only control so much of my own life.

Jamie was visibly nervous, sitting on the edge of the couch, his elbows resting on his knees and his back rod straight. I took his hand and bumped his shoulder with mine. It made him smile, for all of two seconds. I decided to go for broke.

"I want to talk about you and me, Jamie. What we have, where we came from, and where we're going." This didn't abate Jamie's anxiety, and part of me didn't mind. Most of the time when Jamie was feeling out of sorts, he went blank and didn't show any emotions at all. He clearly felt that he didn't need to hide from me and that made me happy. I still felt I needed to make him feel better, though. "I want us to have a long life together, Jamie, but to do that we need to talk about what we want out of this relationship. Both of us."

A smile broke on Jamie's face and then he started chuckling. He didn't let go of my hand, even put his head on my shoulder, and although it made me marginally less nervous, I still didn't understand why he was laughing.

"So you're not throwing me out?" Jamie asked after he stopped laughing.

"This is your house, Jamie. If anything, I should be the one leaving." This made the happy silliness disappear from his face. "No! Jamie, I'm not leaving!" The glee didn't reappear. "I know we didn't start out like other couples. I didn't choose you and you certainly didn't choose me."

"Yes, I did," Jamie said. He smiled at my questioning face. "Nick had been looking for you for a long time. He invited a lot of men to this villa, but I turned them all down. Every time he would tell me I was right to do so, because he could only think of one guy he'd trust me to."

I chuckled as I let what Jamie told me sink in. "Next thing you'll tell me he made that volcano in Iceland erupt so I'd be stuck here."

Jamie shook his head. "He was pretty good at a lot of things, but his grasp on nature was not quite so… godlike."

"So it was coincidence?"

"He started looking for you as soon as he knew he was dying. He left messages with your assistant, but you never returned his calls."

"Clark? What did he tell him? Clark screened my calls. Why did he think Nick's call was irrelevant? I need to ask him about this!"

Jamie squeezed my hand. "Jez, don't. It's not important now."

Of course, Jamie was right. It no longer mattered. Clark wasn't my assistant anymore, and Jamie was with me now, despite of all the hurdles.

"Now that's cleared up…," Jamie said, staring at our entwined hands. He didn't finish his sentence right away. Instead he grabbed my other hand and added it to the pile. "You didn't choose me, did you? Nick persuaded you to take me on, and it took all of his talents. Even after he died, you still weren't sure."

I turned my hand around so I was holding both of Jamie's. "You're right. I didn't choose you, and I was never sure I could do it. I'm still not sure I can be the man you need." I was holding my breath, bracing for Jamie's reaction. I didn't know what to expect, but it wasn't what happened next.

Jamie disentangled one of his hands and brought it to my chin, pushing my face up so I was looking at him. Then he kissed me. It was the most tender of kisses, like he wanted to tell me he loved me, but was almost afraid to. Or like he felt I was too fragile for anything more passionate. Or maybe I was just projecting my own feelings on the situation. Despite all my apprehensions, my earlier feelings of arousal resurfaced. I wanted more. I wanted Jamie to really kiss me, passionately, invasively. I wanted to rip his clothes off and pin him to the couch so I could have my way with him. I wanted to possess him, bend him to my will. I wanted to feel alive. I wanted to be assured that he loved me.

I knew if I let my passion rule, I'd lose control and I'd lose sight of the bigger picture and forget about what Jamie wanted. So I needed to give up control, which wouldn't be easy since Jamie could only be in charge if he didn't think he was. Or when he'd had alcohol.

Jamie had rested his head on my shoulder, and I could feel his breath ghost my neck.

"Jamie? Tonight when we go to bed, I want to do more than sleep together."

Jamie looked up at me.

"I want us to make love, J. It's been so long. I need you."

Jamie kissed me again, but it was no less chaste than earlier. I grunted in frustration.

When I opened my eyes, Jamie was sitting next to me, his hand resting on my knee. "I'm scared, Jez. When I found you, I thought you'd died. I can't lose you like I lost Nick, like I lost everyone else who mattered. My granddad, my mom, Alex at the shelter. Every time I trusted someone, they died."

So the shelter guy had died as well. I put my hand over his. "I can't promise you I'll live forever, J. You have your HIV, I have a heart that skips a beat occasionally, but like you're doing fine with it, I got the green light from my doctor too. There are no guarantees."

Jamie smoothed himself against me. "I know."

Jamie felt comfortably warm against me, and I couldn't stop thinking about how I was going to change his mood from broody and sad to turned-on enough to make love. I knew one way was to command him to do it. I knew how much he loved it when I told him in no uncertain terms what I expected from him, but that would mean getting into my Dom headspace. The problem with that was that it worked well enough with strangers, but always felt a little uncomfortable with someone as familiar as Jamie. Also, I wanted Jamie to do it of his own volition. I wanted him to want it. Want me.

I raised my arm so I could hang it over his shoulder, my hand caressing his chest. It always surprised me that his chest was so toned, because I never saw him work out. I closed my eyes so I could recollect the image of what his chest looked like, getting ready for bed, or swimming in the pool.

"What are you doing?" Jamie asked. His voice was soft and seductive.

"Feeling you up."

"You're way off course."

I chuckled. Was I already getting to him? "I can't reach the rest. I could if we moved." I brushed over one of his nipples and Jamie turned enough for me to be able to kiss him.

"We won't be able to stop, Jez."

"Who said anything about stopping?"

"Mmmh, Jezzie," Jamie moaned. It sounded like protest, or frustration, but he didn't stop kissing me and as he turned more, I could feel his erection digging into my thigh. I pulled him closer to me, but I knew if I managed some patience, I would be rewarded. His tongue invaded my mouth and I sucked on it, intermittently letting it go. He ground his groin against my leg. Then his hand found its way to my erection, which was pushing against the zipper of my khakis. I wanted his hand on my skin, but I knew that if I unzipped now, I'd end up getting a fast hand-job and that would be it. I wanted him naked and lying against me in bed before I let him do that.

"Open it up," he murmured against my mouth as he fumbled with my pants.

"Let's get more comfortable first," I suggested.

Jamie grunted in frustration again. I was getting worried I was expecting too much of him, but then he said: "I don't want to stop."

Chapter 37

IT TOOK some finagling, but I finally got both of us off the couch and standing up. All this was complicated by Jamie's reluctance to stop kissing me, but it wasn't like I fought him hard. Even when I tried to direct him up the stairs, he wouldn't let go of me, so I coaxed him to walk backwards. I wasn't doing badly until he managed to insert a hand down my pants. I missed the door to the bedroom and pushed him against the wall instead, grinding him into it.

"Oh, yeah," Jamie moaned. "Do it right here. Fuck me here."

"No. Fucking. Way."

"Come on, Jezzie." He pushed me away and turned around, but I stopped him, grabbing him roughly.

"I'm too old for this," I grunted.

Jamie snorted. "No, you're not."

Still holding him by the wrist, I pushed Jamie into our bedroom until the back of his legs hit the bed. I could see how dark his eyes were. I didn't even need to ask him whether he wanted this as much as I did.

"I want skin," I demanded.

Jamie rushed out of his clothes. As he pulled down his cargo pants and boxers at the same time, his cock jutted up, ready for action. He saw me staring. "You too," he commanded coolly, a teasing smile on his face.

Oh, how much we'd progressed in a few months. Then again, I didn't have a problem remembering our first time and the blowjob he'd given me. Even then, Jamie was one hundred percent in charge. And I had no problem admitting I liked it that way.

I didn't rush my disrobing. Yes, I was eager, but I liked the build-up, and it gave me the added bonus of seeing him touch himself. He was cupping himself with his left hand while spreading the precum around the head of his deliciously uncut cock, and it practically made my mouth water. I had to stop looking at what he was doing to himself, though. I didn't want quick sex. I wanted the whole damn sensual experience of feeling his skin against mine, of making him tremble, of making him beg for release after hours of kissing and touching. Okay that was probably something I wouldn't even have the stamina for, but a guy needs goals and that was mine.

"Stop touching yourself," I ordered.

"Why?" Jamie was throwing me his most defiant look, and he didn't stop the movements of his hands.

"Because I want you to last."

Jamie cocked his head. "I'll stop if you take those pants off."

It was all I was still wearing and my cock was demanding to be released from its cotton prison anyway, so I pulled them down.

"Nice," Jamie teased.

"That's all you can say?"

Jamie didn't reply. Instead he slipped from the bed, sank to his knees, and swallowed my cock as if it was the most delicious food he'd ever had. It felt so good I let him suck me for a little bit, but I liked it too much so I pulled him up until he was standing again. I grabbed the back of his neck and drew him into a scorching kiss.

"That mouth is mine," I said, panting as I reluctantly pulled away from Jamie's delicious lips.

"It was yours when your cock was inside it too," Jamie replied playfully.

I shook my head and started turning down the covers of the bed. When I stood up again, Jamie pressed himself against my back and I couldn't resist leaning into the touch. "You want to top?"

Jamie shook his head, but didn't move, so I grabbed his hands and pulled them tighter around me. It felt good to hold him close, to feel his buff body envelope mine. "Nice."

"Nice?" Jamie asked, imitating my earlier protest. "That's all you can say?"

I chuckled and reluctantly moved him around to my front, feeling my back go cold instantly. "It feels amazing, but I want to lie next to you in bed, our bed, and make love to you. I want to feel you there, your skin touching mine, touching you until your skin is on fire and you can't take it anymore."

Jamie looked like he was trying hard not to laugh, and my courage sank. I wondered if he was going to accuse me of being too soppy, too soft, or whether he was simply going to laugh in my face. Instead he said: "Maybe you *are* getting old, Jezzie." He then leaned closer and whispered in my ear, "But I like it." He stepped away from me and sat on the bed before scooting to his side. I joined him and realized I was quite relieved that he wanted to follow me here.

We started kissing again, slowly and not all that passionately. It felt good, though, and judging from the fact Jamie's erection hadn't waned one bit, he wasn't exactly having a bad time either. Being the young eager buck that he was, he was grinding against me in no time. I tried to distract him by pinching his nipples, but it only made him moan more. And he was by no means passive. His mouth latched onto my neck and after a little bit of licking and a nick of teeth, I felt him suck and mark me. It wasn't like I had any important meetings to go to anyway, and I actually liked it. I'd get an earful from the boys working at Pablo's, but I could take that easily. Especially since I got what I'd dreamed of since long before the hospital: Jamie in my arms, stark naked, aroused, and both of us just enjoying the intimacy without fucking the stuffing out of each other. Maybe I *had* gone soft. There was no doubt in my mind we'd get off, but feeling so close to Jamie, his buff body undulating against mine, was a feeling I'd missed in all those weeks we did barely more than share a bed.

Now I could take the time to feel his muscles move underneath my hands, to rake through his sparse, but definitely there chest hair, and to feel his strong, lean back. From time to time he'd stop kissing whatever piece of skin he had his mouth on to simply look at me with his aqua-blue eyes, his gaze even more innocent than when we first slept together. For the first time I was no longer jealous of Nick, because I knew Jamie was completely here with me.

"What do you want, Jamie?" I asked, looking him in the eye.

"Anything," he answered. "Everything."

I smiled at him. "I do love you, you know."

"I know." Jamie looked between our bodies and took both our erections in his hand. He'd been doing a lot of yard work, so he had calluses that added to the friction that felt so good to me. I tried to look at us, his uncut monster of a cock and my ample cut one, but I couldn't stay focused. Jamie was looking at me as if to gauge if he was doing a good job, and then something changed in his eyes, as if he suddenly realized what power he had over me. And he liked it, judging from the sweet smile that broke all over his face.

We'd stopped kissing, both because I couldn't stay focused and he preferred to watch me lose it. Then without warning he grunted, fought against closing his eyes, and then thrust into his fist. I felt hot jizz squirt over my cock and against my belly. Jamie dove down, latching onto my mouth, and while he gave me the most scorching kiss, I lost it completely. I wrapped my arms around him, squeezing him against me as we both endured the aftershocks of what were unexpectedly massive orgasms.

We stayed together like that, him mostly on top of me, our bellies stuck together with spunk, until we could both breathe again.

"I should do this more often," Jamie remarked. He must have seen my questioning look. "Fuck sober."

"I don't think I've ever seen you drunk," I replied.

Jamie rested his head on my shoulder. "Even with Nick, I always needed something. It's a double-edged sword. Alcohol makes me unbelievably horny, but also makes me relaxed enough to let someone inside. Without, this is all I'm capable of. Some juvenile rutting."

I looked down at him. "This didn't feel juvenile. I don't adhere to the Bill Clinton school of sex ed that teaches that it isn't sex unless a penis is stuck into a vagina."

Jamie snorted. "That would get us off the hook entirely. 'Look, Mom. It's not sex. A US president said so!'" He giggled as he rolled to his back. "So you like this?" He gestured between us. "What we did."

"Yes, I did. I do." Jamie didn't look like he believed me. "I'm not joking. I used to be all about the fucking, too, but fucking is okay with strangers. This," I too gestured between him and me, "feels good because we know each other, because we have this bond that requires it to be more than just getting each other off."

Jamie turned back on his side, brushing his stubbly chin against the soft skin of my shoulder. His eyes went a little glazy. "I liked it too, Jez."

I raised my arm, running my hand over his hair. "But you and Nick…." I didn't finish my sentence, but he didn't either. "Nick wasn't all about the fucking either, was he?"

"Once he couldn't get it up anymore, he became more cuddly," Jamie admitted. "Once he'd gotten over his hang-ups. But before that it was sex morning, noon, and night. Not that I minded. He was good in the sack, I had to give him that. Although he couldn't always come. Made me feel inadequate sometimes."

I smiled at him. "The downside of working in porn. You get so used to not coming that once you can it takes special measures."

"Why didn't he ever tell me that?"

"Because he was a proud man, Jamie."

"He was."

Jamie cuddled closer to me, still ignoring the stickiness and smell of sex clinging to our skin. He seemed utterly content, and I didn't want to tell him I wanted to take a shower. This was the most intimate conversation I'd ever had with him about Nick, and I was glad to see he could talk about Nick without going rigid or blank on me. I enjoyed the fact he could think back with fond memories.

Chapter 38

SOMETHING changed between us after that night. It was subtle, so it took me a while to notice it, but Jamie seemed more confident and somehow happier. He wasn't just chatty around me, but around Pablo as well, and he even talked to the young guys working the vineyard when he had to. It wasn't casual conversation with them yet, but it was miles from the guy who couldn't talk to strangers at all.

The summer months were sweltering hot, and Pablo was teaching Jamie how to see when the grapes were ready for harvest and how to turn them into wine. Jamie seemed very adept at it, taking to it like he did his cooking. I could tell Pablo grew tired more quickly every day. I didn't tell Jamie, though I had the feeling he saw it too but refused to acknowledge it.

The harvest started at dawn with a small field of grapes for white wine. Pablo showed us how to handpick them, and the neighbor's son and his boyfriend clearly knew what they were doing. As Pablo went back to the cabin, Jamie and I followed Eduardo's and Fabian's directions and by the time it got warmer, we had several crates full of ripe grapes ready for the crusher, which I'd given a last scrub just the day before. This was the first of a number of fourteen to sixteen hour days we were going to experience until the harvest was over. I almost fell asleep at the wheel driving home that night.

I reveled in the hard work, although it was manual labor and I was used to pushing papers across a desk and talking to people, not lugging crates, shoveling grape skins, and funneling juice. Jamie had made sure Pablo had a comfortable chair to sit on in the winery, and we found him there asleep more often than not, but we needed his expertise and he wanted to be a part of the process he'd managed with just the help of a few people all his life.

I also immensely delighted at seeing the enjoyment in Jamie's face. When I first met him, he was quiet and trying hard to blend into the background. He spent his days cooking and cleaning, swimming in the pool, and weeding his garden. He needed to-do lists to get through his day, and whenever something out of the ordinary happened, he was taken out of his comfort zone. The Jamie I saw now pretty much organized the whole winery. He took care of Pablo's house, made sure he ate, told me what to get at the supermercado so we all had something to eat while we worked, and he made sure Pablo told him all there was to know about the winemaking business, while making sure the man got the rest he needed. I was just the muscle, and I didn't mind it one bit.

One day as the harvest was coming to an end and I was cleaning out the winepress for the last time, Jamie walked into the winery and I immediately knew what was wrong. Jamie's face was blank, almost. He couldn't quite hide his emotions.

"Pablo?" I asked him. Jamie nodded quickly.

I crawled out of the crusher and tried to wipe my arms, which were red from the grapes, while I ran to the house with Jamie next to me. I immediately realized Pablo was still alive, but he didn't react to either Jamie or me. His breathing was extremely labored and the grimaces on his face told me he was in a lot of pain.

"We need to get him to a hospital, J."

"He doesn't want that," Jamie argued feebly.

"He's in pain. We can't leave him here to suffer!"

Jamie's decision-making prowess went out the window, and I knew it would be up to me to decide. I couldn't see Pablo suffer, so I chose the middle ground: I called Nick's old doctor. To my surprise, the man arrived in about fifteen minutes and decided right away an ambulance was needed.

When they took Pablo away, Jamie crumpled, and I saw the vulnerable man I hadn't seen in weeks reemerge. In the driveway we stood holding each other for long minutes, me caressing Jamie's back in an attempt to soothe him. I hated to see him miserable, but I also knew this was progress from the blank stares he exhibited when Nick died.

They took Pablo to the local hospital. When we were allowed to see him, he was asleep and looked a lot more comfortable than at home, so we left again.

In the car home, I was wondering what would happen to the winery. I was pretty sure we could finish getting the juice into the vats to ferment into wine, but I had no idea if our hard work would be worth it.

Jamie, of course, was thinking of Pablo. "He's not going to be able to taste his wine, is he?"

I was driving back to the winery, and took Jamie's hand for a moment, until I had to shift gear again. "No, he probably won't."

"Is he going to die soon?"

"Yes," I answered truthfully. "He probably won't be coming home, J."

"Who's going to take care of his vineyard?"

I sighed, thinking of all our hard work. "I don't know."

"Someone has to take care of the vines, Jez. They've been growing all of Pablo's life. We can't let them die." And Jamie was thinking of Pablo's life work.

"It's not our call. Pablo probably has family somewhere, so it will go to them."

Jamie put his hand on my thigh and looked out the window at the darkening sky. We returned to the winery to put all the perishables away, but nothing more.

At the villa, Jamie crawled into my arms and fell asleep while I stroked his back.

THE next few days, we did what needed to be done at the winery. I could tell Jamie was putting up a brave face and I tried to console him as much as I could, but he kept telling me he was fine. Every evening we'd drive to the hospital to see Pablo, but he was always asleep. He did seem a lot more comfortable than he had been in the last weeks.

Jamie didn't cave in until Nick's doctor brought us the news that Pablo had died quietly in his sleep. He managed to stay on his feet for as long as the man was in the driveway, but as soon as he drove off, Jamie turned around and dove into my arms. I could feel him leaning on me heavily as he buried his face in the crook of my neck.

"Go on with your work, boys," I told Eduardo and Fabian. "I'll make sure you get paid." Eduardo took his boyfriend and the other young guys who'd come to help with the harvest into the winery, leaving Jamie and me alone in front of Pablo's cabin.

"Let's go inside, okay?" I told Jamie. At first he wouldn't move, but then I managed to coax him inside. Once we got out of the sun and I parked him on the old, worn-out couch, I was surprised to see he wasn't crying. Maybe my feeling that he was getting better at dealing with grief was premature. I got him a glass of water and sat down next to him. I knew I had to be patient, but I hoped it wouldn't take him four days to start talking like after Nick died.

"J, darling, I know this is hard, but we can't—" I stopped talking because Jamie shook his head.

"We need to finish the wine and clean up the cabin, so when Pablo's family arrives, they won't see this mess."

I couldn't resist smiling as the tension dropped away. I'd had all sorts of scenarios running through my mind about having to take Jamie home because all he'd do all day was sit and stare into nothingness, or not be able to do anything because he needed consoling and wouldn't stop crying. I'd never expected him to take action.

"Why don't you fix the house, and I'll whip the guys into shape to get that grape juice in the fermenting vats?"

"Pablo showed me what to do with the late wines, the ones that need to age," Jamie said.

"If you want, I can clean the house?"

Jamie shook his head. "You hate cleaning."

I shrugged and smiled at him.

"Just come get me as soon as the pressing is done."

I kissed his forehead. "It's a deal."

Jamie had other ideas. He grabbed my head and pulled me into a heart-stopping kiss. When he pulled away, my head was spinning and I was horny as hell. He pushed me out of the door, though.

"Just don't work too hard and drink plenty of water." I must have looked puzzled because he continued, "You're all I have left. You better take care of yourself."

"I will," I said. "I promise." I kissed my fingers and blew it at him. It made him smile and that's all I needed.

THAT evening when we came home, Jamie barely gave me the time to make it up the stairs before he devoured me. Except for our slow and easy making out session, we were always too tired to do anything when we came home at night, and it had been weeks since we'd had full-blown sex, so despite my physical fatigue, I didn't resist. Jamie clearly wasn't tired, despite the fact he'd spent the day mucking out Pablo's cabin more thoroughly than he'd dared to do when Pablo was still around. He was also more than fine with me taking on the passive role. So I let him suck me off while I laid back and feasted my eyes when he rode me like a bronco. He was gorgeous when he let himself be overwhelmed by lust, and I enjoyed my front row seat. As usual, seeing him shoot his load over my belly, his head tilted back and mouth slightly open, sent me over as well, and I loved how he collapsed in my arms.

"You okay, J?" I asked as soon as I had enough breath.

Jamie nodded sleepily.

"Did you get into Pablo's secret wine stash?"

Jamie shook his head. "Nope, stone cold sober." He yawned. "I needed this so badly," Jamie murmured just before he fell asleep on my chest, leaving me to get rid of the condom and do as much cleanup as I could with Jamie draped all over me. I didn't mind.

Chapter 39

WITH all the grapes in the fermentation vats, our work wasn't over yet, but we no longer needed the extra workers, so I paid them what we owned them from my own account and sent them on their way. Eduardo and Fabian still came by to help us with the siphoning and punching of the wine, but we were glad the sixteen-hour workdays were over. The extra free time also seemed to fire up Jamie's furnace. We went through entire boxes of condoms in record time, and I couldn't say I objected in the least.

The day before Pablo's funeral, I walked into the cabin and found Jamie sitting on the bed, going through pictures. "What did you find?"

Jamie pulled me to sit down next to him. "Look." He showed me a photograph of two young men, the colors slightly off and the corners bent. They had their arms around each other and they were smiling widely. "I think that's Pablo." He pointed at the one with dark, curly hair and I could see the resemblance. "And look at the other one."

The one with the straight, dark hair looked vaguely familiar, but I couldn't place him.

"He looks exactly like Eduardo," Jamie said, handing me another picture, this time face down. There was writing on the back. "Eduardo 1968." This time "Pablo" was kissing Eduardo's temple and Eduardo was smiling shyly at the camera.

"Didn't Eduardo say he was named after his father?"

Jamie nodded, clear amusement on his face.

"So you think this is Pablo with Eduardo's father?"

Jamie nodded more fervently.

I swayed the picture at Jamie. "This only proves they knew each other. You know these Mediterranean men by now, J. They're all touchy-feely and hug and kiss for no reason at all."

"I guess we'll never know, but there was nobody else in Pablo's life, and he only had to call Eduardo next door and he sent his son over to help."

I wasn't convinced, but didn't want to push. I'd met Eduardo senior and his wife when I picked up dinner from their house a few times, and I didn't sense the vibe, but then Eduardo did have his wife nearby. I could give Jamie the benefit of the doubt, especially since it seemed to make him happy.

THE next day at the funeral, they were there: Eduardo and his wife, Eduardo junior and Fabian, and Jamie and I. There was only one stranger there, who introduced himself after the service in the small local church.

"I am Dion Vega. Pablo was my mother's brother," he said in a heavy Spanish accent.

I heard Jamie's breath hitch. So there was family. At least now we knew who we'd done all the work for.

I shook his hand. "I am Jeremy Robinson and this is Jamie Kendrick."

He nodded at Jamie and then looked back at me. "You are American?"

"Yes, but we live at the top of the Cami Dels Xiprers, in the Casa Feliz."

"The villa?" Dion asked.

"Yes."

"Eduardo told me you worked the viñedo?"

"Pablo was a friend of a friend," I explained. "When he fell sick, he was desperate to get his last harvest in, so we helped."

"I talked to Pablo's lawyer," Dion admitted. "I am to get the viñedo, but there are too many debts. I am but a simple man, Señor Robinson, and cannot pay off the debt I will inherit together with the land. If I let it go to the state, Tio Pablo will come to haunt me."

I felt Jamie grab my hand and squeeze it, and I knew exactly what he meant with that gesture. "Would you consider taking me to his lawyer? Maybe we can come to an arrangement? Say, I pay off the debt Pablo left and I get the viñedo in return."

"Are you interested in working the viñedo?"

I looked over at Jamie and saw him smile. I knew I had his blessing. "Pablo taught Jamie here everything there is to know about the grapes he grew. He showed me his books, and I've already been working at trying to save as much of it as I could with what limited means Pablo had."

"Not to mention, you paid the harvest workers and arranged for his funeral. The family is very grateful."

"It was our pleasure," I said sealing the deal with a handshake. "Pablo was a wonderful man. His viñedo will always carry his name."

Dion said his good-byes after I gave him our phone number, and he promised to call us with an appointment to see his lawyer.

When I walked away from the churchyard, Jamie wrapped his arms around me and I put my arm around his shoulders. "Happy?"

Jamie nodded. "Can we stop at the grotto?"

"Of course."

I drove us to the grotto and stopped in the turn of the road. As always, I stayed in the car, but Jamie walked around the car and dragged me out. He sat me down on the bench where the old lady always sat and looked up at the Virgin.

"He doesn't believe this works, but I asked you to make sure the vineyard would end up in good hands, and I asked you to arrange something so Jez and I could stay living at the villa. I never figured you'd be able to fix everything in one go, but you did it. Thank you." He squeezed my hand and then looked at me. "Oh, and you made Jez get better too. I tested him and he passed with flying colors."

"So that was what all the sex wa—" Jamie cut me off by clamping his hand over my mouth.

"Jez, she isn't called the Virgin Mary for nothing. You can't tell her about that!"

I couldn't stop a giggle, which turned into a laugh, which ended up with tears of happiness streaming down my face. I was so in love with this naïve man, I couldn't contain it.

"She won't mind this," I said, pulling Jamie closer and kissing him on the mouth.

When we broke apart, Jamie was smiling. "Now I want to learn how to drive."

Instead of telling him I didn't see that happening in the near future, I kissed him again.

Epilogue

IT TOOK us four years to produce a wine that passed muster at the wine cooperative that organized distribution for all the wines in the area, but we made it. Who knew it was so difficult? No matter how much we learned and experimented, we never managed to produce the strange but delicious Rioja that had brought us to Pablo's vineyard in the first place. I guess his secret died with him.

What we did do was bring the process into the 21st century, so we had a more efficient process and bigger revenue. It took a big chunk out of both Jamie's inheritance and my savings, but our hearts were fully invested in it, and neither of us had any regrets.

Looking back, I only now realize how unhappy I was before Jamie came into my life. I thought the job I did made me happy, but I couldn't have been more wrong.

And Jamie blossomed too. He was still shy, but talked to strangers when needed and even picked up more Spanish than I did, especially after he got his driver's license and would go into town for groceries on his own.

He rarely drank our wine, except to taste it, but made one exception: for our marriage.

We got married in the town hall of our village, with half the village and Lakiya and her family in attendance, and Eduardo and Fabian as our best men and Lakiya as my witness. This is where Eduardo told us about his father's and Pablo's relationship, and I thought Jamie was going to beam right out of his skin.

"You know, they were both there, during our wedding," Jamie said unexpectedly, when we sat on the second floor patio of our villa, overlooking the garden and the swimming pool and enjoying the amazing starry sky above us.

"Who?"

"Nick and Pablo."

"Together?"

"No, you silly." Jamie stabbed my side and made me double over. "But they were okay with it."

"Of course they were," I agreed, although I knew Jamie meant he actually knew they were there, and I didn't believe in that sort of thing. "They both tried very hard to keep us together."

"So unnecessary!" Jamie shouted, and then he kissed me.

ZAHRA OWENS is a multilingual globetrotter who loves big cities but also has a weak spot for the wide-open spaces that are so rare where she lives.

She likes her men every which way they come and never tries to change them. Men who are tough on the outside but have a huge soft center get extra credit, though, as do the strong, silent types who think they hide their damage well… but don't. She makes it her personal goal to find them their happily-ever-after, even if the road toward this leads via hospital beds, villas with gorgeous vistas, or ranges full of horses.

Zahra is a proud member of the Rainbow Romance Writers, a special interest chapter of the Romance Writers of America, and won't quit until M/M romances are treated like every other romance story. RWA allowed her into its Professional Authors Network, but she hasn't quit her day job yet since it allows her to work in a man's world. And what girl can resist that?

If Zahra had her wish, a day would have at least thirty-six hours, because how else would she find the time to finish all the novels still inside her head?

You can find Zahra at http://zahraowens.com.

Also from Zahra Owens

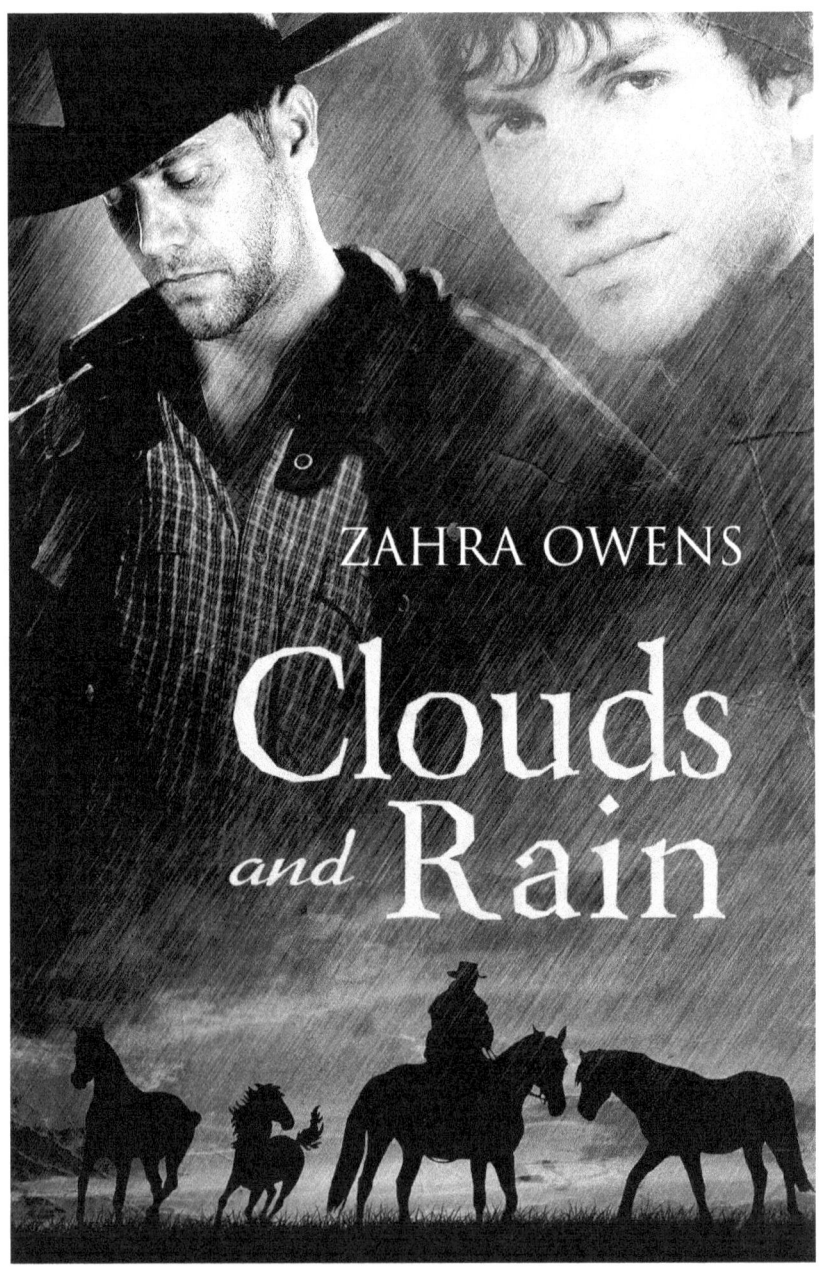

ZAHRA OWENS

Clouds
and Rain

http://www.dreamspinnerpress.com

Also from ZAHRA OWENS

http://www.dreamspinnerpress.com

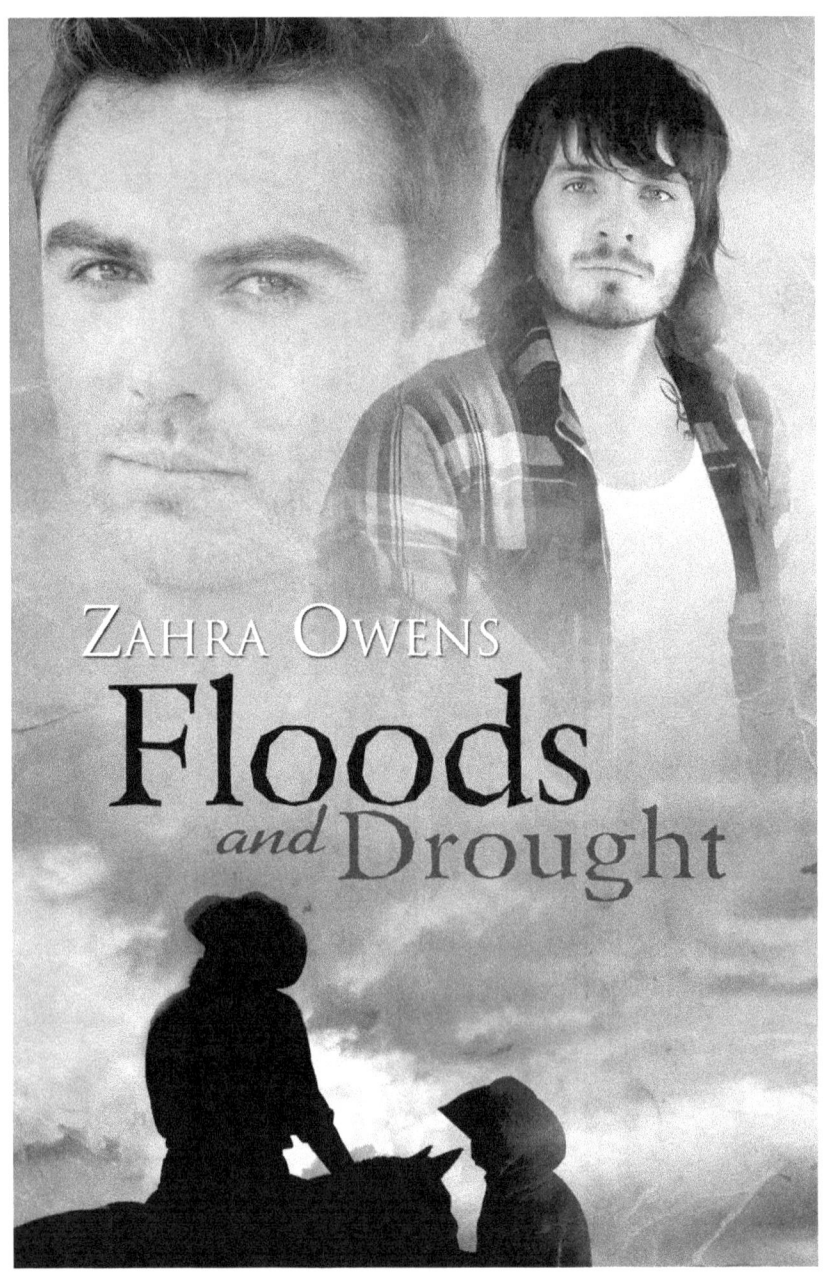

Also from ZAHRA OWENS

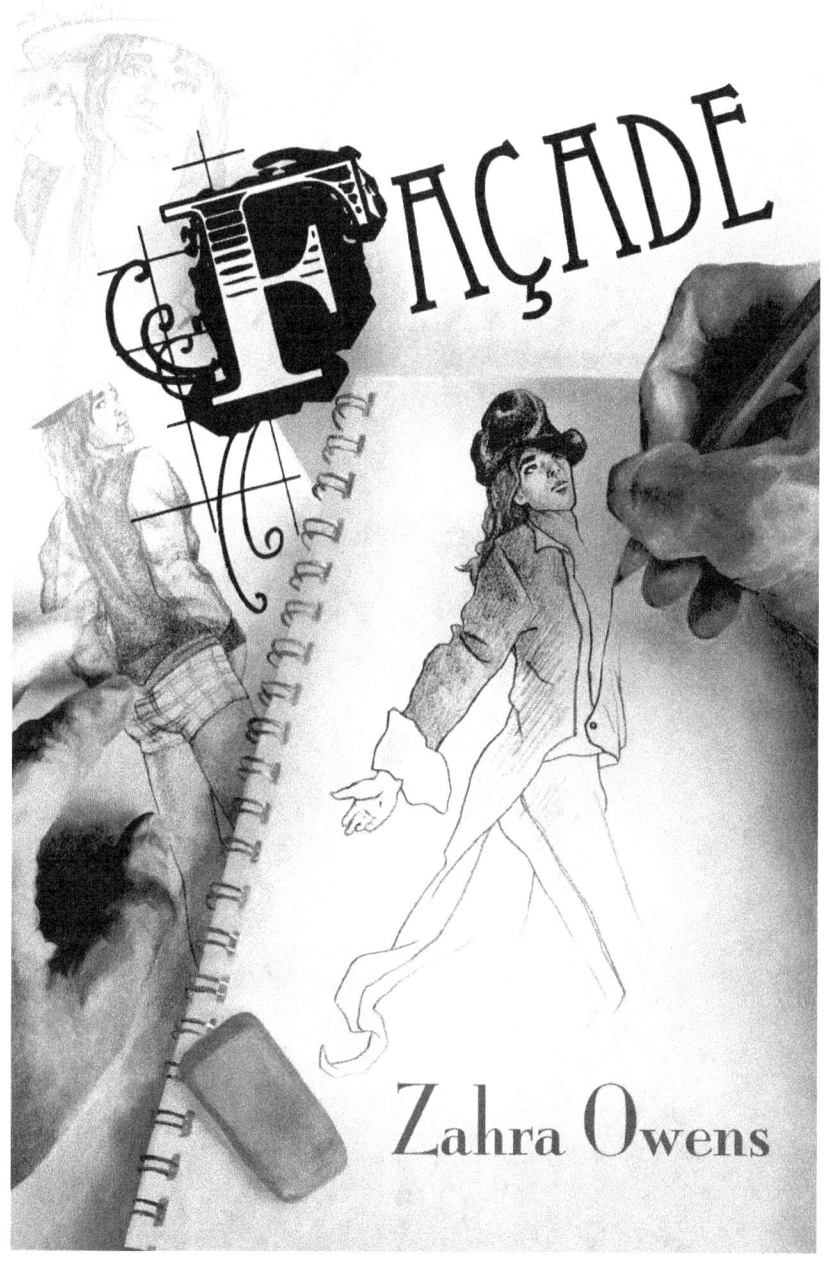

FAÇADE

Zahra Owens

Also from ZAHRA OWENS

You Can Choose Your Friends

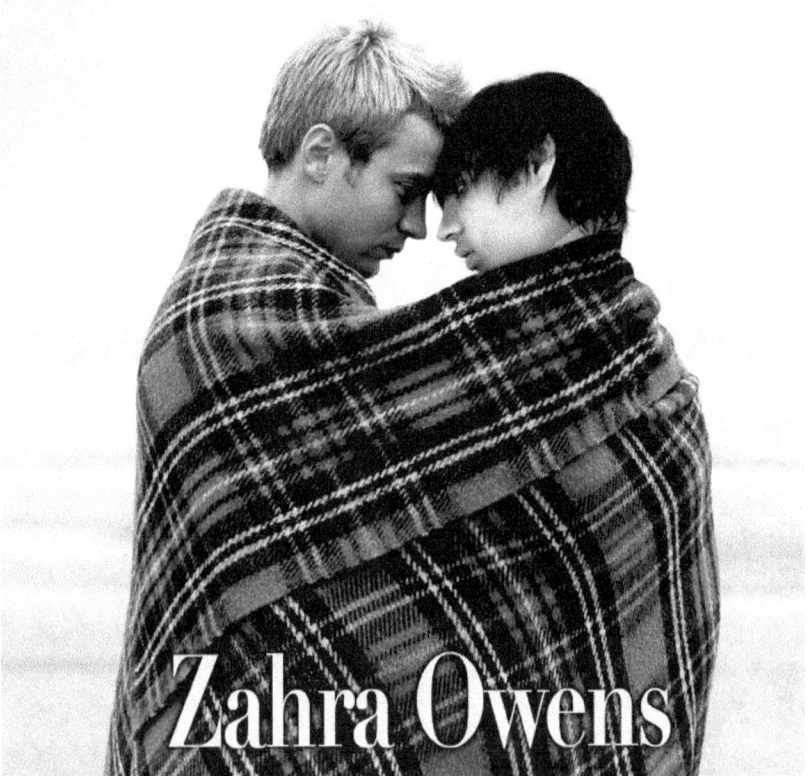

Zahra Owens

http://www.dreamspinnerpress.com

Also from ZAHRA OWENS

You Can't Choose Your Family

Zahra Owens

http://www.dreamspinnerpress.com

www.ingramcontent.com/pod-product-compliance
Lightning Source LLC
Chambersburg PA
CBHW051638260626
47170CB00004B/1231